MUST LOVE CATS

ANGELA ADDAMS

Must Love Cats
ISBN # 978-1-83943-739-7
©Copyright Angela Addams 2021
Cover Art by Erin Dameron-Hill ©Copyright September 2021
Interior text design by Claire Siemaszkiewicz
Totally Bound Publishing

MUST LOVE CATS

Dedication

To all my fellow Cat Keepers.

Chapter One

Lucki

Cat Keeper of Weeping Falls. It sounds like a joke, right? Cat Keeper... What the hell kind of job is that?

"The best job in the mothereff" — *burp* — "ing world!" Lucki Collins raised her almost empty pint of beer and cheered the crowd of rowdy townspeople who were seated all around her. The burn of too much booze heated her cheeks, and the ache from so much laughing had her cradling her side. She was being treated like a queen and didn't care if she was making an ass of herself.

"Cheers to our new Cat Keeper. May your time here be ever filled with joy." Mr. Rose an elderly man with a bright red nose and long white whiskers, raised his glass, which was filled with...milk. It was the only thing he'd been drinking all night.

Lucki figured it had to be mixed with bourbon or something. The man was way too cheerful to be sober. *They're all way too cheerful.* The entire town of Weeping

Falls, a population of a hundred at most, had welcomed her with open arms the second she'd cleared the town line—and hadn't stopped welcoming her.

"To our blessed Cat Keeper!" Everyone cheered, raising their glasses, thumping on the tables, laughing, singing.

They were in the tavern, a throwback to the old West, complete with its swinging doors and long curved bar, plank wood floors that were scuffed and dented and an old-time piano that one of the residents had been playing since Lucki had gotten there. Everyone was dressed in the fashion of the time too—from the cowboy hats to the heel spurs, corsets and billowing skirts. Lucki truly felt like she'd stepped into the olden days—and she loved it.

Weeping Falls had been an actual mining town back in the day. Now it was barely hanging on as a ghost town tourist attraction—the Wild West in Alaska. There wasn't much in the way of bookings, from what she'd gathered. The only visitor was her, and she was soon to be a resident too. She'd be Lady Clover's Cat Keeper, responsible for tending to a massive cat colony who'd been bequeathed a mansion and a trust fund and who called Weeping Falls home.

When she'd been offered the job, she'd thought she'd heard wrong.

"Cat keeper? What kind of job is that?"

Scout, the man who'd found her, had answered her simply and honestly. *"We can't afford a trained vet to come. You have almost all the requirements and a lot of experience working with animals. You'll do."*

Lucki had been working at shelters her whole life. Always a tender heart around those injured or in need of love, she'd solely manned a cat sanctuary in her hometown until a fire had taken out the entire colony the past summer. It had nearly destroyed her heart to lose all those precious lives.

Scout had come knocking on her door one morning, claiming he'd heard about her compassion toward the felines and had wanted to offer her a new job as Cat Keeper for Lady Clover's Cat House in Weeping Falls, Alaska.

It had seemed like a good idea at the time — a windfall, actually. Everyone knew she was destined to be a crazy cat lady anyway, and now she was going to be paid to fulfill that dream. It sounded pretty freakin' perfect to her.

Besides, she had another reason to leave home — a big, six-foot-two, built-like-a-brick-house reason whom she wanted no reminder of ever again. He'd be in jail for another year at least, and by the time he got out, he'd find no trace of her. That gave her some measure of peace.

Her heart had been crushed, battered and beaten enough over the last ten years. She needed this escape, and Scout's offer had come at the perfect moment. Time would heal all wounds — or so she'd heard — but cuddling with a bunch of cats would make that time sweeter.

And there hadn't been a moment of regret — not one. She'd spent more than a day on the road with only a brief stop to rest, travelling all the way from her hometown in northern British Columbia.

It was a long way to come for a bunch of cats.

Best decision ever!

She downed what was left of her beer then snorted in the most unladylike way when another full pint slid in front of her.

"Oh boy, no way!" She laughed. "You people are going to get me totally wasted."

"Aww, lass, no harm," Andy Crawlie drawled. "We're just happy yer finally here. We've been waitin' on ya fer a vera long time."

That had been what it had been like the entire night. They'd fed her delicious food until she was stuffed, then they'd started pouring the beer, keeping her glass full while they sang and laughed and told stories. There were enough people in the tavern that she lost track of all the names and keeping everyone straight. But she had plenty of time to learn them.

Lucki giggled but pushed the glass away. "Thank you for all your generosity, everyone." She had to raise her voice to be heard over the music playing. "I think I should head back to Lady Clover's, though. It's late… Wait! How late is it?" Her phone had stopped working at some point during the night. She imagined that cell service was spotty at best around here anyway. She made a mental note to ask someone about it in the morning when her thoughts were clearer.

"Oh, it's hardly after midnight, dear," Sandy Evernight said as she picked up Lucki's beer and took a sip for herself. "But if you must go, we'll send you with an escort, to make sure you get back to the house in one piece."

"An escort?" Lucki pushed her chair back. The wood feet thudded across the floor, giving Lucki a bit of a fight to stand.

"It's always a good idea around here." Sandy shrugged, her cheeks bright. She had a glint in her eyes that made Lucki question if there was a punchline coming. "'Cause of the wild animals and such."

"Wild animals?" Lucki frowned, her good mood taken down a notch. *Not a joke, then. Right, because you're in the middle of freakin' Alaska! Spring is coming. Of course there are animals roaming around.*

"Och, Sandy, quit scaring the girl. You want her to pick up and leave before she's even settled in?" Mr. Rose said. "Rueben's out there watchin' for her. He'll make sure she gets home safe."

"Oh, Reuben's around?" Sandy winked, aiming another sly smile at Lucki. "Didn't know. Hadn't seen him."

"Don't be daft, woman." Andy *tsk*ed.

"You'll be fine, Lucki," Mr. Rose said with a reassuring pat on her arm. "Just be sure to put your coat on. The nights are still bitter cold around here."

Someone handed Lucki her giant parka as she stood on wobbly legs, the beers rushing through her system worse than she'd first thought. "Thanks." She slipped herself inside the warm down coat and instantly shivered as the heat embraced her. It would soon be too hot to be wearing inside the tavern. That was for sure. "I'll see you all in the morning."

Everyone mumbled something at her in response, but as she moved toward the door, she realized they just as soon returned to their drinking and joking, seeming to forget all about her. Looking over her shoulder at the group, she smiled once again. *Such a fun bunch of folks.* Unusual, sure, but also warm and embracing. Their unquestioning friendliness was like a comfort blanket around her heart. And that was something she really, really needed.

She pushed through the doors and blinked against the cold bite of the air. Icy wind shot up her nose and stung her brain. Sandy had said it was spring and she wasn't wrong, calendar wise, but the weather up here was not any kind of spring that Lucki had ever experienced. Even in Canada, where the winters could get brutal, May usually came with milder temperatures, even at night.

But today was only May first, she reminded herself. *Beltane.* The familiar stir of longing rattled through her. In years past, Beltane was always a night she'd enjoyed with others. *With him.* Marking the coming of spring, Beltane was a celebration of new growth and fertility, and usually involved a night of ritual, song and dance, bonfires and, in her adult life, a lot of sexual exploration. This was the first time in many years that she would be alone.

But the past is the past, and it's better to be alone and happy than with someone and miserable.

"Blessed be," she said with a sigh.

She let her eyes adjust to the night then looked up at the impossibly bright stars overhead. She'd never seen so many in her life. She scanned the sky, hoping to see the Northern Lights, which she'd read about when she had been trying to research what to expect in Alaska, but the only light was from the stars and the moon, which was near full. *Beautiful.* She took in a deep breath, ignoring the burn of the cold air as it ripped up her nose again, freezing her nostrils. *Refreshing, sure, but also painful.* She chuckled to herself then took a few steps off the porch.

The gritty earth crunched under her feet. It was a strangely comforting sound that broke up the silence of the night and gave Lucki something to focus on other than the shadowed buildings.

The town consisted of a main strip with all the old ghost-town amenities—a barbershop with its candy-cane stripe, a hotel down the road, grocery store, shoemaker, blacksmith and even a church. There was a carriage without its horses and bundles of hay off to the side. It was so old-world and yet not. There were modern amenities as well—like the streetlamps, which were a little too far apart for Lucki's liking, and a few cars parked here and there.

She flipped up her hood, suddenly feeling the cold worse as it whipped down the back of her neck, making her shiver right to her bones. Lady Clover's Cat House was at the other end of the strip. The lights of the mansion shone from almost every window, a guiding beacon, so it would be impossible to not find her way there.

My new home. Hard to really fathom. It was three stories of old-world charm. Painted yellow like the sun, it had stained-glass multicolored windows with white shutters to frame them and a wraparound porch that could fit a hundred people with no problem. There was even a swinging chair there for her to lounge on in the warmer months, and she so looked forward to reading a few books out there with some cats on her lap. It was a house she could only dream of living in one day, and here she was walking down a dirt road, on her way to spending her first night in a castle of cats. *Bliss.*

Although this particular bliss included a pretty frosty walk. The cold bit at her cheeks and stung her eyes, so she walked faster. The noise from the partiers dimmed behind her. The silence of Alaska greeted her with each step she took toward her new home. She could fall in love with a place like this. It was so peaceful. So simple. She didn't miss the buzzing white noise that she'd grown accustomed to back home or the constant urgency to check her phone for messages. She was unplugged. Calm. At peace.

"Meow."

Lucki stopped in her tracks. *Ohhhhhhh, one of the cats?* She hadn't met any of them yet, but she was eager to.

"Kitty?"

"Meeeeeow."

She shifted her hood so she could look all around. "Here, kitty. Come here, kitty. Let me see you!" She felt no shame in her excitement over meeting the cats. She looked forward to bonding with each of them. She'd been warned it was quite a large colony, a hundred at least. "Here, kitty!"

"Meow!"

She felt a nudge against her boot and shifted her hood to look down. The coat was so bulky that she could hardly see her own feet.

"Mr. Whiskers?" she said, as she swooped down to pick up her own cat. "What are you doing out here all alone, baby?" The only cat to have survived the fire was one of her favorites, a mangy brown tabby she called Mr. Whiskers. She'd brought him with her to Alaska but had left him safe and sound in the house—or so she'd thought. "How'd you get out here?"

"Muuuuurrrrow!" He purred like an engine and nuzzled into her arms as she stroked him.

"Well, you silly boy, let's get you back inside where it's warm."

She walked, the *crunch* of her feet on the gravelly dirt road a distraction again. She pulled her attention from the ground and scanned the buildings around her.

"It's awfully dark." In between the streetlights was pitch black, and unusual shadows had collected in those places, keeping just out of reach from the lights. In each of those in-between spaces were alleys that were so opaque that they were impenetrable without a flashlight.

Creepy. The sobering reality of being completely alone in the middle of a town where she didn't really know anyone slithered down her spine. If she called out, would anyone hear her?

The faint sound of music from the tavern drifted toward her. *Nope…probably not.*

She also kind of felt like she was being watched. *Paranoia? Maybe.* The tickling at the back of her neck had her scrunching her shoulders, and she picked up her pace all the same.

"Where's this Reuben guy everyone is talking about?" she whispered to Mr. Whiskers, but he didn't say anything back. He just purred in his contented kitty way. No fucks given.

The cat house was only about thirty feet ahead, if that. The urge to bolt the rest of the way poked her from all sides, but she was scared that if she did that, she'd drop the cat or freak him out enough to make him claw his way over her face.

Just one more alley to cross. She moved a little to the center of the street, putting some distance between her and the black maw of nothing on her left.

As she crossed the alley, she heard a noise. Low and quiet at first, it was a rumble of sound that she didn't know quite how to place. It froze her in her tracks, though. There was definitely a menacing tone to it, like a warning. A growl.

"Do you hear that, Mr. Whiskers?" She couldn't keep the quiver out of her voice. *Keep walking.*

Mr. Whiskers stopped purring. In fact, he stopped moving and was frozen in her arms, his body rigid as he stared down the alley, a murmur of a hiss growing in his belly.

The growling from the alley came again. It was definitely not friendly. *Oooooh nooooo…*

Something dazzled, a blink of light, then twin orbs of blue appeared to be floating in the darkness. *So pretty.* The slow grind of gravel under foot, deliberate careful movements, didn't bring Lucki any comfort. "What is that?"

She unlocked her knees then took a step back. Then another. The sound got louder. The growl grew in strength with each step toward her until it was a warning she couldn't ignore. She moved back quickly, almost stumbling on her own feet. Out of the shadows came a giant dog, its teeth bared, eyes menacing.

No, not a dog.

A wolf!

"H-h-holy shit," Lucki stammered.

The wolf crouched, ready to pounce.

I'm going to die.

Mr. Whiskers hissed a growl of his own then leaped from her arms and she, the stupid fool, chased after him—right up to the wolf, within feet of the menacing beast. Mr. Whiskers stood between them, his fur fluffed out and back arched. He gave a hiss of warning with a paw raised, ready to strike.

"Mr. Whiskers, are you nuts?" Her voice was barely loud enough for anyone to hear. It was a croak instead of a scream. No one would come to her rescue. "Help!" Her voice failed her once again, coming out as a half whisper, strangled by her fear. The wolf watched her, its eyes searing deep inside. It ignored the cat completely.

What is the right move? Why didn't I research this?
What to do if a wolf stalks you...yeah...that.

The wolf took a menacing step in her direction, its predator glare never wavering. Lucki's legs shook with an alarming sway. Her knees were literally knocking together. If she tried to run, she'd fall flat on her face for sure.

Running with a predator giving chase was probably not a great idea anyway.

The cat launched itself, jumping toward the wolf.

Her voice unlocked. "Mr. Whiskers, *no!*"

But it was too late. The cat struck a clawed paw against the wolf's muzzle, causing it to growl and lower its head. Lucki thought for sure Mr. Whiskers was gonna lose all nine lives in one go, but Mr. Whiskers didn't get the memo on that. He struck again, quick and determined, a claw swipe against the wolf's nose.

Lucki quickly calculated the odds of snatching the cat up as she ran. It didn't look good. She was not that coordinated.

She sucked in a deep breath, then opened her mouth to scream.

The wolf took a step back, its head bowed...in... submission?

What the...? Her scream died on her tongue.

Mr. Whiskers, still all puffed out, still defending his human, was no longer on the attack. He even seemed to have a smug grin as he tossed a glance in Lucki's direction. The wolf stayed down, muzzle lowered to the ground, its eyes blinking rapidly.

"Get outta here if you aren't going to be civilized," a booming voice said from behind.

The wolf flicked its eyes up, looked behind Lucki for a moment, then it bolted away into the darkness of the alley.

"Sorry, hon. Got caught up in a conversation and didn't realize you were leaving so soon."

Lucki glanced behind her, then did a double take. A huge, burly man stomped toward her. He had to be at least six-five, six-six. He wasn't wearing a coat, just a blue lumberjack shirt, rolled up at the sleeves, that showed some impressively muscled forearms. His brown hair was parted to the side and his soft eyes crinkled with what kind of looked like amusement. The lower half of his face was covered with a beard, close cropped and well kept. This guy was a bear—a huge, lumberjack bear. He had an easy smile and a dimple, and he was so disarming that Lucki smiled back, that and her panties melted right then and there.

"I'm Reuben." His voice had the kind of husky depth that stroked her soul.

Her legs quivered.

She cleared her throat to get the lusty lump of drool out of the way. "There's a wolf…" She turned her head to the alley, but the wolf was definitely gone. Mr. Whiskers nudged her to be picked up.

"Yeah, I saw." Reuben radiated heat. It literally steamed off him. He came up next to her then placed a firm hand on her back, which instantly steadied her legs. "Let's get you to the house before you freeze to death."

"A wolf, though…" She turned her head from side to side, scanning the area as she bent down to pick up the cat.

"He's gone now. Don't worry about him." Reuben's voice was so sure, so confident, so soothing. "Happy to finally meet you," he added.

"Was that real?" The adrenaline that had coursed through her body crashed out of her in a whoosh. She took a step but her legs crumbled out from under her.

"Whoa there!" Reuben swooped in and held her upright. "They been pouring drinks into you? Those beasts don't ever learn."

Her head was clear. Any buzz she'd had from the booze had burned through her. It had to be shock that was making her dizzy and disoriented now. She could have died. Mr. Whiskers had done his best, but really, that wolf could have eaten her in a few bites.

"I got ya." Reuben picked her up then cradled her and the cat in his arms.

She gasped, more to herself, as she looked up at him. "You're a big guy." She was in the arms of a mountain.

He chuckled. "I am." He hitched her up higher. "Let's get you home, shall we? Then we can properly introduce ourselves. It's Beltane, you know, a good night for introductions." He smiled, his dimple popping and his eyes glistening.

His wink to follow undid her completely.

Chapter Two

Lucki

He carried her right up the steps of Lady Clover's and straight into the house like he owned the place, knowing exactly when to twist and turn so that he didn't bonk her head on any doorframes.

A fire blazed in the living room. *How'd that happen?* Lucki hadn't had much of a chance to look around the house before Sandy had come to snatch her up and take her for a bite to eat at the tavern, but all the same, she would have remembered if the grand fireplace, with its gaping mouth and lion-head mantle, had been lit.

In fact, she had stood inside the fireplace, just to see if she'd hit her head, but her whole five-foot-seven self had fit, with room to spare. That was how big the thing was.

With the fire blazing, Lucki shivered against the sudden warmth. It seeped through her coat and into her frosty skin.

"Mmm-m, that feels good."

Reuben chuckled, a rumble she felt against her body, warming her in a different way. He'd stopped walking and she realized he was looking down at her with an expression that almost seemed wistful. His eyes radiated a heat all on their own.

"So pretty," she gasped, mesmerized by his eyes, which were such an unusual color. She'd never seen anything like it. The contrast of such a rich amber encircled by a ring of black was breathtaking, remarkable, almost otherworldly. His chestnut lashes softened his stare, but even so, Lucki knew he was reading her, searching into her soul to find her truth.

"So are yours." Reuben's husky voice tickled all her girlie parts. "Pretty, green, like an emerald."

"My name is Lucki."

"I know who you are." His gaze trailed from her eyes to her lips. "Lucki Collins, our new Cat Keeper."

She wiggled a bit in his arms. Not that she didn't enjoy being there, but it did seem odd that he hadn't let her down yet, and she was getting a little overheated with the blazing fire and her coat still on. Mr. Whiskers had abandoned ship the moment they'd stepped into the house.

He chuckled again then slowly lowered her to the couch. Kneeling in front of her, he unzipped her coat and helped her out of it.

"And you are?" The heat of the fire on her face overwhelmed the burn of a blush rising in her throat to her cheeks. "I mean, I know you said you're Reuben, but what do you do around here?"

He stripped her coat free and tossed it over the back of the couch.

"I'm Reuben Bear, your protector." He said it like she should understand, like she should know what that meant.

"Protector? Like a bodyguard?"

He touched her hair, teasing a hunk of it between his fingers. His forehead was so furrowed and his eyes so intent that she thought maybe he was seeing something that she couldn't.

"Reuben?"

He snapped his eyes to hers. As if caught being naughty, a sly grin exploded on his face. "Mmm-m?" He moved his fingers to her cheek. "I wanted to see if you're as soft as you look." He caressed her bottom lip with his thumb. She closed her eyes and leaned into it.

Maybe he hadn't been staring into her soul.

Maybe he'd been stripping her naked.

Maybe he'd been thinking about how Beltane should be celebrated.

Please be thinking about getting naked.

She gulped, opened her eyes and tried to keep her shit under control. She'd just met this man. Even though he exuded all sorts of hot-guy, cinnamon-roll vibes, still…it was a little presumptuous of her to think he wanted to jump her body. "You're my bodyguard?" Her voice came out wispy, like she was some kind of siren. *Oh well, no hiding my desire.*

He moved his thumb over her bottom lip again. "Yeah, something like that."

He smelled like a lumberjack should – a hint of pine, a little clove.

"What do I need protecting from?" She shifted a little closer, questing for more of his touch.

"Up here? A great many things," He rumbled deliciously.

Feeling brave, she lifted her hands, one to place on his forearm, to caress the hard muscle and sinew, and one to the side of his face where his beard was the thickest. It was soft, his beard, not at all scratchy or rough.

He snapped his eyes wide for a moment, then he smiled again, his dimple just above her thumb. "Lucki, would you mind very much if I kissed you?" As he asked, he moved closer, his hips between her knees, spreading her apart even more, so she had to wrap her legs around him. She had to. There was no other reasonable choice.

"Kiss me...? Yes, okay." All the melty tingles flushed through her, from scalp to toes and everywhere in between.

His eyes sparkled, he parted his lips, the smell of mint wafted toward her and his dimple deepened. That damn thing was going to permanently derail her brain from now on.

He leaned in more, draped his arms around her then brought her closer so she could wrap her hands over his shoulders. Her pussy was nestled hard against his waist, wedged in so pleasantly.

"Mmm-m." *Is this too forward? Maybe.* But years ago, when she had been younger and before all the bad stuff had happened, she'd been carefree like this. She'd enjoyed Beltane with a stranger—a near-stranger. Reuben was her protector, and everything about that rang true.

His lips on hers were soft, gentle and electrifying, all at the same time.

The fire crackled behind them, the room suddenly so warm that sweat began beading between her breasts. His kiss started a fire deep in her belly too, stoking the ache she'd been denying for months now — the longing, lusting and lonely pain. Gosh, she'd been so very alone.

"You taste like nectar," he said as he pulled away. "Sweet, just as I imagined."

"I'm hot," she blurted. "I mean, is it getting hot in here?"

He did that throaty chuckle she was growing to love. "Yes, we can fix that."

He made a move to pull away and she clenched him harder, keeping him in place. "No!" She smiled, suddenly a little shy, as she loosened her grip on his neck. "I mean, it's Beltane. The fire is appropriate, don't you think?"

"Indeed." He motioned between them and she reluctantly released her hold. "I was just going to get more comfortable."

She watched as he slowly unbuttoned his shirt, his big fingers moving deftly from one to the other to reveal a chiseled chest full of swirly curls of chestnut hair.

Her body coiled. Her pussy throbbed. Her panties were soaked.

Doooo it! "I should...maybe..." She should leave. She should snap out of it. She didn't know this guy—had just met him, in fact. And yet...and yet, what was life if it wasn't meant to be lived? Her mother would have called her a fool for denying the sexual impulses she felt toward Rueben.

"He's a hot hunk of a man, Lucki! Indulge! Live life, darling! You don't know how long you've got!"

As if Lucki hadn't spoken a word, he continued to strip off his shirt, pulling it from his upper body, his muscles flexing, moving so fluidly that she was mesmerized.

"You're hot too?" He motioned to her top.

She nodded, her throat dry, and gripped the bottom of her sweater, pulling it, with his help, over her head. Her hair cascaded against her back as it fell into place. She always loved that sensation. It was long enough to sweep the base of her spine, and that sent a chill through her that raised goosebumps.

He put his hands on her waist, his calluses abrading her just right, then rubbed his fingers against her skin as he pulled her closer into him. "You're so soft." He dipped his hands lower, gripping her ass so that her breasts were crushed against his chest. The hair there tickled her nipples through the lace of her bra.

He dipped his head and kissed her again.

"So soft," he murmured.

She ran her hands along his back and followed the cut of his muscles. The press of his bulging dick between her legs made her curse the clothing that blocked her from feeling more.

He kissed her again, probing with his tongue for entry, which of course she allowed. He was in her now, exploring as their tongues collided, their kiss deepening. He moaned into her mouth as he stroked her, making her vibrate on high frequency, making her want to pull him closer, deeper.

"I want to taste you," he said, panting as he broke their kiss.

Wait! Hadn't he just been doing that? Her fuzzy brain was lust-rattled.

He popped the button of her jeans and she understood.

"Yes, do that," she said with a gasp, helping him slip her jeans over her hips, her panties going along with them.

When he put his hands on her bare ass, her body clenched even harder. His touch was electrifying. She was near naked, her bra the only thing left, and she felt no self-conscious nervousness at all. Being a pagan and part of a Wiccan family, she was used to being sky clad and was comfortable in her skin. She was even comfortable with a near-stranger between her thighs. That was what her Beltane used to be like…until she'd met Shane.

Shane.

He had a dampening effect on her mood, so she pushed the memory of him away hard and focused all her attention on Reuben. Perhaps he'd be a good distraction for her, a way to overcome the sorrow she'd been feeling all year. *Too much loss for one heart to bear.*

His tender caresses made her shiver. Everything Reuben did was gentle, like he was honoring her body with each stroke—his lips against hers, trailing his fingers down her collarbone, pulling at the strap until it slipped from her shoulder, all so maddeningly slow, so deliciously torturous that she wanted to tear it off and offer herself for him to devour. He moved his mouth from hers, along her jaw, nipping playfully before licking a fiery path down her chest, tugging on the cup of her bra to expose her breast. She twisted her hand behind her back then flicked the clasp, letting it slide from her body so he could access what he wanted, whatever he wanted.

And he did.

Dear Goddess, he did.

Sucking her nipple deep into his mouth, his moan was a rumble against her flesh. He rubbed a callused palm against her skin before tenderly stroking, rolling the hardened nub between thumb and fingers, making her groan. She tilted her head back, her legs spread wide and invited him there next. *Goddess, please, move this man along.*

While he licked and sucked away at her nipples, he slid his hand down her side, caressing along her hip, until finally, *finally* he glided over her sensitive clit. She jolted like his fingers were high voltage then rolled her hips so he'd do it again.

Yes! Yes! Yes!

He chuckled but didn't stop, dipping his finger inside her, wedging it in like she was super tight, a virgin to his massive digits. He moaned again, moving his lips away from her breast so that he could suck her cream from his finger, locking eyes with her as he did, clearly savoring her taste.

It made her giddy to watch him — her body hot with desire, his attention intoxicating.

Who is this guy?

Does it really matter?

Yes.

No.

She reached forward to run her fingers through his hair, pulling him toward her so that she could kiss him. He obliged, moving into her once again, his lips on hers, delving his tongue deep, so intensely that it took her breath away. She tasted her cream in his mouth and she liked it. He moved his fingers back inside her, slipping along her pussy lips. He rubbed the heel of his palm against her clit, making her writhe into him.

"You are so beautiful, Lucki," he cooed, pulling his lips away with a smile and a wink.

She bit her bottom lip. He groaned. Then he licked her straight down from her neck, over one breast, along her stomach, right to her pussy.

"Ahhh, yeeeessss," she moaned, sinking back on the plush cushions of the couch.

She brought her fingers to her breasts, molding her hands to briefly cup herself, gliding along her skin — which *was* super soft — and up to her nipples, which were hard and achy. She pinched and flicked while Reuben did the same to her clit, thrusting his talented tongue inside her then twitching her clit, nipping with his teeth, then sucking her there too. It was maddening. It was blissful. She arched her back, hardly able to contain herself.

It didn't take long for her to come all over his face. Her orgasm rose swiftly, like a thunderstorm in her body, cascading over her with shuddering gasps of pure pleasure. And the look of satisfaction on his face made her want to giggle uncontrollably.

But it also made her want to return the favor.

So once her legs stopped quivering and he sat back, she pulled him up her body with a tug on his arm, her sensitive skin on fire as he kissed his way back to her lips. The smell of her all over his beard made her body whimper with need.

"My turn," she said against his lips, nipping there before pushing him to the side, making him take her place as she kissed her way down his torso, licking and sucking his nipples, snaking her hand down to pop the button on his pants.

She didn't hesitate, not even when his cock popped out from his pants and fell across her palm with a heavy thud. Okay…it didn't make a sound, but it sure felt like it would thud. The thing was huge, hard and beading pre-cum, which made her mouth water even more.

She looked up at him, her eyes wide, a smile tugging on her lips. "Well, you don't see that every day."

Reuben's eyes were heavy with lust. He nodded, urging her to continue, his hand in her hair, stroking through the strands as he moved off the couch to lie on the floor.

She nodded too, moving with him, straight to the tip of his dick, dabbing with her tongue, teasing, tasting that beading pre-cum.

"Mmm-m." She parted her lips, letting some saliva drip down as she cupped the tip of his dick with the ridge of her mouth.

His balls were massive too, heavy and silky, his hair trimmed neatly there. She appreciated a man who groomed. She palmed his sac, using her fingers to stroke gently as she licked her way down to the base of his cock, lubing him up with a mixture of his cum and her spit, flattening her tongue against the salty flesh of his dick until she got to his balls. She cupped him with her mouth, breathing around his sac, heating his flesh, soaking his skin as she stroked him with her tongue. He undulated his hips, rocking gently. His moans made her pussy weep all over again.

Goddess, I could do this all night.

She sucked on his sac, giving it all the attention before finally making her way back up his rigid dick, slipping over the tip once again and attempting, which was near impossible, to take him all in. Her mouth was big enough to accommodate the girth, but even she wasn't sure that she could deep-throat his length. So, she took in what she could, rolling her lips down as far as she dared, pushing on the gate of her throat, stroking the flesh below with her fingers. He didn't seem to care that she couldn't take him all. His eyes were on her, a lusty stare that had her reaching down to stroke her clit. But he stopped her before she could reach her goal. He delved his fingers into her pussy, so she flipped herself around, her ass in his face, earning her a groan that sounded like appreciation, then devoted all her attention to getting him off.

She sucked, he stroked, she rubbed, he flicked. Before long, both of them were a writhing, moaning orchestra. Her body coiled in tune with his. He arched his back and bellowed. Her climax matched the beat of his cum as it spurted in her mouth, hitting the back of her throat. She swallowed as she rocked her hips, riding out the last of her orgasm, panting as she sucked everything he had to offer and took everything he had to give.

She collapsed next to him, her head at his hip, watching as his dick pulsed and his chest heaved. He laid a hand on her calf, rubbing her skin with tender strokes.

"I like your taste, sweet girl." He heaved himself up, his hand on her knee then slipped down her body. "I'd like to taste you again."

Lucki giggled, then she parted her legs with a smile. "Be my guest." No way would she turn down another orgasm. "I'm all yours."

"I'm going to eat you alive." His eyes flashed with a predatory hunger that made Lucki shiver. He licked his lips, then did exactly what he'd promised to do.

Chapter Three

Reuben

"You didn't waste much time, did you, Reub?" Wren had an edge to his voice, as usual.

Too early for that. Reuben smiled in response, knowing it would get under Wren's skin more than anything he could say. He poured himself another coffee, indulging in a long-neglected treat.

"She's young." Wren huffed, crossed his arms and leaned against the doorframe of the kitchen. He'd turned his nose up at the coffee, but Reuben knew that the smell of frying bacon had piqued his interest.

"She's not *that* young." Her license said twenty-nine. A ripe age if Reuben said so himself. His mind drifted to the night before and the way she'd moved her body for him, how she'd purred under his touch. His cock came to life and Reuben's smile was impossible to contain. She was gifted with her tongue. He could only imagine what sinking himself in that sweet pussy would do to him. They hadn't gotten that far, though.

She'd been exhausted after her long day of travelling and he'd insisted she get some sleep.

There was time. Not much, true…but enough. She'd been a willing partner last night and he guessed that she would be so again.

"Her name… It's foolish," Wren scoffed.

Reuben shrugged. "You're nitpicking." He returned to the bacon on the skillet, moving it around so it wouldn't burn. The cats were taking an interest in the smell of cooking meat as well. They wouldn't eat it, finicky things, but they liked to nose around all the same. "She's perfect."

Wren came up next to him, plucking an uncooked strand of bacon right out of the pan and gobbling it down.

"That, my friend, will make you sick," Reuben said, pointing the spatula at his nose.

Wren swatted it away. "You wish." He moved to the other side of the counter, not offering to help in the meal preparation, which was probably for the best since they both knew Reuben was the better cook. Rusty, perhaps, but at least he knew his way around a kitchen, and he enjoyed the domesticated routine he'd abandoned years ago.

"She's a redhead," Wren said.

"You like redheads."

Another scoff.

It had been so long since they'd had a young woman in the cat house. Too long. Wren had obviously given up hope about three Cat Keepers ago. The selection of chosen ones that Scout kept sending had been laughable…until it wasn't. After the last recruit, a sixty-five-year-old with a nasty temper, Reuben had had to wonder if they'd done something to offend the old man — or perhaps he'd just lost his mind completely.

"She's sweet and earnest." Reuben moved the bacon around. "Give her a chance at least. The cats like her." And in the meantime, Reuben would take full advantage of Wren's hesitation. Lucki was a vibrant woman who seemed to enjoy sexual exploration — something he would never shy away from.

"The summer solstice is less than two months away. You think you can secure her commitment by then?"

Reuben only smiled in response. *Piece of cake.*

"Mm-m, something smells delicious."

Lucki walked into the kitchen, wearing a pair of purple pajama pants slung low on her hips and a tank top that didn't leave much to the imagination. Her nipples were perky this morning, not that Reuben minded.

"Oh...hi!" She stopped short at the sight of Wren.

And he was a sight. Tall, almost as tall as Reuben, with long, tousled hair, a scruffy day's growth of beard and piercing blue eyes. Reuben had seen what passed for models these days in fashion magazines, and Wren had them beat by a mile.

But the attitude...sheesh... The attitude was what killed it all.

"Wren Wolf," he grumbled, hardly looking in her direction as if he couldn't care less, when they both knew that she was the center of all attention right now.

"Hi, Wren, I'm Lucki." She held her hand out to shake, her chipper mood not dampening in the least.

Another reason to like her.

Wren looked at it for a second, turned his lip up then walked out of the room.

"Ahh, did I say something wrong?" Lucki's pretty face twisted, confusion and hurt shining, her hand held limp in midair like she couldn't actually believe that had happened.

"No, ignore him. He's not a morning person." Reuben put the tongs down and turned to face her fully, getting all up in her space so he could kiss her good morning.

She put her hand on his chest, giggled a little then ducked away. "Sorry." She bit her lip and pointed toward the sunlight streaming into the window. "Morning brought a reality check."

Reuben's smile faltered. "You didn't enjoy last night?"

"Oh no, don't think that." Her face reddened, her freckles popping as she laid her hand over her chest. "No, I enjoyed myself a lot—a lot, a lot. I just..." She waved her hand around. "I'm new here. And I don't want you to get the wrong idea."

He moved in close once again, taking her hand in his and bringing it to his lips. "Nothing to be embarrassed about, sweetheart."

"Oh no, I'm not embarrassed... I just...last night, it was great. Really great." She tugged her hand away once again. "It's just that it was also impulsive and well, Beltane, you know," she said with a wistful smile. "I'm just really looking forward to being friends with you. That's all."

"Friends?" His heart dropped right down to his gut.

"Ya, with benefits, I guess. No turning back the clock on that one, right?" She laughed. "I just don't want to give you the wrong idea. I'm not the kind of girl who's expecting romance after a...well...you know...hook-up."

"A hook-up?"

Reuben heard a faint snicker from the hallway. Wren was listening, gloating in this setback. Wren apparently didn't believe it would come easy—and maybe he was right.

"I see." Reuben turned back toward the bacon. He couldn't keep the disappointment from his face, and he didn't want to upset her.

"Don't get me wrong... I really had a good time last night." She sighed. "Ugh, I'm terrible at this kind of thing... I just...I had a really bad break-up a while ago and I'm not looking for anything more...serious right now."

Someone had broken her heart. Reuben could sympathize with that. He nodded slowly. Securing Lucki's commitment to the Brotherhood would maybe not be such a piece of cake. But he wouldn't be Reuben Bear if he wasn't up for the challenge.

He plated her food, piling it high with something of everything — eggs, toast, bacon, potatoes. He could win her over — of that, he was certain.

"I like to have fun too." He turned toward her, his smile back in place.

Her eyes were wide as she looked from the plate to his face. "Fun?"

"Yeah, things don't have to be so serious around here."

"Oh!" She took the plate from his hands. "Okay, great."

The cats were playing coy with her, hanging around the doorways, under the table, on the windowsill, but not yet harassing her for attention. He hadn't been lying when he'd told Wren that the cats liked her. He could see it in their eyes. Fearful would have them bolting from the room, but curious and intrigued had them checking her out...cautiously optimistic. Considering what they'd been through over the past few Cat Keepers, he didn't blame them.

She smiled as she took a seat at the breakfast nook. Two cats jumped up on the chairs on either side of her.

She looked down at them but didn't force attention on them. *Good sign.*

"I'll give you a tour of the place once you've eaten." Reuben joined her with his own plate piled high.

"I should probably get the clinic set up, so I can give each of them a once-over, to make sure everyone is healthy."

"Oh, no need for that," Reuben said between mouthfuls. "The cats are all perfectly fine."

She looked up at him, her eyes wide, her fork midway to her mouth. "They're fine? But I thought I was here to perform some basic vet stuff. I d-d-don't have my d-d-degree, not completely." She stammered a little, rushing through her explanation as she set her fork down. "But I've had a lot of training. I can perform the basics —"

Reuben put his hand on her hers. "You're perfectly qualified to check them over. I'm just telling you that it would be a waste of time. They're all in perfect health."

"They've been checked out recently?"

Reuben started to nod, realizing that now might be the best time to fill in some gaps for Lucki. He opened his mouth.

"Reub," Wren growled from the foyer, "we have company."

Reuben's hackles rose, and he pushed himself from the table with a growl. "Stay here. Do *not* come outside."

"What's going on? Is someone in trouble? One of the cats?" Lucki rose too then started for the hallway.

He silently cursed his lack of tact. "No, no, nothing like that." He stopped her, blocking her from taking another step toward the door with his bulk. "Just stay put, okay? We have some business to attend to." He motioned toward the cats that had started to file into the kitchen. "Why don't you herd the animals? Take a head count. There should be a hundred felines — plus the one you brought."

Then he left the room, but not before hearing her mumble about the impossibility of herding cats.

He smiled to himself then scoured his face completely to get rid of that evidence. Wren was already outside. Reuben closed the door behind him to keep Lucki from hearing what was about to go down.

"Rafi, Camden, Alessandro, to what do we owe this honor?" These three beasts were the henchmen of Mistress Angelica and not welcome in town. Reuben's muscles rippled under his shirt and anger punched through him, making his heart thunder.

"Don't play the fool, Reuben. You know why we're here." Alessandro eyes glinted as he pulled a card from his coat pocket. It had a wax stamp on it that Reuben knew very well — an emblem of a scrolling A with filigree all around. Quite beautiful, if it weren't so tainted by the hand that had pressed it to the paper.

"Our mistress issues a duel notice to the Cat Keeper of Weeping Falls. Summer Solstice. Midnight."

"Pomp and circumstance." Reuben waved his hand in dismissal. "We are aware of the time of year."

"Well, we could just kill the Keeper now," Camden drawled with his lazy way of speaking, as if he had no cares in the world. "What did your Scout send this time? Another terminally ill human? Or a sixty-year-old past her prime? Or, wait! The best, that prima donna... What was his name?"

It was true. Scout had been sending up some odd choices over the past few decades.

Angelica issued her yearly duel notice all the same, but when the time came for battle, she rarely showed up. This year, with Lucki, would be different. This year, with all things considered, there was an excellent possibility that the Cat Keeper would be bonded to the Brotherhood by Summer Solstice and thus empowered with a magic that would rival Angelica's.

"You'd have to go through us," Wren growled back, his teeth bared.

Reuben winced, wishing he and Wren had strategized about how to handle this. In previous years, there'd been no fuss, and he'd wished Wren didn't act on impulse as often as he did. Alessandro, Rafi and Camden knew of Lucki's arrival but would not know enough about her to realize that she was a viable threat. Wren's malice toward the henchmen was a dead giveaway.

"You like this one, huh?" Camden narrowed his eyes. "I sense a change about you two."

The door opened behind them.

Rafi's eyes went wide and his body straightened, coming to attention like a solider in battle. A flash of fang and the slit of pupil confirmed to Reuben that Lucki had just ignored his instructions.

"Get back inside," Reuben yelled, turning to hit Lucki with a glare, only to see her eyes growing wide as well, her mouth gaping open, her finger pointed and trembling.

"Fuck!" Wren roared.

Reuben sensed the crest of power and it was enough to ignite his own. With one last look at Lucki, he tried to will her back inside, knowing that the shock of what she was about to see might have her running down the porch steps and straight into a predator maelstrom.

Angelica's henchmen were hunched with the agony of their transformation to wildcat warriors.

Reuben's veins pumped full of adrenaline. His muscles screamed as his body contorted, fur erupting down his arms. Fangs dropped from his gums. He lifted his head and roared to the sky.

He was a ruthless hunter, a raging mass of fury and, most importantly, a fierce protector.

Wren's transformation was seamless—one minute human, the next wolf. He launched himself at one of Angelica's wildcats, his fangs extended, claws out to strike. And Reuben, now fully in his bear form, huffed and puffed his chest out to bellow in the direction of his foe, who was leaping toward Lucki.

Reuben caught the cat mid-jump with a swipe to the side, sending him flying to land a few steps down from where Lucki still stood.

Reuben's beastly eyes met hers, seeing understanding shining back at him. There was disbelief there too.

Her piercing scream cut him through to the heart just as another cat jumped on his back, fangs and claws sinking in deep.

He lifted his head and roared as rage shuttered his vision in red.

Chapter Four

Lucki

Lucki had seen a lot of crazy things in her life, but never, never anything quite as crazy as five humans spontaneously combusting into wild animals.

Her first instinct was to scream—not because of the impossibility of shifters, but because those humongous cats were obviously gunning for her and their claws and fangs looked sharp...very, very sharp.

The bear and the wolf were busy battling the massive beastly looking cats, somehow keeping them at bay. Lucki's body had frozen the instant she'd seen the men transform, but that fear just as suddenly turned into an intense need for flight. She started to take steps backward, not daring to look behind her for fear that something would come at her from the front.

The bear let out bone-jarring roar and Lucki's heart stutter-stepped at the ferocity of it. It was hard to believe that this was the man she'd fooled around with the night before. She wasn't the type of person to deny the truth, though, especially when it presented itself right in front of her.

Reuben was a bear.

Wren was a wolf.

Lucki was officially in one fucked-up wonderland.

"Murrrow!" A chorus of cat meows touched her ears, and she dared a quick glance over her shoulder. There had to be at least thirty cats milling together at the door, none daring to step foot onto the porch, despite the fact that Lucki had left the door gaping open. They all looked about as freaked out as Lucki felt and seemed to be beckoning her inside.

Right, because the cats are smarter than I am, obviously.

Lucki turned on her heel then closed the distance to the front door. The cats all moved in a wave of fur out of her way so that she could slam the door closed and turn the lock. Even with her back pressed against it, she heard the guttural roars of the beasts fighting outside. It didn't feel safe and, yet, somehow, she knew that Rueben and Wren would fight to the death to protect her.

"What is going on here?" She wrapped her arms around her waist.

Shifters, Lucki. Right outside the door. That's what's going on.

She blew out a shaky breath then twisted so she could peer out of the stained-glass side panel window. All she could make out were blurs of fur, moving so fast that she couldn't see who was who and didn't know if that meant the home team was winning or losing. She pulled back then pressed herself to the door once again. "What should we do?"

The cats meowed and purred, swirling around her legs in a way that made her move, one unsteady step at a time, away from the door. Her hands shook so badly that when she went to brush some hair out of her face, she nearly poked herself in the eye. One of the cats, a large black-and-white tom, nipped at her pant leg, and when she didn't start moving faster, he latched on with his teeth and gave her a strong tug. "Okay, okay, I'm going."

Strange cat behavior...but maybe not strange, considering what was going on outside.

Lucki and the cats moved en masse down the long hallway that went from the front of the house all the way to the back. She passed the kitchen and the living room, the main staircase, plus a few closed doors that she had yet to investigate, straight to the back door, which led to a closed-in glass portico. "Out here?"

She stepped out into the portico, then shielded her eyes from the glare of the sun. The cats kept swarming her, more and more of them adding to the writhing bunch who were nudging and cajoling her forward. Their meows were more insistent now, a sound so desperate that it made her stomach clench and twist.

They wanted her to open the door that led into the back garden, but outside seemed so much more dangerous than inside.

One of the cats hissed. Another one bit her calf — not hard enough to break skin, but it was enough to send the message. "Ouch! Okay! Okay!" She opened the back door then took a step outside. She had her runners on but didn't have a coat, and the chill in the air was enough to have her all goosebumped within a second. She wrapped her arms around herself but didn't move.

The back garden was brimming with all manner of greenery — shrubs, towering trees, flowers. It was like a dense rainforest of vegetation. "I don't have a coat."

Why am I talking to the cats?

She started to turn back, but one of the cats lashed out and dug its claws into her hand, tearing at the skin with a warning growl.

Motherfuc –

"Ouch!" Blood welled immediately. "Bad kitty!" She covered her bleeding hand with her sweater sleeve. The cats surged forward, hissing and acting all pissed off. Another cat moved quickly, jumping up onto the furniture, coming toward her like it was going to launch itself out of the door and at her face.

That got her moving.

She took a few more steps along the gravel path. Why were the cats turning on her? Rejection battered against her. *This is insane.* Her life was in danger, those three massive wildcats definitely wanted her...so, she had other things to worry about and should not be concerned about the cats pushing her out of the house.

She looked back at the door and found all the cats crowded there, watching her expectantly from the portico. All one-hundred of them, it seemed. The aggression was gone. There was no more hissing. They'd gotten what they'd wanted. She was out of the house. Only Mr. Whiskers dared to venture out with her.

"You won't abandon me, will you?"

He trotted past her down the path and she watched him disappear into the dense foliage.

"That's it?" Now why did she feel like she was the sacrificial lamb here? The cats wanted her out of the house—maybe because they sensed she was the target of the wildcats at the front of the house? Or maybe they knew something she didn't know about the back garden? "It's cold out here." Her breath came out in a cloud, despite the sun beaming down through the canopy. Her hand stung from the cat's swipe. She dared a look at the scratches. The bleeding hadn't stopped, and she would have liked to wash out the cuts, but no way did she want to run the gauntlet of angry kitties again.

She briefly glanced at the path. Her gut told her to run, to get as far away as possible. A pounding sense of urgency had her taking a few more steps down the path.

The cats were all silent and staring, as if agreeing with that instinct. *Run, Lucki. Get as far away as possible,* their silent eyes seemed to say.

Nothing felt safe right now. Her mom would know what to do. She would have swallowed this situation without flinching and would have known exactly what decision to make.

"Trust your gut, Lucki. It'll never steer you astray."

With a gulp, she turned to the path ahead and moved quickly after Mr. Whiskers.

The back garden went from a wonderland of flowers and bushes to dense forest with little warning. One minute she knew she was still close to the Lady Clover's house, on a path that she felt certain she could follow back if she needed to, and the next she couldn't tell which way was the right way and what direction she was actually traveling in. She couldn't even see the sun, and the temperature was dropping rapidly now that she was in the forest. With chattering teeth, she pushed on, desperate to catch a glimpse of Mr. Whiskers and his flash of fur moving up ahead between the trees.

This is foolish. What am I doing?

She scanned all around and saw nothing but trees and more trees. The birds had stopped chirping sometime in the last few minutes, and all Lucki could hear was the crack of her steps on the branches and leaves under foot. She moved a little more slowly now. "Mr. Whiskers?" she whispered. "Where are you?"

The throaty, rough *kee-eeee-arr* of a hawk sounded overhead and Lucki snapped her gaze up. If there was a hawk flying around, Mr. Whiskers might be the target. She'd known hungry hawks to attack the smaller and weaker of the colony she used to take care of. "Mr. Whiskers! Where are you?"

There was a crunch of noise behind her. Lucki spun then froze. Something was moving through the trees — a dark shape that was coming closer and closer.

Kee-eeee-arr! The hawk landed on a tree branch next to her, close enough that she could see blood on its beak, far enough away that she could appreciate its size as being abnormal. "Why do all the predators have to be so huge in this place?"

Was she about to be killed in some freak animal attack? *Stupid Canadian girl gets lost in forest and ends up dead.* Death by? Lexi squinted into the darkness ahead, her ears picking up on the slow, deliberate movements of something stalking her. She took a step backward, trying to put some distance between her, the hawk and whatever was coming for her through the trees. She didn't like the look in the hawk's eyes.

Were they scavengers? Was it waiting for her to die so it could peck at her bones?

Oh, Goddess. Her skin was tight and hot — her heart in her throat, threatening to beat itself out of her mouth, presumably so it could run for its life and get the hell away from her.

A low growl echoed around Lucki, sending instant shivers up and down her spine. *Mountain lion.* "Bad, bad idea to come out here. Bad idea!" She moved backward quickly, pressing herself against the trunk of a large tree. She was *so* going to die.

The hawk made its eerie wail again before taking off, shooting up through the trees. *Oh great, even the predators are on the run.*

Why, why had she listened to the cats? How was that even a thing anyway? Why hadn't she run up the stairs and locked herself in her bedroom? She could be hiding in her closet rather than trying to hold herself up against a giant tree. She took a step. Maybe if she hid in some brush, the lion would keep going? She caught sight of Mr. Whiskers sniffing the base of another tree, seemingly not a care in the world, right in the path of the mountain lion.

"Mr. Whiskers!" she hissed. The cat ignored her, naturally. "*Pspspsp.*" Her desperate voice came out with a croak.

The lion roared again. Lucki jumped, her body vibrating hard and fast. There was no way she wouldn't pee her pants before this was all said and done.

Mr. Whiskers shot his head up, his back fur stood at attention and he slowly, carefully, started to move backward just as the biggest mountain lion Lucki had ever seen broke through the trees.

Its dark eyes locked on Lucki. It licked its mouth and flashed its fangs. It stalked toward her at a steady clip.

I am lion food. Sadly, her inner crazy cat lady was clamoring to reach out and pet the damn beast. *His fur looks so soft.*

She somehow slid her body down the bark, ignoring the bite of it against her back as she frantically searched for a rock or a stick or something she could use as a weapon.

The big cat kept moving. Lucki's search was fruitless. How was it possible that she'd picked a tree that had no debris around it?

Finally, she touched something solid. She curled her fingers around the stick then quickly swung it in front of her. Mr. Whiskers let out a loud, mournful-sounding yowl, but one glance from the mountain lion and his yowl died in his little kitty mouth.

"I don't want to die." She pushed herself to her wobbly feet and held the stick out in front of her as if her arms weren't shaking so badly that she could actually do something to defend herself.

The hoarse cry of the hawk returned, and Lucki tore her eyes away from the approaching lion to watch as the hawk swooped in, as if it was about to go after Mr. Whiskers. A scream lodged in her throat when one minute she was sure her cat was about to become hawk food and the next she was witnessing the impossible... again.

In a flurry of feathers and fog, the hawk disappeared and in its place was a man—a short, lean, completely naked man. He had a crooked smile that would have been totally disarming if there weren't a mountain lion stalking toward her still. He bent down and picked Mr. Whiskers up. "This your cat?"

Lucki frowned. *Huh?* She felt something warm and wet press against her hand, right where her cat scratch was. She looked down in horror to find the mountain lion licking her skin. Its tongue was huge and so were its fangs. It had bypassed her ridiculous stick and was in the process of licking her again.

"Quit it, Julian. You're freaking the poor beauty out." The naked man grinned as he said that, casually stroking Mr. Whiskers' head. "I'm Benjamin Hawk, by the way."

Lucki gulped. "B-B-Benjamin?" *Hawk*. Her brain clicked like the pilot light was trying to snap on. *Reuben Bear. Wren Wolf*. "Oh, Goddess. You're all shifters."

Right before her eyes, in another whirlwind of fur and dust, the mountain lion turned into a blond, buff god of a man. She looked up at him, her mouth agape. *How can they all be so freakin' gorgeous?* She flicked her eyes downward to confirm that he, too, was incredibly well endowed. "What do they feed you guys up here?"

"Julian Lion," he said as he took her hand. "We didn't know whether or not to believe Reuben's message, but the scent of your blood confirmed it for us."

She looked down at her hand, which still bore the scratches from the cat, now clean of any blood thanks to Julian's rough kitty tongue. "One of the cats scratched me," she mumbled.

"Smart feline," Julian said as he rubbed his thumb over her palm before raising her hand to his lips. His lips on her skin, so very gently kissing her, made all kinds of sparks flash through her body. *Cold, what cold?* Her body flared hot, so hot she wanted to take her sweater off. She wanted to giggle. She wanted Julian to kiss her again, but this time on her lips.

Instead, she gulped then cleared her throat. "Reuben sent a message?"

Julian didn't let go of her hand. He lowered it then nodded. "We didn't believe him at first. There have been so many Cat Keepers, you see."

"So many false Cat Keepers," Benjamin added. "We were taking our time getting here, not really sure…" He shook his head. "But we caught the smell of your blood and well, we just knew it was true."

"We raced to get here." Julian entwined his fingers with hers. "The felines drew blood in order to get our asses moving. They must have sensed that we were approaching."

"The cats? The ones at Lady Clover's?" Lucki shook her head. It was a lot to take in, even for someone who was pretty open to unusual things.

"They'll always have your best interests at heart, love." Julian smiled warmly down at her. "So, where is everyone? Why are you out here alone?"

Lucki's thoughts snapped to the battle taking place outside Lady Clover's. "There are beastly cats fighting with Reuben and Wren back at the mansion." Giant, ugly, monstrous-looking wildcats that looked more like deranged, deformed Sphinxes. Lucki shivered. "Reuben told me to go inside. The cats forced me to move out of the back door… I guess to find you two."

Julian shifted a look at Benjamin. "I'll go. You stay with…uh…what's your name, beauty?"

Julian had such green eyes, like the richest leaves, tinted with brown and gold. "Lucki," she croaked. "My name is Lucki Collins."

Julian smiled, lifted her hand to his lips once again and kissed her tenderly. "There are so many wonderful connotations to go with a name like that." He winked and Lucki was sure her panties slipped down an inch of their own accord. "We'll catch up later." In a flash, Julian was gone, the hulking mountain lion in his place.

"You and I will make our way back to Lady Clover's, shall we?" Benjamin held out his hand, while holding Mr. Whiskers in the crook of his other arm. The mountain lion let out a loud roar then bolted, disappearing into the trees in a flash.

"Are you sure it's safe there?" She moved tentatively toward him. He was dark where Julian was light. His eyes were a deep penetrating brown and his hair was a glistening chestnut that seemed to pull all the sunlight so that it almost looked like strands of dark gold were threaded throughout.

"It will be by the time we get back. Alessandro and his guys wouldn't be expecting more than Rueben and Wren, who are quite capable of handling themselves. Add Julian to that mix and they don't stand a chance." Benjamin snorted. "Julian has been itching for a good brawl for years now, so he'll make short work of whatever is left of the battle." He took her arm and encouraged her to wrap it around his. "Tell me everything, Lucki." He wasn't as tall as the others, maybe only an inch or two more than her five foot seven, but he was fit, his body compact and, without question, powerful.

"Everything?" She looked up at him, her brain still muddled from it all. "I just got here. I'm not sure I know everything yet."

Benjamin's laugh was full of warmth. He encouraged Mr. Whiskers to jump down so he could move one arm around her waist and entwine the other with her hand. It was all so strange, considering he was still naked as could be and seemingly unbothered by the cold, crisp spring air. "What I mean is, tell me all about you, Lucki. Where do you hail from? Who are your people? How did Scout find you?" He didn't give her a chance to answer before adding, "We were sure that old bat had lost his marbles completely, what with the last few Cat Keepers he's sent our way — too old, wrong pedigree, no magic whatsoever." Benjamin shook his head. "But you? You have it all. Youth, beauty, magic... You're brimming with all three. You'll be a wonderful Cat Keeper, Lucki. I can tell already."

"Wait a second..." She dug her heels in to stop them both from taking another step. "Magic?"

Benjamin looked at her with seeming bewilderment. "Of course, you'll need some kind of natural base of power in order to take hold of the magic we give you — or else how in the world will you ever defeat Angelica? That'll be a total bloodbath without magic. And to be sure, once she realizes how much power you hold, she'll be gunning for a proper fight."

"Um...defeat who? Fight who? What?"

Chapter Five

Wren

The boys are back. Wonderful. "You came too late...as usual," Wren grumbled as he dabbed at the weeping cut above his eyebrow with a towel. It still hurt like hell, but he'd live.

"Angelica's poisonous magic must be getting stronger if you're still bleeding, my friend." Julian perched himself on the kitchen table then grabbed an apple from the bowl next to him.

Wren waved his concern away. "We've been too long without a Cat Keeper. That's all. I'll be fine."

"I know you will." Julian took a bite from the apple, then talked around the chunk in his mouth. "But it's still concerning, all the same."

"Well, now we have the perfect Cat Keeper, don't we, fellas?" Reuben came into the kitchen all amped up and practically glowing from battle. Of course, he hadn't sustained any injury. The man was an impenetrable tank.

"Whether or not she is the one is yet to be determined." Wren leaned against the doorframe, his arms crossed — not looking for a fight, just stating a fact.

"Why? What's wrong with her?" Julian stopped chewing and snapped his gaze from Wren to Reuben. "She seems perfect to me. Her blood is ripe with magic."

"She doesn't want—" The sound of the back door opening and Benjamin ushering Lucki inside killed any further words coming out of Wren' mouth. He, like the others, all rushed toward the back of the house in order to make sure Lucki was all right. He would have laughed at himself for the reaction, but having a Cat Keeper in town brought out all their baser instincts, first and foremost being her protector. He wouldn't have been able to control himself, even if he'd tried.

"Are you hurt?" Reuben had his big meaty hands all over Lucki, checking for injury.

"I'm fine. Just a scratch." Lucki surveyed the crowd before her. Her pupils were dilated and she was trembling. Her gaze landed on Wren and he jolted like he'd just touched a live wire. "Are you okay? What happened to your face?"

Trapped by her eyes, Wren was suddenly tongue-tied. He wanted to fall into them, to gaze at her for days—just the two of them, with no other distractions. It wasn't just the color, which was an astonishingly vibrant green. It was the expression he saw shining back at him. He wanted to close the distance between them and take her in his arms. He wanted to kiss her for the concern she was showing him alone.

"Oh, no worries, beauty. That's just the way he looks all the time. Right, brother?" Julian gave him a hearty slap on the back to go along with his deep belly chortle.

A wisp of a smile fluttered on Lucki's lips while all the men got a laugh at Wren's expense. "I like his face," she said as she shifted a little closer to Wren. "I've got a medical kit in my room."

Wren gulped when she closed the distance and laid her hand on his cheek. Her touch was full of electricity, not because of any magic she was wielding but because he wanted so badly for her to be the *one*. "I'll be fine," he grunted. If she had control over her powers, she would have been able to heal him with that touch alone. But she didn't control her powers. She didn't even know they existed—and that meant she might not be the one to save them after all.

She frowned.

"Don't waste your time with him, beauty." Julian swooped in and wrapped his arm around her waist. He winked at Wren before hauling her away. "He's a surly one at the best of times."

"You two have been delinquent in your duties with Miss Lucki." Ben re-entered the back room after having slipped out to throw on a pair of track pants. Why Ben and Julian insisted on shifting naked was beyond Wren. Sure, it took a little more concentration to shift the clothing, but upon return, there was never any problem with the clothes rematerializing. "She is unaware of her duties as Cat Keeper."

"She just got here," Wren growled, not liking the accusation that he couldn't do his job properly. "Then Alessandro and his men arrived. They wasted no time this year." Which gave Wren a spark of hope that Lucki was indeed holding enough natural magic within her to make Angelica take notice. She'd all but ignored the last three Cat Keepers.

"I really have no idea what's going on." Lucki shrugged in a helpless way. "I thought I was just coming here to tend to the cats, but that's not what's really going on, is it?"

"It's a bit more than that, beauty." Julian guided her down the hall toward the front of the house. "Let's get you in front of the fire and warm you up. Your teeth are practically chattering."

* * * *

Reuben, ever the homemaker, insisted on tea and cookies as well as some fresh fruit and finger sandwiches. None of them needed the food, except for Lucki, but Rueben had always loved entertaining guests, forever clinging to his long-lost humanity.

They'd all piled into the less formal sitting room, which was more like a den with a rolltop desk and bookshelves lining each wall. Everyone, except for Wren, jockeyed for position next to Lucki. It was pathetic, to say the least. They were all coming off as desperate schoolboys looking for attention. Reuben, being the biggest, managed to bully his way next to her on the leather couch and took up nearly half of it with his size. Benjamin perched on the arm to Lucki's other side and Julian had pulled up an ottoman so he could sit as close in front of her as possible. Wren hung back, taking his usual spot leaning against the doorframe. He crossed his arms and waited for the posturing to stop. Their behavior was enough to send her running.

"I put a little of everything on here for you, Lucki." Rueben handed her a heaping plate of finger food.

"Thank you." Lucki took the plate and set it on her lap but didn't eat anything right away.

"Sugar in your tea?" Ben had a spoonful of sugar ready to go.

"Oh no, thank you. Black is fine."

"Are you still cold, beauty?" Julian started to get up, ready to stoke the fire to an inferno, no doubt, intent on everything and everyone in the room melting.

"Oh, no, I'm okay now."

Lucki glanced from Julian to Ben to Reuben with a weak smile. Wren could see that she likely wanted to run the hell out of there and hide in her room. *So much attention from such overwhelming personalities.* Even the damn cats were crowding into the room, taking up various spots all over, high and low, vying to get close to Lucki.

Wren shook his head. If he left it up to the lot of them, they'd run her off before nightfall. "You likely have questions."

Lucki snapped her eyes to meet his, an expression that Wren took as relief crossing over her face. "I do."

"We weren't expecting Angelica to send her beasts so soon." Rueben took her hand, his expression solemn. "I should have explained everything to you last night."

And why didn't you? Wren bit his tongue instead of blurting out that thought. He didn't want to call attention to Rueben and Lucki's activities the night before, because he knew it would only lead to the others becoming even more competitive for her attention. He also didn't want to embarrass Lucki. She was a sweet girl, and there was nothing wrong with celebrating Beltane however she saw fit.

"Who is Angelica?" Lucki asked. "Julian mentioned that I'll have to fight her or something?" Her voice rose with the last question and her gaze moved from man to man. It was obvious to Wren, by the way her fingers clenched on the side of the plate and how she darted her eyes so frantically, that she was barely hanging on to her calm demeanor.

"She's a wicked sorceress and she wants, more than anything, to take possession of the cats." Ben squeezed her hand. "The cats are very special creatures, you see."

"They would bolster her power, kind of like familiars to a witch," Rueben added. "She wants them, has wanted them for a very long time."

"What does that have to do with me, though? I mean, I agreed to come and care for the cats, but I didn't know there'd be some crazy sorceress wanting to steal them or battle me for them."

"As the centuries have gone on, the training of the Cat Keeper has slipped away, and the stories have been lost. Lady Clover's direct line of descendants ended sometime in the last hundred years, and since then, Scout has been searching for a suitable genetic match." Wren pushed off from the doorframe and moved into the room. "It's like finding a needle in a haystack. I don't know how he came across you, but it appears as though he may have found a match suitable for the role."

"Julian told me that Scout was the one sending Cat Keepers here—that he'd sent the wrong ones the last few times."

"Well, Julian wouldn't know beyond rumors, since neither he nor Ben bothered to meet the last few Cat Keepers who had been sent," Wren said dryly as he cut a hard glance in Julian's direction. "This is the first we've seen of the two of you in, what? Fifty years or more?"

Julian scoffed. "We came. We saw."

"We knew the last ones were without magic." Ben shrugged. "Why waste the time?"

"Some of us take our vows to heart," Wren bit back.

"Now, now, boys." Rueben took Lucki's other hand and patted it. "Let's not hash out our family qualms in front of Lucki." He looked down at her kindly. "We've been brothers in vows for a very long time — so long that old arguments refuse to die."

Lucki nodded, but Wren knew she was still so very confused. There was so much to teach her, so much to train her to do. The longer she went without the bonding magic the men would provide, the more time was wasted and the greater risk she was at from Angelica.

"You're the first Cat Keeper in a very long time who has magic," Wren said.

Lucki looked down at her hands, her legs, then back up at him. "How do you know? I mean, *I* didn't even know. How would Scout have figured it out?"

Wren had no idea how that old coot functioned on a daily basis as it was. "It's like an aura around you." He cleared his throat. "You shine." And he should have seen it right from the get-go. Even last night, when he'd been watching her in his wolf form, he should have noticed the spark to her aura.

Lucki smiled then, and it was the first real smile Wren had seen on her face all morning.

"He's right. It's emanating off you. The cats feel it. We feel it." Ben leaned forward. "You're the one."

"The one for what?"

"To finally defeat Angelica and end the curse that has kept us all trapped, tied to this place." Julian waved his other hand around. "You'll save us all when you win the battle, Lucki."

"This is crazy. I'm no hero." She shook her head. "I can't do any spells or anything. I mean, sure, I grew up in a pagan house with Wiccan worship. Mom and I, we did little incantations, used candles, gems, crystals...but that was mind over matter, you know? Nothing actually worked... If I had magic, wouldn't those spells have worked...like *really* worked?"

"Your magic is within you, beauty," Julian said, his expression indulgent. "You just need the right catalyst to bring it to the surface and the right bond to hold it steady."

Wren felt the collective intake of breath. Julian had thrown the word 'bond' out there so casually and Lucki hadn't even flinched. Maybe she wasn't all fun and games. Maybe she would accept what they had to offer.

Lucki sighed before covering her face with her hands. "When exactly is this battle supposed to happen?" Her voice was muffled as she rubbed her fingers down her face before looking up at them expectantly.

"At midnight of the Summer Solstice."

"What! That's in two months!" Lucki straightened, her spine suddenly like a ramrod. She passed her plate back to Reuben. "How in the world? I mean...not that I'm even agreeing to this...or believing that this is real...or that I'm capable of using magic in a responsible way. No. No. *No.*" She stood up, bypassing Ben so she could pace. The cats did their best to move out of the way, but there were so many crowded around that they could only give her a short circuit to move. "This is insane. You all are shifters! Shifters! I know I grew up seeing some weird as hell shit, but this is too much! I don't think my brain can handle all this today—or ever."

"Yes, we're shifters. Have been for a very long time. Our primary job...the very reason for our existence right now, is to protect you." Reuben jumped up then put his hands on her shoulders, halting her pacing. "We'll prepare you. We'll make sure you're ready. Don't worry, Lucki. You'll win this fight. We'll make sure of it. You're powerful...so, so powerful."

"I don't feel powerful. I don't feel any magic. I don't see what you all see. I'm not the one. How could I be?" Her voice cracked as she looked up at Reuben, and Wren's heart cracked a little along with it. She was so lost—within herself, to herself. He could see how shattered she was, too. It mirrored his own broken pieces.

Which was why, it was now occurring to him, he hadn't seen her magic shine before now. She was so lost that she couldn't even be true to herself. Her magic was so muted by her tumultuous thoughts that it dulled her very essence. It made him want to peek inside her mind to find out what was troubling her so much that it had rocked her off her axis.

Two months wouldn't be enough time to prepare her. She was right about that.

"You will—once we've marked you." Ben stood up too and walked toward her.

"*Marked* me?" She shifted to look at Ben, then Julian, then, finally, Wren. "What does that even mean?"

And there it was. It wasn't that she'd swallowed the word 'bond' that Julian had thrown down moments ago. She hadn't registered it.

"For you to be powerful enough to beat Angelica, you first need to have a natural base of magic, which you have, whether you believe it or not," Wren said. "But you'll also need our marks on you."

"In the bonding ceremony, we'll all mark you with our symbols. Then you'll be able to really feel your magic...and wield it properly." Lucki's mouth gaped open and Julian, finally sensing that he was sending Lucki into a panic, hastily continued with his explanation. "They're like tattoos. Girls your age love tattoos, right? These ones will fade when not in use, though. Cool, right?" Julian was aiming for enthusiastic, but again, Wren felt he was coming off as desperate...or maybe insane. "You'll be able to—"

"Hang on!" Lucki brought her fingers to her temples and closed her eyes briefly. "Bonding ceremony?"

Wren winced. *Moron.* This was a topic that needed to be dealt with in a different way, with a little bit of finesse.

"Of course, beauty, in order to receive our marks, we need to bond."

"Bond as in—"

"Bond the magic so you can manipulate it—bond to us so we're connected, lives intertwined, partners with us, beauty, for eternity."

Wren smacked his forehead. *Idiot!*

"For *eternity*?" Color rose fast and furious to her face, and even her ears turned bright. She crossed her arms and set a glare on each of them in turn. She was definitely ready to blow.

Great work, team.

"To all four of you?"

"One of us for every mood," Julian joked. "Why have one man when you can have more?"

Could this get any worse?

"Oh, no. No. No. No. *No*." Lucki clasped her hands to her head and beelined right past Wren, straight out of the room, mumbling about a pack of men being the last thing she needed in her life right now.

Wren slow-clapped. "Your wisdom in matters related to women once again shines through."

Reuben sighed as he rubbed his hand over the back of his neck.

"What? What'd we do?" Julian had his hands out like he really couldn't guess how he'd messed up.

"She got out of a bad relationship not long ago," Rueben said, his expression defeated. "She's scared of commitment…of being hurt again. I got the impression that the wound she carries is very deep."

"So, throwing an eternity with four men at her probably wasn't the best idea," Ben said.

"Do you know anything of the women of this time?" Wren barked. "Throwing an eternity with four men at any modern woman would get you slapped."

Julian shrugged.

Ben shook his head but didn't look particularly contrite.

Arrogant pukes. "You two spend all your days running in the forest, ignoring your duties here, and leave us to keep house. You know nothing of these modern times. You know nothing of Lucki, barging in here like you have everything all figured out. Now you've sent her running. It wouldn't surprise me if she didn't just pack her bags and leave right now."

Rueben shook his head. "That could have gone better."

"Ya think?" Wren snapped.

"She's young, sexy, open-minded," Julian said. "The way she was looking at Ben and me? Well...it was definitely simmering. There's interest there."

"Oh yes, she's quite happy to be friends with benefits." Rueben slumped down onto the couch.

"Friends with benefits?" Ben screwed up his face.

"Casual sex. No strings attached. No commitment." Wren started walking toward the door. "Like I said, she may seem perfect, but she's likely not going to be 'the one'. We can't force a relationship with someone who doesn't want one, and we come with a lot of baggage. It would be better if we encourage her to leave, escort her out of town so she can escape before it's too late. Keeping her here is a death sentence."

"Fellas" — Julian raised his hands like that would calm the room — "we're centuries-old protectors, and we come from a time where women were wooed with just a few gestures. We know how to convince someone to want to be with us."

Wren scoffed but stopped walking.

"With all four of us turning on the charm?" Julian said. "She doesn't stand a chance."

"We can't manipulate her, Julian. If she's been hurt by a bad relationship — "

"We show her what a good relationship can be like," Julian insisted. "Two months to make her fall in love? I'm up for the challenge." He looked at Reuben. "You in?"

Reuben seemed dubious but nodded all the same. "I'm in."

"Ben?"

"You don't even have to ask. I'm in."

"Wren?" They all looked at Wren expectedly. "It's the closest we've come, man. Lucki has enough natural power to give Angelica a run for her money."

The possibility of that hung heavy in the room. To be able to end a two-hundred-year curse? To give the men freedom, no longer bound to Weeping Falls — no longer feeling the intense pull to protect the felines year after year? To have, after so long, the possibility of finding love, true love, with a gorgeous woman? Was hope for all that worth the heartbreak?

"A fool's mission." He shook his head then shrugged. "I'm in, for what's it's worth." Not that he thought they'd succeed. He'd heard Lucki when she'd said she wasn't looking for a relationship. He heard the truth in her words, along with the pain. "At least, I won't get in your way."

"Like I said, she won't be able to resist our charm. Trust me." Julian grinned and Wren got the feeling that they were about to start something that none of them were even remotely prepared to handle.

Chapter Six

Lucki

Lucki paced her room, moving from her suitcase to the closet, back to her suitcase, then to the dresser, but each rotation ended up with her taking clothes back and forth, not actually packing, not actually staying.

This was all too much. *Shifters. Eternal bonds. Magic. Some kind of battle?* Yeah, not what she'd signed up for.

A tentative knock on her bedroom door made her freeze mid-step. "Lucki?" It was Reuben's voice.

Lucki knew he wouldn't come in unless she invited him. He didn't come across as the kind of guy who would do anything without consent. "I just need time to think." Time to pack. Time to find a way to leave town without anyone trying to stop her. And yet...she kept cycling back to the words the men used..."*release us from the curse and save us all.*" Ugh! Damn her incessant need to help. Why in the world did she have to have a bleeding heart for hopeless causes? Everything about this was a hopeless cause. *I'm doomed.*

Reuben cleared his throat and it sounded like a bear grunting. Because…of course it did.

"I know that when I'm feeling overwhelmed and need time to ponder things, I often go for a walk."

Lucki stared at the door, a bundle of T-shirts in one hand. "Is that even safe?" Were there wildcat beasts roaming the town? What about the sorceress?

"It's safe for you to walk. Angelica can't step foot in town until the Summer Solstice, and her minions won't take the chance of venturing too close, not with all four of us here—not after this morning."

Lucki gulped back the lump in her throat. A walk would be a good way to sort out her thoughts, and she could use some advice from the townspeople. Sandy would tell her what was going on, and if not her, then maybe Andy would—or even one of the other people she'd met the night before. She had a gut feeling that if she could just talk to someone else, not one of these shifters, she could get her head straight about things.

Of course, she wished with every part of her that she could turn to her mom for advice. Her mom would know what to do. She'd weigh the pros and cons. Gosh, Lucki would love one more minute with her mom, just to see her smile. She would kill for an hour to have tea and chat.

Either way, Reuben was right. She needed out of this room and out of the house.

"Okay, maybe I'll go for a walk then." She put the shirts down in the drawer of her dresser. "Alone."

"Of course," Reuben said with an awkward-sounding laugh. "The town line is marked and Wren,

Julian and Ben are patrolling the perimeter, so you'll be safe."

And you? Lucki wanted to ask, knowing full well that Rueben had been left behind to keep an eye on her...or to maybe woo her in some old-fashioned gentlemanly way. She sighed. Part of her wanted to embrace what these men were offering her, the part of her that still believed in such foolish things like love and fated mates and building families that didn't come from blood but from something much more profound—respect, choice and a genuine desire to care for one another. Lucki's mom had indoctrinated her into the wider world of Wicca, and she'd been part of a coven from the time that she'd been a baby. That had all ended when her mother's illness had become too much for the coven to handle—too much for Lucki to handle, in all honesty. Lucki had rejected the coven just as much as they'd rejected her, and by the time it was all over, she had been way too immersed in her boyfriend's world to turn to the people she'd considered her family years before.

She'd grown up believing in all kinds of things that the average person wouldn't dare think, though—fairy-tale things that promised eternal love and belonging and magical relationships where everyone was blissfully happy and eternally content. She'd been raised with stories of love that transcended time, couples who defied death to be together, lifetimes of pure, uncomplicated joy. Magic had been woven into all those stories and fairytales, magic that Lucki had believed would manifest in true love—that prince in shining armor, the hero to slay the dragon. She'd believed that magic like that would come for her one day, and she'd thought she'd found it in Shane.

But now, there was a bigger part of her that believed in stone-cold reality...and her ex was her reality. She had baggage. She had pain. The fairytales she'd grown up with had primed her for a guy like him, a predator. During the time her mother was dying, Shane had pounced...like he'd had a homing ability to find the most vulnerable girls who were ripe for his charm. He'd found her and he'd swept her off her feet. She'd fallen hard. She'd fallen deep. And she had paid so dearly for that.

The fear of falling into that kind of hole again, after the battle she'd waged to pull herself out? *Yeah...no thank you.* She'd as soon be alone...with a hundred cats to keep her company and no men to be seen.

And yet, these men were different in so many ways. Obviously as shifters, but in other ways too — ways that she found intriguing. Like Reuben with his domesticated homebody warmth and Ben with that twinkle of mischief in his eyes. Julian and his school-boy energy and Wren with his impossible-to-ignore brooding that had already given her a glimpse of pain that matched her own.

She slumped down onto the bed. Tears burned the back of her eyes. A scream lodged in her throat. She wanted to punch something. She wanted to lash out. Scout had definitely left out a few details when he'd offered her the job as Cat Keeper.

Too good to be true. *What an understatement.*

Reuben moved away from her door. She'd been intimate with him the night before and felt no shame at all because of that. What she felt was disappointment, really. She was attracted to him. Hell, she was attracted to all of them in one way or another, and if it had been a normal situation where four guys were offering to bring her intense pleasure, she'd be all for it. Why not? She was a sexual woman with cravings of her own that she liked to indulge. She just didn't want the eternity of bonding that came with a relationship with these guys. So much hinged on that...so much that she still didn't really understand.

Ugh, her head hurt.

Fresh Alaskan air would probably help.

She pushed herself off the bed then grabbed a bulky fleece sweater. The sun was shining, and she needed some time to think. She opened the door to find a crowd of cats all milling there. They looked up at her expectantly, so she crouched down to pet each of them. "You're a bunch of pretty kitties, aren't you?" She ran her fingers over one of the tabbies' heads and got a loud purr in thanks. "I've heard you're all special kitties." She gave a little chin scratch here and a head rub there. What a dream! To have all these cats around her who wanted attention. It filled her heart with so much joy.

Too good to be true.

The cats left, one by one, after they got a good petting, so Lucki made her way down the front staircase, half expecting Reuben to appear.

She made it to the foyer without being noticed, so she put on her boots and grabbed a tuque and scarf, as well as some mittens, then opened the front door. "I'm going for that walk now." But there was no response, not from bear or cat. "Okay then." She stepped out into the crispy day and immediately knew it was the right decision.

Her lungs welcomed the fresh air. Her eyes adjusted to the brilliant spring sun and the rush of something close to peace seeped into her pores. She walked down the porch steps expecting to see signs of the battle she'd witnessed between the shifters, but there was no evidence of it having taken place, and for that, she felt even more relief. It was easier to pretend nothing was wrong when there were no signs to be seen. If she could just go back twenty-four hours and reclaim the unbelievable happiness she'd felt.

The best way to clear her head would be to take in the tourist attractions offered by the town. Even though Scout had told her it was off season and there would be very few tourists visiting, she paused in front of the tavern. That was another lie, wasn't it? Weeping Falls wasn't a tourist attraction. There would be no visitors from around the world coming here. Lucki shook her head. Had anything Scout told her been the truth?

She beelined straight into the tavern and was met with…nothing…nobody. *What the…?* It was right around noon. Why wasn't this place bustling with townsfolk?

"Murrreow?" A gray longhaired cat jumped onto the bar and regarded her as cats do, with its head titled to the side and its eyes narrowed.

"Where is everyone?" Lucki couldn't imagine the entire town sleeping in this late.

The cat started to lick its paw then groom its head. Lucki walked back to the swinging doors and peered out. There was no sign of movement anywhere—not in the barbershop or the apothecary, and not on the street either. If she craned her neck, she could see the town's border on one side, but no one was walking there either—not Wren or Julian or Benjamin. For all intents and purposes, Weeping Falls truly did feel like a ghost town.

"What is going on around here?" she wondered aloud.

"I guess I owe you an explanation."

Lucki spun around with a scream on her tongue. "Scout?" His name came out like a rockslide, crashing with too much noise.

The old man sat stooped at the bar, his long gray hair draping partially over his scruffy face, and Lucki realized that maybe she *had* completely lost her mind. He hadn't been there a second ago. "How did you—? Where did you come from?"

Scout shrugged one shoulder as he clasped his hands in front of him. "Been here the whole time."

Lucki's mouth dropped open. She looked from one end of the bar to the other. The gray cat was gone. "I didn't see you. It was just me and the cat—"

Scout cocked an eyebrow. "I'm one of the few who can change at will."

Lucki pulled a chair out then slumped into it. She didn't trust her legs to hold her up right now. "Are you saying that you're the cat who was just here a moment ago?"

"Lucki, after everything you've seen so far today, are you really asking that question?" Scout turned on the stool and braced his elbows on his knees.

Right. "So, you're a shifter too."

"All the cats here are," Scout started. "I'm just the only one who can change at will. Helps in the search, I guess. I can travel fast as a cat, get into small spaces, don't have to pay for transportation." He chuckled a bit. "That's how I found you, actually. Started hearing some whispers from the feral cat communities of a human who seemed special."

Lucki put her fingers against her temples. "This is all so strange."

"Which part?" Scout chuckled again.

"All of it?" She lowered her hands and shook her head. "The cats I'm caring for, Lady Clover's cats, are all shifters?"

"You're wondering where all the townsfolk are, aren't ya?" Scout nodded toward the tavern doors. "All one hundred of them?"

Lucki's eyes widened. "The townspeople are...the... You mean, Sandy and Mr. Rose are cats?"

"Yep. Cats by day, humans by night. It's part of the curse."

"I'm so confused."

"Yes, I would imagine that's a natural reaction for someone who doesn't know about this place." Scout shook his head. "It was easier when I was bringing Lady Clover's descendants up here. At least they had heard the stories and weren't as shell-shocked to learn that those tales were true. The last few Cat Keepers, including yourself, have been too far removed from the line to have heard any of the stories. Makes it harder to digest."

"Somewhere in my DNA is a link to Lady Clover?"

"Yes, it was another thing that drew me to you — that and the magic." He rubbed his hand over his face. "You're the first one in a very long time who has such natural power."

"Reuben and the others said the same thing." Lucki's thoughts flashed back to that conversation. "They said I can free them from the curse."

"Possibly." Scout shrugged. "It's a complicated curse, and you do have the raw magic in you. Depends on whether or not you'll commit to them."

"I don't understand why I have to do that? I mean, don't you think it's a little old-fashioned? We're talking an eternity here, right? What kind of crazy curse asks a woman to commit herself forever?"

"Old-fashioned!" Scout laughed and slapped his knee. "Well, the curse was cast over two hundred years ago, so yes, I guess the details of it are antiquated. No changing them now, though, and it is a curse, so by nature it isn't meant to be accommodating or easy on anyone."

"Two hundred…years…so Reuben and the others… the townspeople… Everyone has been existing this way for that long?"

"You can imagine why they are so thrilled to have finally found a Cat Keeper who can help." Scout stood then walked behind the bar. "Tea?"

"Um…sure, thank you."

Scout got busy pouring water into the kettle before setting it on the burner of what looked like a hot plate. "Angelica cast the curse two hundred years ago over a misunderstanding." Scout set out two teacups and saucers. "I can't rightly remember after all this time what caused it all, but it was something involving Lady Clover, I think. The boys would know." He moved around the bar area, collecting sugar, pulling out a container of milk and spoons. "Anyway, Angelica was a strong spell caster at the time, feared for her magic by many people but perhaps not feared enough for her liking—or maybe it was respect she was after." He shrugged. "Either way, she became enraged over some dispute and cast this incredible curse on Weeping Falls. As with most curses, though, there are unintended consequences for everyone involved, including the spell caster. For most of us, it's being at the mercy of the sun and moon. The cats, excluding me for whatever reason, are bound to the motions of the day and night.

When the seasons change and it's nighttime for twenty-four hours, they remain human for all that time. In the summer—"

"Oh, they stay cats for the whole time there is only daylight?"

Scout nodded. "You've got it." The kettle started to boil, so he moved around again and brought back two teabags. "Lemon?"

"Sure, I'd love some." She frowned. "So, Wren and the others were cursed to be shifters as well?"

Scout got to work cutting up a lemon. "No. They were already holding that magic as part of some kind of ancient brotherhood. They were just in the wrong place at the wrong time. A lot of them got trapped here. Some have been able to wander off, push the limits of the curse, perhaps live in misery farther away."

"Many of them? Like more than the four shifters who are here right now?"

"Oh yes, according to Rueben, there are quite a few in the Brotherhood and more than four who were here at the time the curse was cast."

Lucki's mouth went dry. They were crazy if they thought she'd bond with four men, let alone possibly more.

"But those others haven't been seen or heard from over a century. Well, other than the ones who went bad. You met Alessandro and the others?" He didn't wait for a response. "Anyway, Reuben and Wren stay here year-round, serving as the cats' protection, while Julian and Benjamin roam as far as they can, testing the limits of the curse's boundaries, monitoring the perimeter, I guess. We don't see them more than once or twice every fifty years or so." Scout poured the tea then slipped the lemon wedges onto the edge of each cup. He piled everything onto a tray then made his way over to her table. "The curse affected Angelica as well."

Lucki accepted her cup but waved away the offer of sugar and milk. "Thank you." She squeezed the lemon and waited for the tea to cool a bit. "So why do the cats need protection?"

"They're a source of great power. Little bundles of magic. You see, when Angelica cast her curse, she didn't know that it would draw on her power the way it does. The curse's demands weaken her, because when she cast it, something fractured, broke apart, split from her. She wants the cats because they're like a battery boost, a coming-home of her powers. One cat can sustain her for a while. This town used to have twenty thousand souls."

Lucki gulped. Now they had one hundred cats plus their protectors.

"Angelica has taken that many — stealing them away during the daylight when they are in their most vulnerable cat-like consciousness. They have magical power, yes, but not necessarily the wit to avoid her traps. Not all of them anyway."

"So, when the day turns to twenty-four-hour sunlight, Angelica has more opportunity to catch them."

Scout nodded, lifting his cup to his lips for a taste. "Like their feline counterparts, they do fall prey to curiosity, and they love the hunt. Some are wily enough to avoid capture, but still, every summer, we lose a few more."

"That's awful."

"It is believed that the only way to break the curse is to match its power on the same night that it had been cast all those years ago. That's where you come in.

Angelica only follows through on a duel notice to the Cat Keepers she feels might be strong enough to generate enough power. All others she ignores."

"Wait! Angelica wants to break the curse?"

"The shifters think she does, but I have other thoughts." Scout tapped his head. "Breaking the curse would free the cats from the spell that makes them magical, so I believe that she wants to transfer the curse. She wants to shift its draining properties to a new conduit."

"Me."

Scout nodded, his expression solemn. "I am sorry for that. If I'm right and she transfers the curse, she'll no longer be drained of power, but the magic that traps the cats in their forms will continue to build. She'll be able to pluck away the rest of the cats at her leisure and use them to fuel any number of devious spells she plans to cast." He reached over and took her hand. "But I do believe you can defeat her."

"And if I do? I free the town from the curse?"

"You'll weaken her to the point of obliteration is the hope, and yes, free us all from the curse."

"But I have to bond with the men for the rest of my life."

"For the rest of your *eternal* life." Scout had the sense to look ashamed about that and withdrew his hand from hers. "I know I've burdened you with a heavy load."

"You plucked me out of my life. You didn't give me all the information. It's more than a burden. You've cursed me too."

"It's possible that a shifter would have found you eventually, drawn to your innate magic. Being here, with these shifters who are trapped, does put a certain sense of obligation to it, I suppose." He sighed. "You can leave at any time, Lucki. Nothing is holding you here. You can get right into your car and drive away, never look back." He sipped his tea like this was the most natural conversation ever. "But you have to admit... You weren't exactly living your life back there, were you?"

His question hit like a hammer and she deflated. She couldn't argue that assessment of how she was handling things back home. Her mom had died years ago, but she'd never really come to terms with that grief. Her relationship with Shane had ended abruptly a year before. Then the cat sanctuary — her beloved job, her life — had burned to the ground and almost all her precious cats had died. When Scout had found her, she'd been existing like a zombie — hardly eating, not sleeping, barely functioning as a human. She hadn't been living, true, but she had still deserved full disclosure.

"You obviously know nothing about me if you think I can walk away from someone in need." She put her hands on her head and leaned into the table with her elbows. She was a bona fide bleeding heart — which meant she'd do many things to help, even if she didn't like the methods.

"And you may not have to bond with them. You might just be powerful enough to fight Angelica on your own."

Lucki snapped her eyes to meet Scout's.

"Lady Clover was." He shrugged. "At least, that's what I remember."

"If she was so powerful, then why is the curse still working?"

"She was powerful enough but ran out of time. She was building a spell, you see — one that she believed would counter the curse. On the fiftieth anniversary of the casting, she thought she had enough of the spell done to win the battle with Angelica, but something went wrong, and the spell wasn't quite right. She needed more time to test it. She realized that at the last minute and decided to sacrifice herself so she could cast a protection spell around the house and the town. It weakened her so much that Angelica made short work of her. At least she died knowing that the cats would be safe if they stayed in the town, more specifically in the house, where the spell is the strongest."

"But they don't stay in the house if so many of them have been taken by Angelica over the years."

"Well, they are cats, Lucki. How many cats have you known who obey all the time? And they're magical creatures, so they can open doors, unlock locks, even free themselves from cages if they want to. There's no one here with enough magic to stop them."

"Until now."

Scout nodded. "Until now."

"What if I find the spell Lady Clover started and finish it? Do you think I could stop Angelica then, without having to bond with the men?"

Scout regarded her closely. "You'd be better off with their marks. The power they can help you master is tremendous, but yes, I do believe you could defeat her if you train properly and devote yourself to harnessing the power that you have. You'll need to visit the circle, of course, to unlock your own power. If you finish the spell she started, it may work."

The circle? It was too much to filter through. "So where is the spell? How do I find it?"

Scout shrugged. "It's been lost since her death, I'm afraid."

Because...of course it has. "So how do I find it?"

Scout shrugged again. "Maybe start by asking the cats to help you. They know that house inside and out. Maybe they'll have some idea." He put the teacup down and yawned. "Enough chatter for the day. I need a cat nap. Good day, Miss Lucki."

Between one blink to the next, Scout went from a full-grown human man to a gray long-haired cat. The cat arched his back in a big stretch before jumping from the chair and sauntering off out the door of the tavern, leaving Lucki with a cup of cold tea and a whole lot of thinking to do.

Chapter Seven

Benjamin

"Where's Lucki?" The only thing on Ben's mind all day had been the deliciously tempting redhead and all her budding power. Even while in his hawk form, his mind had been whirring around just what to say, what to do, in order to convince her he was the guy for her.

"She's in her room." Reuben had been stress-baking all day and the house smelled amazing for it. He'd already created plates of cookies, two cakes and what looked like some kind of filo pastry. It had been many, many years since Ben had tasted something so decadent.

"I'm impressed that she can withstand the smell of all this." Ben waved his hand around while using the other to snatch a cookie. It was still warm. He popped it into his mouth and let the chocolate melt over his tongue. Gawd, it had been too long since he'd indulged in such a basic human joy.

"I took her up a tray. She hadn't eaten all day." Reuben kept kneading the dough in front of him. He had flour in his hair and a splattering of something else on his apron. "She didn't eat it all."

"How is she doing?" Julian walked into the kitchen wearing a low-slung pair of cut-off jeans and nothing else. His chest glistened with sweat. He froze mid-step at Reuben's scowl. "What? I was chopping wood for the fireplace."

Ben shook his head. He'd been chopping wood right under Lucki's window, probably hoping she'd catch sight of him working his muscles for her benefit.

"She's taking time to herself." They were likely all thinking it was a good sign that she hadn't cut and run yet. Reuben motioned with his head in Julian's direction. "Maybe put a shirt on? We do have a lady in the house."

"And this isn't the Victorian Era," Julian scoffed but left the kitchen anyway. He thumped his way up the stairs, presumably to get some clothes from his room.

"The cats were whispering." Reuben kept his eyes on the dough. "Something about her talking to Scout."

Ben didn't know the why or how of it, but Reuben had always been more sensitive to the cats. They spoke to him in their weird way. He'd explained once to Ben that it was a mix-and-match of language, images and emotions. It wasn't always coherent, but sometimes they told him things that mattered.

"The old coot is in town?" Wren rolled in looking exceptionally brutish with his hard eyes and tussled hair. "I'd like to talk to him."

"I'm sure he'll make that exceedingly hard to do." Ben laughed. For whatever reason, Scout was the only one of the townspeople who could change form at will.

Even so, for the time he did spend as a cat, just like the rest of the town folk, a bit more of his humanity disappeared.

After two centuries of cycling from human to cat and back again, the towns' people had seemed to develop fewer verbal communication skills and more animal-like behaviors. Ben had seen it with shifters too. If a shifter spent too much time in animal form, he tended to become more like the animal at all times and less like a human. Like Ben, Wren spent a lot of time in his animal form. Unlike Ben, his attitude showed for it. Scout wouldn't be offering himself up for a conversation with Wren any time soon.

Smart cat.

Wren grumbled something under his breath before heading up the stairs himself.

Ben watched him go, wondering if Wren would be the weakest link when it came to wooing Lucki. Ben might have spent the last fifty years or so living in the forest, but that didn't mean he'd forgotten that some women liked the rough and rugged Neanderthal type. Lucki didn't come off as that kind of woman. Then again, Ben had only had a handful of conversations with her. Would Wren scare her off or pull her in? Would they be able to balance out his abrasiveness with their charm? "Something I said?"

"He likes to shower after he shifts." Reuben shrugged. "We've gotten used to some of the modern conveniences."

They'd gotten used to being recluses, more like.

Too long without a woman around had all of them acting like rogues in one way or another. Julian was acting like a teenager, showing off his muscles and trying to impress her that way. Wren was being his usual dark and dreary self but now layered with a burning so intense that they could all feel it. Ben was itching to get Lucki naked so he could really show her what he was good at. Reuben was the only one who seemed to keep his emotions in check—trying to make sure Lucki was comfortable, not chomping at the bit to get her to make the commitment. Time was wasting away, and they all felt the pressure to protect her in the best way possible, but Reuben? He was holding it all together like a master.

A door squeaked open upstairs and they both looked expectedly to the back entrance of the room where a second set of stairs accessed the kitchen. By the light footfalls on the steps, it was obvious that Lucki was venturing down.

She looked like she'd gotten some sleep. The dark circles under her eyes were less obvious. Her skin had a healthier hue. She stood tentatively at the base of the stairs, one arm wrapped around her slender body and her hair cascading down her back.

Ben wanted so badly to run his fingers through all those silky-looking waves. He wanted to inhale her scent and bury himself in her. Everything about her was compelling, from the magic she had wafting around her like tendrils of ribbon to the way her lips curled into the sweetest of smiles.

"I'd like to cook dinner for you all," Lucki said quietly. "Then I'd like us to talk as a group. Together."

Reuben's eyes lit up. Talking was something Reuben always advocated for. "Of course! A conversation would be good, I think. I'll help you prepare dinner."

Lucki merely nodded in response.

"The pantry is fully stocked. The fridge and freezer too." Reuben talked so quickly that it was almost hard to follow what he was saying. He moved around the kitchen like a tornado, cleaning up, putting dishes in the sink. "I wasn't sure what you'd like so I ordered a store-full."

"Are you making bread?" She nodded toward the dough on the counter and took a few steps toward Reuben.

Reuben moved toward her too, closing the distance so that he was almost touching her.

Even that small action had his competitive instincts rearing into action. "I'll help too! I love to cook."

Reuben snapped his eyes up to meet Ben's, his forehead furrowed with a clear *what the hell?* He was lying, and it looked like Reuben was just about to call him out on it when Lucki put her hand on Reuben's and all eyes swiveled to that tiny gesture.

Ben's heart ramped up. His body coiled in an uncomfortable way. He wanted her to touch him. He wanted her to look at him the way she was looking at the bear. He narrowed his eyes. *Wait a minute...* She was looking at him like they'd shared something together. Like they'd —

"Reuben?" Lucki's soft voice and light touch sent a clear message. For Reuben there was tenderness already.

They had been intimate. He was sure of it. *That sly bastard.*

"Uh, yes, rolls, actually." Reuben cleared his throat. "I was getting ready to make some rolls."

"Perfect. I was thinking I could make my famous giant meatballs with spaghetti." Lucki didn't move her hand right away, and Ben smoldered with jealousy.

Something significant had already happened between Reuben and Lucki, some kind of emotional bonding or maybe some kind of sexual play. It had been Beltane the night before. Lucki and Reuben may have celebrated.

"I hope you're all okay with garlic." Lucki shifted her eyes to his, snapping Ben out of his envious thoughts.

"Sounds delicious." He moved around the island, wrapped his arm along Lucki's waist and tugged her toward the pantry. "Come on. Let me show you what we've got in here. Consider me your slave for the night."

Lucki didn't hesitate. She let go of Reuben's arm and molded herself into Ben like she belonged at his side.

* * * *

"So, you don't need to eat. That's what you're telling me." Lucki was washing up the dishes now that her meatballs were in the oven. Ben was at her side, having bullied his way into dish duty. He hated doing chores like this. He found them tediously boring, but he'd do just about anything to keep Lucki close by his side. Watching her delicate hands move in and out of the water had him thinking about all the things she could do with those hands that would hold his attention so raptly.

"We don't," Reuben replied before Ben could. He was standing at the stove, stirring the pasta, shooting quiet glares Ben's way every time Lucki wasn't looking. "But we love to eat."

"It's just amazing to me. You're all so big and powerful. I would think you'd need some sustenance." Lucki swept her gaze over Reuben in a way that made Ben want to growl.

"You don't have to be big to be powerful, beauty. Isn't that right, Ben?" Julian popped up out of nowhere, his hair damp and face shaved. He was fully dressed, looking refreshed where Ben suddenly felt unkempt and dirty.

Maybe he should have slipped upstairs for a shower too, but then he'd have missed his chance to be close to Lucki. "Compact guys can have a lot to offer." Ben flexed his biceps, which earned him a giggle.

Julian clapped Ben hard on the back as he swooped into the now-cramped space. "This smells delicious." He dipped his fingers into the bubbling sauce, pulling a gasp from Lucki.

"Julian, that's too hot. You'll burn yourse—"

Julian pulled his fingers out, a cunning grin on his face. "No worries, beauty. I'm impervious to pain." Which wasn't totally true... They all felt pain. It just took a lot to bring them down. Julian slipped his fingers into his mouth, somehow making that action seem so sensual that Ben could practically see Lucki melting. Julian closed his eyes as he circled his tongue around his fingers. "Mmm-m....so good." He opened his eyes to lock on to Lucki's and somehow made that seem sultry too. The message was clear and the heat in the room ratcheted up a few notches.

Ben watched Lucki's chest rise and fall rapidly, like she was trying to keep her emotions in check. She didn't look away from Julian, not even as a blush rose to her cheeks. *Brave, daring, intriguing.* This woman had it all.

"What a nice family portrait," Wren drawled from the doorway.

All eyes turned to him. He was fresh from the shower as well. His hair was drying, left loose to cascade over his shoulders. He hadn't shaved, though a few days' beard growth only added to his dark and dangerous look.

"I thought we could sit down together for a meal." Lucki turned fully so she could face Wren. "But then I found out you guys don't actually need to eat." She laughed awkwardly.

Wren's eyes softened for a split second before returning to his usual hardened glare. "No, we don't." That was it. No other words, just a sharp exclamation of fact.

Reuben winced. "Wren, why don't you pour some wine? Lucki wants to talk to all of us. Together."

"I have some things I'd like to say." Lucki's voice was barely audible.

Wren regarded her like she was a foreign object to study. Ben understood why Wren was so skeptical — he did — but the guy could ease up for the sake of the rest of them.

"Brother —" Ben turned toward Wren. If he had to, he'd slap some sense into the man.

Wren sucked in a deep breath, then pushed himself off the doorframe. "Red or white?"

Twenty minutes later they were all seated around the dining room table, platters of fine-smelling food all around them. It had taken some overly manly side conversations to work out where Lucki would sit and where each of the men would be in relation to her. Wren was the only one who didn't seem to care, so he got the chair opposite her and farthest away. Ben and Reuben were on either side of Lucki, and Julian, when he was seated, which wasn't very often, was next to Ben.

"I'm sure you all know that I spoke to Scout today." Lucki had only eaten a little bit of her food when she'd started talking. Ben knew that Reuben was worried about her keeping up her strength. Until she bonded with them, she would be vulnerable to all human frailties.

"Word gets around quickly here," Reuben said. "Can I butter a bun for you?"

Lucki smiled at him. "That would be nice, thank you."

Reuben got busy selecting a bun, the biggest one of the batch. "Did he give you some insight?"

"He did." Lucki looked at each of them in turn. "He said that Lady Clover had been working on a spell that could break the curse."

"Yes, that's true," Reuben said as he buttered her bread. "She didn't get a chance to finish it, though."

Ben shifted his gaze to Wren to measure how he was reacting to this conversation. He was looking down, his hair partially hiding his expression, but the scowl was firmly in place.

"He said that she was powerful enough to defeat Angelica." Lucki leaned forward, pulling all their attention toward her. "That she was powerful enough without bonding to any of you. So, I'm thinking that if I find the spell she'd been working on, maybe I could finish it...maybe I could end the curse like she had wanted to." Lucki smiled. "I mean, you all said that I'm powerful, right? I have natural magic in me. So maybe I can finish what she started and free you all without having to bind myself to you."

"You've never used your magic." Wren all but barked those words. "It's dormant and useless right now."

"Enough!" Reuben growled.

Lucki visibly tensed.

Ben winced and patted her hand. "What Wren means is—"

"I meant exactly what I said." He snapped his gaze up and stared at each of them in turn, skipping over Lucki completely. "Her power is untapped. We need to unleash it first. We need to—"

"She just got here." Reuben laid his hand on the table and glared at Wren. "It's too soon."

The room was silent for a moment and Lucki took them all in. Her expression shuttered. "I don't mean to offend anyone." She shrugged, frowned and her eyes grew sad. "And yes, you're right, Wren." She shifted her eyes briefly to Wren but his glare didn't falter from Reuben's. "I've never actually used my power, not that I know of anyway. I just can't bond with you, if that's what you're talking about. If that's what it takes to unleash it—" Her voice cracked. "I've just been through a lot...with someone who promised me eternity." She let out a bitter-sounding laugh. "Maybe not the kind of eternity you all are offering." She lowered her eyes. "I just can't do that again. I lost myself for a long time. Maybe I'm still a bit lost. So, if that's what it takes to unleash my power, then—"

Her words fell like boulders. Everyone was quiet for a few minutes. Reuben shifted his eyes away from Wren to look at Lucki with obvious sympathy, his hand already cocooning hers on the table, his expression mirroring her.

Lucki cleared her throat, sniffled a little, then looked up with a bright, but unconvincing, smile on her face. "I'll practice for however long it will take. If the magic is inside of me, I'll figure out a way to get it out. If there's a spell that can break the curse, like Scout said, then I want to find it."

Wren scoffed.

"Scout is remembering wrong, beauty." Julian had his elbows on the table, his expression grim.

Lucki's smile faded. "There isn't a spell?"

"No, he's right about that. She was working a spell." Ben reached over and took Lucki's other hand. "But she wasn't powerful enough on her own."

Her expression crumbled. Ben entwined his fingers with hers and opened his mouth to continue, but it was Wren who spoke next.

"She was bonded to one of us."

Lucki's expression was troubled once again. She locked in on Wren, who stared right back at her with such intensity that it was as if he were shooting sparks out of his eyes. "She bonded herself to one of you?"

"Happily." Wren grunted, his eyes challenging her to form the conclusion everyone else already knew.

"To you?" Lucki whispered.

The whole room grew quiet once again.

"Yes, to me." Wren pushed his chair back and it made such a loud noise that Lucki jumped. "And it wasn't enough to save her."

Chapter Eight

Lucki

Lucki felt every thump as Wren pounded his way up the stairs. She followed Reuben's gaze as he tracked Wren's movement, watching the ceiling until there was a long *cre-ee-eak* followed by a door slamming shut. She wanted to get up and leave too—lock herself in her room and never come out again. She pulled her hands away from Ben and Reuben then wrapped her arms around herself.

"Don't let him upset you, beauty," Julian said.

"I, um, well, I don't know what to say." She really didn't. Her brain was all clogged up with confusion, like a cotton ball was wedged in there, making it impossible to think clearly.

"Wren has never forgiven himself for what happened to Isabel." Reuben eyes were glassy. He left his hand lying empty on the table, half open and looking lost, like he just couldn't understand why her hand wasn't entwined there still.

Impulse nudged for Lucki to reach out to him, to take his hand again, but she dared not. She couldn't have these men thinking the wrong thing. There would be no commitment from her—not for an eternity, not for even a second, not at any point.

That didn't stop the knot from forming in her chest, though. She wanted to help. She just didn't know how.

"He wouldn't let anyone else bond with her." Ben downed his glass of wine then motioned for Julian to refill it. "Too possessive."

"They possessed each other." Reuben frowned. "It wasn't just Wren. It was Isabel too. She wouldn't let him out of her sight."

"Thick as thieves and always whispering." Julian gulped down more wine.

"After Angelica had cast the curse, we were all stunned for many long months. Power like that being thrust upon a town and its people? Well, it makes it hard to think for a while." Reuben tapped the table.

"A long while," Ben agreed.

"Awareness came slowly. It took us a while to figure out what she'd done and why," Reuben said.

"Scout said there was a misunderstanding."

Julian snorted. "We've never found out what caused her anger, but she targeted the entire town, so we've always assumed it was more than one person."

"Isabel had been here already, a settler with a lot of money and also a witch with powers. Both were assets that she'd used to live independently, which at the time was unusual in this rugged land," Ben said. "She'd felt Angelica's magic before the curse but hadn't had any reason to interact with the woman. Like the rest of us, being in the wrong place at the wrong time had meant that she'd been swept up in the curse as well."

"Why were you all here? You shifters, I mean. Scout said that there are more..."

Reuben heaved a deep breath. "We're attracted to magic signatures. On the hunt for magic to bolster, to protect those witches in need."

"Like a familiar."

"Yes, exactly like a familiar." Ben nodded. "We're incomplete without a partner. The magic of this place? It was so powerful that it beckoned many of us—Isabel, Angelica, both powerful witches in need of familiars. Many of the Brotherhood came to investigate. Many left before the curse was imposed. Many more were trapped here."

"But they somehow left, right? I mean, it's only the four of you here now."

"Over the decades, then a century, many did find the strength to leave, to search for a way to break the curse or to hide away in a magically induced hibernation that would protect them from the deep sorrow of being incomplete."

Lucki flinched.

"We were new to the Brotherhood, new to our existence, when we arrived in Alaska. Our primary objective was to find our witch and to secure the magic that would make us whole." Reuben flexed his fingers. "We were trapped here along with the townsfolk and Isabel."

"I'm so sorry." Lucki could hardly fathom the reality of what they were telling her—centuries-old shifters, familiars in shapeshifter form. To have one sole purpose and to be thwarted by a curse that was out of one's control? To be trapped for hundreds of years without ever feeling whole because of being in the wrong place at the wrong time?

On some level, Lucki understood the kind of loneliness that came from being incomplete. When her mother had died, a chunk of her heart had died too. She had tried to fill that space with Shane, but he'd taken even more of her heart. Now she was almost empty. She was incomplete like these men were, but unlike them, she wasn't searching for something to fill that hole. She couldn't bear to lose any more of her heart.

"If you somehow manage to break the curse..." Julian started.

"You'd free us," Ben finished.

"So, you'd be able to find your partner? To be made whole?" She wanted these men, these shifters, to find their mates—but at the same time, a tug of jealousy had her frowning. "If Wren and Isabel were bonded, why wasn't she able to defeat Angelica?"

Everyone grew silent as she put the pieces together.

"She needed more than one bond. That's what Wren meant when he said it wasn't enough that she'd been bonded to him."

"As the first year of the curse slipped by, Isabel and Wren fell in love, then they bonded." Reuben rubbed his hand down his face. "They were intensely passionate and possessive of one another."

Lucki didn't need Reuben to spell it out. Wren and Isabel hadn't wanted anyone else to join their bond.

"Angelica began stealing the cats almost immediately, and we soon realized that she was rebuilding her power. We spent all our time protecting the townspeople from her, attempting to keep the cats safe, and we thwarted her efforts to take more cats for years." Reuben shook his head. "Isabel spent her time, when she wasn't with Wren, trying to figure out how to break the curse."

Julian opened another bottle of wine and refiled the glasses that were in need of it.

"The first fifty years slipped by quickly." Reuben nodded thanks to Julian then picked up his wineglass. "Hard to imagine, but it did." He took a deep drink before continuing. "Angelica became bolder. She somehow captured and transformed some of our brothers from protectors to the beastly wild cats that you met earlier. She found a vulnerability. She somehow removed their conscience. That's when we knew she was planning an attack. One of the other brothers suggested that more of us bond with Isabel. That if we bolstered her with enough of our magic, maybe she could take out Angelica, along with the curse."

"But she wouldn't." Lucki closed her eyes.

"We all thought Isabel was stronger than Angelica." Reuben touched her hand, and she opened her eyes to see worry etched on his face. "And she didn't want to bond with anyone but Wren. We didn't fight them on it because it was obvious that they were so in love, and we didn't know if it would even take or if it would be what she'd need." Reuben motioned for Julian to fill his glass too. "We didn't know then, of course —"

"We were all fools." Ben clinked Lucki's full wineglass. "Drink up. It'll make that knot in your chest ease."

Lucki looked at him with a mix of shock and awe. "How did you —?" She cleared her throat and scraped her knuckles over her sternum, pressing in hard to relieve the tension there. "Never mind." She picked up her glass and took a few huge gulps. Even though it was smooth, her throat was so dry that it burned like hot coal all the way down to her empty stomach. "So, you don't actually know if multiple bonds would work."

"We have good reason to believe..." Ben touched her hand. "It was because of Wren that Isabel was able to cast her protection spell around the town to keep Angelica out except for one night a year. Isabel used Wren's magic when she did that."

Lucki wasn't going to even pretend to understand how it all worked. The bond. The magic. It was all so...surreal. "I don't mean to cause you all trouble." She wiped her mouth with her fingers. "I...just... My ex...he...um—" She just couldn't sputter her way through telling this story again.

"It's okay, beauty." Julian topped her glass once more and she didn't argue. She was going to need a good numbing to get through the rest of this day. Maybe if she drank enough, she'd fall into oblivion and sleep away the rest of this nightmare.

"The protection spell she'd cast weakened her. We believe that if she'd had more bonds from us, she could have used our magic to bolster her after what Wren had given her waned."

"She died here, in the house?" Lucki croaked.

No one answered but she didn't need them to. The expressions on their faces said it all. Anguish. Loss. A deep cave of longing for someone they would never see again. Even after so much time, this woman still haunted them all. And they were expecting what from her, exactly? To take the place of this ghost? To step into the shoes of a woman they'd all coveted but had never gotten the chance to be with?

"I can't do this." She started to push her chair back, her head already spinning from the few gulps of wine she'd had and also from the reality that once again, the man...*men* in her life were asking too much of her.

Reuben stopped her with a gentle hand on her shoulder. "We understand, Lucki." His voice was a deep rumble and he speared her with a look that said he wasn't lying, shooting sincerity like laser beams. "No one wants you to do anything you aren't comfortable with."

And yet, the obligation still sat heavy in her thoughts. She slumped. She didn't really want to go to her room again anyway. It was a nice room, sure, but it was lonely up there.

"I remember the spell book Isabel was working on. She would never let us near it, but I know what it looks like. It's got to be here somewhere." Reuben picked up her plate. "I'm going to warm this up. You need to eat something if we're going to put our heads together and figure out a plan to find her spell." He flashed her one of his giant disarming smiles and she couldn't help but smile back. It was maybe not as wide or as brilliant as his, but a smile did tug her lips in a way that lifted her heart a bit.

She watched him walk into the kitchen. Her stomach was a hollow cavern with wine the only thing sloshing around. Sure, she'd eaten some cake and cookies earlier, but she needed something more or she'd be a blubbering mess of wine-infused thoughts. *Who knows what I'd spill then?*

She picked up the bun that Reuben had buttered for her, took a bite and instantly regretted not doing it sooner. The bun was still warm, the butter fresh and it all tasted like home. She shoved the entire thing into her mouth.

"We'll figure this out, Lucki. We'll keep you safe, even without the bond." Ben reached over and rubbed her arm. "We won't push. You control what happens next."

She smiled through her chewing, but her mouth was too full to say anything.

"I remember the spell book too." Julian motioned a rough outline of the size of the book, which was maybe a bit bigger than the average one, but not by much. "It was thick, full of her writing."

"Her grimoire." Ben held his fingers open wide. "I'd say about five inches thick with inked spells stuffed inside."

"That would need a particular kind of hiding spot." Lucki's mom had had a grimoire of sorts herself and she had hidden it—under floorboards, behind the bed, in the closest under stacks of boxes—never the same spot twice. Now it was with her in the afterlife, because Lucki had put it in her coffin before her cremation. As much as she'd wanted to keep the book as a memory of her mother, it didn't belong to her. It was her mom's talisman anyway, and she might have need of it wherever she went.

"She didn't have her spell book with her that day." Julian had given up on filling glasses and was drinking straight out of the bottle. "Whatever she did, however she cast the protection spell, it came from her head."

"From her heart." Reuben was back with Lucki's plate steaming once again. He put it down in front of her and the smell of home hit her, this time like a sledgehammer. She longed for normality, for days long gone when she'd make this meal for her mother and they would drink wine together and talk about all kinds of things. She longed for her dearly departed cats that she'd taken such good care of. She longed for what once had been but would never be again.

Reuben hovered over her, like he was waiting to make sure she'd actually eat this time. She was worried he might try to feed her.

Her stomach yowled. Reuben's fingers twitched toward her utensils.

"Thank you." She picked up her fork and dug in.

Reuben seemed satisfied that she was eating, so he settled back into his seat. "That day was all chaos from what I remember, but Julian is right. She didn't have her book with her."

"So, it could be in this house? Hidden somewhere?" Lucki asked between bites, a trickling of hope curling through her body. She was a skilled treasure hunter. Missing a sock? Lucki would be the one to find it in the lint trap. Misplaced the keys? Lucki would find them wedged between the closet door and a pile of shoes. Looked everywhere? Lucki would find the place the person hadn't seen. This was something she could do, and when she set about a task, she always finished it. "I'm good at finding things. I can start looking today."

"We can all start looking today, beauty." Julian downed the rest of the bottle then wiped his mouth with the back of his hand. "Let's partner up. I'll—"

Ben put his arm around Lucki's shoulders, delicately trailing his fingers against her arm. "I'll be your partner. I know all the secret hiding places—all the nooks and crannies." He winked and she couldn't help but laugh.

"I bet you do." The tension in her body evaporated. Maybe it was the wine or maybe it was the way these three men were willing to help her, even if she couldn't help them — not the way they needed her to. She wasn't against exploring each of them alone or together — no way would she turn down a chance at pleasure like that — but she wasn't going to lead any of them on, and she really got the vibe that they respected that.

"I propose we all have an opportunity to partner with Lucki." Julian pushed his chair back and rose with a finger pointed in the air like he was about to give a presidential speech. "A partner for each floor." He turned his finger toward Ben. "You start in the basement."

Ben pointed his finger too, the middle one. "You think you're being clever, but I know of many comfortable but tight spots down there that Lucki needs to see. The book can be hidden anywhere. We might just have to squeeze into tight places together to look."

Lucki covered her mouth with her napkin but couldn't help the sputter of laughter from escaping.

"Sure, if you like getting dusty." Julian stuck his tongue out in a grossed-out kind of way.

"I'm sure Lucki doesn't mind a little down and dirty treasure hunting. Do you, love?"

"I'll have you know that I keep a very clean house," Reuben huffed. "You won't find dust on any floor, not even the attic. You two might have been living like beasts in the forest but we certainly have not."

Lucki couldn't contain herself a moment longer. A volcano of giggles erupted with little control. Reuben was so obviously offended by the notion that the house was dirty that he didn't seem to care that Ben was really talking about getting down and dirty with her.

Soon enough, all three of them were laughing and Lucki suddenly knew that even if she couldn't let herself go enough to embrace them all in commitment, she could at least embrace them all as friends...maybe even with benefits.

Chapter Nine

Julian

After sort of helping Reuben clean up the kitchen, which was a total buzz kill, Julian set out to search for Isabel's book. He would have preferred to start in the basement with Lucki, but every time he even so much as pointed his body in the direction of the staircase that would take him downstairs, Reuben did one of his deep throaty growls to warn him away. The man had eyes at the back of his head...or maybe in every room. Rueben didn't even have to be near Julian to know when the magnetic pull toward Lucki got overwhelming and he had the urge to seek her out.

"It's Ben's time to be with her," Reuben grumbled, his hands on his hips and a damp-looking dish cloth over his shoulder. "To get to know her."

"Yes, I'm sure he is...getting to *know* her." Julian flopped down onto the couch and remembered just how uncomfortable the thing was. The sitting room was always a mystery to him. Isabel had insisted every great mansion needed one. It was a posh-looking room for guests to sit and take tea, but she'd never actually used it for that. The pink couch was stiff and hard as a stone slab. The furniture, with all of its fine wooden designs, needed constant dusting. The fine china tea set, which perpetually sat on a rolling tea caddie, never got used. It was a total waste of a room, if anyone asked him. And he usually avoided it altogether.

It was just the kind of place Isabel might hide something she didn't want him to see.

"Do you even remember what the book looks like?" Julian pushed himself up from his attempt to sprawl on the unyielding cushions and sat as he was meant to. Back straight, hands on his lap, looking for all intents and purposes like a gentleman.

"I do." Reuben stepped into the room. His reflection almost filled the entire mirror on the opposite wall. "I helped her fashion it." He tore the towel off then whipped it into the kitchen before moving to the Queen Anne chair across from the couch.

Julian stifled a wince when the chair groaned under Reuben's weight. "I didn't know you helped her with that." The usual flare of jealousy that Julian might have felt upon hearing that one of his shifter brothers had helped Isabel and had left him out didn't cut so deep anymore. Sure, it had been a hundred and fifty years since she'd been with them, but that had made no difference in the past.

"She wanted the right animal pelt to make the leather."

"Let me guess? Bear?" Julian drawled.

Reuben raised one shoulder in a so-what shrug. "It's the strongest."

It was true. Reuben was the largest of the Brotherhood and, by his accounts, the strongest, but there was much debate about that. Would Julian want to go head-to-head with Reuben's bear? Not for fun, no, but as an almost two-hundred-pound lion, Julian knew he could hold his own if it came down to it — not that it ever would.

"So, it was encased in brown leather," Julian prompted.

"And embossed with a cat eye." Reuben motioned with his fingers the rough size of the design on the cover. "The pages were made with birch bark."

"Oh yes, that I remember...the smell of her preparing the bark." Isabel would spend countless days preparing each page of her spell book as she needed them. Each one, she'd said, had to have a particular signature in its making so it would hold the magic she was going to put on its pages. "And she used a special ink, I remember."

"Baneberry and blood." Reuben leaned forward to rest his elbows on his knees and steeple his hands under his chin. "To bind the spells to the book."

"So, where is the damn thing?" Julian swept the room for the millionth time. There were so many places she could have hidden it — under floorboards, behind shelves, one of the hundreds of secret nooks. But knowing Isabel, it was probably hidden in plain sight.

"I've asked the cats," Reuben said. "Out of all of us, they'd have the best idea."

Julian had no idea how Reuben was able to understand the cats. Whenever Julian got a hint of communication from them, it was garbled and indecipherable. "Do they even know what you're asking them?" Because over the years, as the curse continued, the cats had become more and more cat-like, losing their humanity bit by bit.

"They do."

Julian blew out a long breath, unclasped his hands then stood up. "Well, with all of us looking, we're bound to come across it at some point." He moved to the far wall then ran his hands along the seam of the wainscotting, looking for a trigger that might open a secret hiding hole. It wasn't the first time he'd wished there had been some kind of plans drawn up, a map of all the secrets in this house.

"Maybe we will. It's possible that Isabel cloaked it with one of her spells." Reuben stayed where he was seated, making no effort to join the search. That was enough to tell Julian that for all his assurances to Lucki, the big guy didn't really think they'd be successful in finding the book. Which meant they'd have to find another way to protect Lucki from Angelica.

"Do you think Wren is right? Should we take her to the circle now?" Julian knew there were dangers in exposing Lucki to the magic circle too early on, but it was the best way to ignite her powers.

"She has never so much as made a wish with intention, Julian. How could we put her in that place and expect her to survive it?"

"Well, it wouldn't kill her, would it?" Julian was appalled at the idea that the sacred circle of stones could harm their Cat Keeper — or worse, kill her.

"It depends how untapped her power is. Is it possible that she has unknowingly used magic in her life? Yes, but I'm fairly certain she's never made a conscious attempt to control it." Reuben shook his head. "Without our marks, stepping into that circle could be too much for Lucki to handle."

The sound of an upstairs door creaking open followed by thudding footsteps coming down the stairs had both of them looking toward the wide arched doorway of the sitting room. Wren stepped off the last step and took in the two of them with eyes of steel. "You're wasting your time. Isabel didn't want us to stumble onto that spell book, so she hid it well."

"Even from you?" Julian bit back.

Wren eyes didn't waver from his steady glare. "Even from me."

The cats began milling around Wren, nudging him toward the front door. Reuben took the cue and hoisted himself up from his chair. "Twilight is upon us."

"Don't let Lucki wander the town tonight," Wren barked. "Reuben and I are going to patrol the forest to make sure Angelica isn't setting up any of her usual spring traps for the cats."

Julian gave a two-finger salute as Wren and Reuben headed to their duties.

"And leave Ben and Lucki in peace!" Reuben said before shutting the door behind him.

Julian slumped into the Queen Anne Reuben had just vacated...and promptly jumped back up. "Ugh! Why does everything have to be so damn uncomfortable in this room?" Seriously, the chair felt like it was made of marble, despite the pillowy-looking cushion.

A waft of Lucki's sweetly melodic laughter floated down the hall, followed by Ben's deep-throated one. Julian curled himself around the sitting room door frame and gazed at the door that would take him to the basement. Lucki and Ben had been down there a while...*alone*. They might need some refreshments. A bottle of red maybe...some finger foods perhaps?

Besides, it would be better for the three of them to tackle that ginormous space so they could check it off their list if the book wasn't found.

A very wise course of action.

Julian beelined for the kitchen. Reuben had a plate of snacks made up already, so he might as well put it to use now.

* * * *

"Break time!" Julian hadn't been in the basement of the cat house in fifty years, so he was somewhat surprised to find that Reuben and Wren had renovated in the time he'd been gone. While most of the space still resembled a dark, classic horror-film kind of place with exposed rafters and wires, visible plumbing and discarded furniture, Reuben and Wren had transformed a huge section into what Julian could only describe as a modern-day man heaven.

He walked into the space with his mouth agape. The carpet was plush, the walls wood paneled, the TV bigger than the moon. There was a fully stocked bar, complete with a small fridge, leather-wrapped stools, a pool table and darts. He wandered in, trying to see everything at once.

"Oh, wine, what a great idea!" Lucki came in behind him.

"Snack time! Good thinking, Julian!" Ben slapped him on the back hard enough to send a message.

Julian chose to ignore him. "Man, have you seen…? I mean…this place…" He set the tray he was carrying down on the bar. "Where the hell did they find all this stuff?"

"It's a mystery." Ben waved his hand around. "I can't imagine Bill or Scotty putting together anything like this, despite being damn fine furniture makers." He pointed to the wine, his eyes hot and steady on Julian. "Since you appear to be staying, why don't you pop that open so we can have a drink?"

"I'm sure they just ordered it all online and had it delivered." Lucki smiled like that made total sense then settled herself on the massive couch and promptly sank into the pillowy cushions.

"Whatever 'online' is, it must be mighty powerful magic to create such a comfortable space." Ben seated himself right next to her...practically on top of her, actually — as if there wasn't room for him to spread out. Lucki didn't seem to mind, though. She just laughed it off then snuggled into him when he draped his arm around her shoulders.

"I forgot you two were in the forest for a long time." Lucki reached forward and grabbed the TV remote. "You have watched TV before, right?" She clicked it on.

"TV, yes. Maybe not this huge or flat-looking, but we are familiar." Julian got busy opening the wine.

When Lucki turned the TV on, Julian was unprepared for the vibrancy of the picture and found himself mesmerized all over again. *How can they get such color to happen?* The people on the screen seemed so real that it was as if they could actually step right out and join their little party — and the sound? It encompassed him.

"It looks like Reuben and Wren have a few subscriptions to streaming services. We could take a real break and watch a movie if you two wanted."

Ben had pushed himself forward, leaving Lucki behind so he could stare at the screen, just as Julian was.

Every time Lucki scrolled to the right, more options presented themselves. All manner of shows…movies… all so compelling.

"Or we could just watch the trailers," Lucki laughed.

Ben looked over his shoulder at her. "You pick, love. My head is spinning from what you've just shown us. I don't know why we've been prowling in the dank forest all this time when we could have been sitting down here, watching endless hours of TV."

Julian snorted a laugh then brought a tray over with three full wineglasses now balanced along with the plate of food Reuben had prepared.

"Why did you two spend so much time in the forest?" Lucky motioned to the room. "I can't imagine it held the comfort that this place did."

Ben cut a look at Julian. *How much truth is too much?*

Julian set the tray down on the coffee table. "After Isabel's death—" He paused, because how could he put into words what Isabel's death had done to them all?

"The curse was designed to trap us here," Ben said, his eyes pointed at the TV as if he was actually paying attention to the flashing screen when really, Julian knew, Ben was cycling through the memories of that time, just as he was—*the darkness, the depression, the desire to end everything.* "After a hundred years of protecting the cats with limited success, Julian and I decided to test the limits of the curse's boundaries. Other brothers had succeeded in getting away somehow."

"It was too heavy here," Julian blurted. "Too hopeless, especially after so many Cat Keepers failed to break the curse."

"We felt more at peace in our animal form, less burdened by sorrow. So, we kind of slipped away."

"It was cowardly." Julian held Ben's stare. "But we wouldn't have survived with any semblance of sanity if we hadn't."

"Not cowardly." Lucki patted the couch next to her. "I've always been a strong believer in self-care. You have to do what's necessary to protect yourself from further harm."

Taking Lucki's cue, Julian plopped himself on Lucki's other side. "You're very gracious in forgiving our actions."

Lucki smiled at him and it warmed his body like she'd lit a fire in his belly. "Just as gracious as you all have been to me and my commitment issues."

Julian handed Lucki a glass of wine. "Did you two make any headway in the search for Isabel's book?"

Ben shook his head, wineglass in hand, then leaned back so he could drape his arm around Lucki again. "It's going to take us a while to even make a dent. We've searched the most obvious places, but the thing could be anywhere."

"For all we know, it's behind these walls," Julian said with a wave of his arm.

"It has to be somewhere accessible, right?" Lucki sipped her wine. "Isabel used the book often enough that she'd need to be able to get it quickly, wouldn't she?" She snuggled closer to both men somehow, seemingly content to have them both pressed alongside her.

She smelled like magic, lavender and lily, ginger and pine. She smelled like nutmeg and mint and vanilla all mixed together. Julian took a deep breath in, testing the layers of her unique signature. He wanted to run his tongue along the creamy skin of her throat. He wanted to taste the sweet nectar of her lips.

And when she turned her beautiful face toward him, he thought, *Yes! This is it! My turn!* Only to see the confusion in her eyes…because of course, she'd asked him a question.

He cleared his throat. "She did use it often, if not for casting spells then for creating them." Julian downed his own glass then cursed himself for leaving the bottle on the bar. He didn't want to get up and leave Lucki behind, not even for a moment.

"So, it must be somewhere she could get to quickly if needed," Lucki said. "I say we tackle all the obvious places first before we start thinking about going deeper than that." She drank a few sips of her wine.

"Tomorrow." Ben slipped his fingers up the back of Lucki's neck and into her hair. "But tonight…"

She turned her head, effectively blocking Julian out, and leaned into Ben, parted her lips then kissed him. Not a chaste kiss, either. It was full of heat that told Julian a story of just what they'd been up to down here while they had been searching.

Disappointment crushed him, like heavy boulders dropping into his gut.

Julian knew he had to leave. Lucki and Ben had something going on and he'd obviously interrupted them. Without a word, he started to slip off the couch.

Lucki's firm grip on his thigh stopped him.

He froze, uncertain but extremely hopeful of the message she was sending. He put his glass down on the table, then took hers as well. When she broke her kiss with Ben then turned to face him with moisture on her lips and hot desire in her eyes, Julian knew without a doubt that they'd finally found the woman for them.

For *all* of them.

Chapter Ten

Lucki

Lucki wanted this. She wanted these strong, sexy men to ravish her. She wanted them to banish the memories of her ex that still lingered, the ones that had left scars in her heart and had broken her in so many different ways. She wanted these two gorgeous shifters to leave her body with memories of pleasure. Although the scars she wore on the inside ensured that she couldn't give them commitment, she could give them spectacular memories too.

Ben lifted her sweater, so she had to break her kiss with Julian to get the thing off. She was smoldering anyway and wanted nothing more than to be naked with these two. As soon as the cooler basement air hit her exposed skin, a shiver rippled over her body with goosebumps following in its wake. Ben immediately got to work kissing the shiver away, down the side of her neck, across her shoulder, deftly unclasping her bra and sliding his hands forward to cup her breasts.

Julian, whose eyes were hooded, his lips parted and breaths ragged, leaned in to kiss her again while he also unbuttoned her jeans. He stroked her tongue with urgent probing and sensual tangles. He ran his hands along her waist, pushing her pants and her panties down as he glided over her hips.

Ben discarded her bra, tossing it to the floor, then molded his hands to her breasts again—kneading, cupping, teasing her nipples with the barest of flicks. He ran his tongue along the column of her throat.

Her body was a rolling wave of sensation, her nerve endings pinging as if every kiss, every lick, every touch ignited small fires that blazed with want and need.

Julian moved down her body, leaving her lips aching for more, which Ben immediately satiated. He devoured her mouth, gliding his fingers over her pebbled nipples again and again while Julian licked every inch of her skin as he made his way over her hills and valleys. He paused to suck on each nipple, kissing his way down the underside of her tits, one after the other, while Ben continued to pinch and flick in Julian's wake.

By the time Julian made it to her pussy, she was a writhing mess. She couldn't help but offer herself to him, to beg with her body for him to suck her clit as hard as he could. With his hands on her ass and his eyes on her pussy, she all but came right then and there. When he flicked his eyes to hers and she saw the hunger burning on his face, she knew she had to hang on for as long as she could, because this man was going to make her scream while he ate her alive.

She reached her hands behind her head, questing for Ben's cock. He was wearing loose track pants, which were tenting in a spectacular way, giving her a homing beacon straight to his dick. As she grazed his erection, Ben's moan reverberated along her skin. With his body curled over hers, his lips on her collarbone and fingers strumming her nipples, their positioning was too awkward. She wanted to do more before Julian finally made his way to her pussy and her brain was obliterated. She put her foot on Julian's shoulder and pushed him back — or tried to anyway.

He stilled. His eyes flashed with dangerous heat, like she had interrupted a predator on the hunt. He dug his fingers into her hips. Ben stilled too. It was almost enough to make Lucki stop moving as well, almost enough to freeze her in place. But she wanted to taste Ben and later Julian, to make sure everyone got their happy ending.

She opened her mouth but her words jammed up in her throat. She was staring into the eyes of a hunter. If Julian had fangs in his human form, he'd be baring them right now. She slowly took her foot off his chest then wiggled her hips to loosen his grip. Something soft flickered in his eyes and he released her in an instant. She rolled over, curving her back and stretching her body, sending the message that she wasn't ending their play but extending it. Julian clearly got the drift. He ripped his clothes off, and by the time Lucki had fully positioned herself, on her knees, ass in the air, elbows holding her up and Ben's dick in her face, Julian was right back where he'd started. He gripped her hips and his hot breath cascaded over her soaking pussy.

Ben may have been a compact man, shorter than the others — who were all toweringly above average — but he was no less cut and powerful. His abs had abs. His cock was…well…proportionally bigger than the rest of him — and that was saying a lot.

Pre-cum glistened on the tip of his steel-rod dick. Lucki licked her lips, flickered her eyes up so she could stare into Ben's then opened her mouth as wide as she could and took him in. He fluttered his eyes closed and arched his back, jutting his hips toward her, and he moaned such a guttural sound that her body quivered in response.

Julian took that moment to lick his way over her pussy lips, sucking her in as he moved toward her clit, and it was her turn to moan. She knew he wasn't a lion right now, but his tongue was rough and soft all at the same time, his strokes against her sensitive flesh mighty thrusts that made her toes curl and her body rev. Two glorious men were worshipping her body. Two primal men wanted only her.

Only me.

Two powerful men who could be four powerful men, all wanting to pleasure her, to protect her, to make her stronger than she already was. She wanted all of it. *Now.*

Reality rapped its knuckles against her brain. She couldn't let herself get overwhelmed by their attention. She had to keep focused on the pleasure of it all, because if she let her heart get involved then she was screwed — and not in a good way.

Julian's tongue lapping against her clit brought her back to her body and away from anything else.

She slurped and sucked on Ben's cock, taking him all the way back until his tip nudged against the gate of her throat. Julian stroked her clit, flicking her on like a hundred-watt bulb. Her body vibrated, pulsing with tremors.

Ben reached under her to cup one breast while Julian reached from the side to grab her other. The sensation of having two men touching her was incendiary.

Her nerve endings pinged in rapid succession, her body coiled up tight, her breath hitched and all the while she licked her way back down Ben's dick and Julian stroked his way deep inside her pussy.

She didn't stand a chance.

Her climax exploded like an atom bomb. It shot her straight up into the sky and kept her there. Wave upon wave blasted through her, making her pussy spasm, making her nipples harden so they could cut glass. Every part of her skin was on fire, burning hot and wanting more.

Ben's cock jolted and he rocked into her, pistoning her mouth as he squeezed her tit. His cum erupted with little warning, hitting the back of her throat so she had to swallow quickly to keep the flow from spilling out. Her orgasm seemed never-ending and so did his, his dick pulsing along with her pussy.

Her legs were shaking by the time her climax eased and she collapsed to the couch, licking a stray bit of cum from her mouth. She flipped herself over and grinned up at Ben then Julian. "Definitely more fun than watching a movie."

"Oh, love, we're not done with you yet. I want a taste." Ben lifted her shoulders. "If you're up for it, that is."

Lucki scrambled to follow his direction. "Of course I am!" And she wanted to suck Julian's cock too. No way would she give up a night of multi-orgasmic play.

By the time they had her positioned exactly as they wanted, her head was supported at the end of the couch, her body spread wide, Julian was on his knees, his dick hovering above her face, and Ben was on the other end, his hands on her thighs, his focus on her pussy, his lips pulled into a hungry grin.

She ran her tongue down the back of Julian's dick, savoring the salty taste as she made her way to his balls. He moaned with approval, his eyes telling her just how much he loved what she was doing. With her body like this, her hands were free, so she gripped his shaft with one hand and cupped his balls with the other, licking and kissing him all over.

Gliding his hands down her thighs, Ben then parted her wider before slipping his fingers along her slit then into her hole. He cupped her pussy like that, rubbing his palm over her clit and pumping her pussy at the same time. *Delicious pressure. Tantalizing friction.* Her body was so sensitive already that she writhed immediately, arching into him, urging him to pump her harder, faster.

He reached up and flicked both of her nipples, rolling the hard nubs this way and that between his fingers then lowered himself between her legs, his hot breath sweeping over her slick flesh. Lucki was busy working Julian's dick, using her hands to stroke him, taking his balls into her mouth so she could heat him up, soak him with her saliva. When Ben latched on to her clit, she cried out, creating a vibration against Julian's balls that made him groan in a wholly animalistic way.

Ben slipped his fingers back inside her. He sucked and licked her clit while he pumped her pussy, rubbing against her G-spot, making her writhe. She wasn't even sure if she was on the same planet anymore. Her pussy quivered. Her body shook. Her brain misfired again and again.

She popped Julian's balls out of her mouth then licked up his shaft to his tip. His eyes were locked on hers the whole way, so when she took him down to the back of her throat, a shudder went through him that she both felt and saw.

With Ben pumping her and Lucki pumping Julian, there seemed to be a cascading wave that started at one end of her body and rolled to the other then back again.

Where her first orgasm had sparked through her like a flint to steel, this one started as a slow vibration, like plucking a guitar to test its sound before playing the real music. Every touch, every lick, every stroke against her body was another chord being tested. She liked the way these men teased her climax out, stretching it until she thought she might snap in two. As Julian's cock began to pulse inside her mouth and his cum rolled along her tongue, her body unleashed its song.

When the shuddering, spasming shockwaves had subsided, they lay in a tangled mess of limbs. Ben's head was on her hip, her head on Julian's lap. He was stroking her damp hair while Ben ran his fingers along her thigh in a pattern that made her shiver for all the right reasons.

"Thank you, beauty." Julian's voice was no more than a hoarse whisper. "It's been far too long since we've enjoyed a night like this."

"For me too," Lucki said with a crooked smile. The last man she'd been with was her ex—and that had been over a year ago. Until coming to Weeping Falls, she hadn't had any interest in being with anyone else. Reuben had unlocked something inside her the previous night and now Julian and Ben had opened the door wide. She felt closer to her true self than she had for a very long time. Although she and her ex had been broken up for a while, it had been many years before that that things hadn't been okay for her. He'd made a million tiny cuts, hard to notice as they were happening, devastating to her well-being all the same.

"You are a spectacular woman, Lucki." Ben flattened his hand against her belly.

"I'm in a house full of spectacular men." Lucki sighed. And she was. It was obvious that each of these men wanted her to be happy and satisfied. None had pushed her into anything she didn't feel comfortable doing. And yet…and yet, her thoughts began to circle around the one man in the group who had so far kept his distance.

She knew that just as she wanted him, Wren wanted her too, but also just like her, he had baggage of his own weighing him down and keeping him at arm's length.

Chapter Eleven

Lucki

Weeks passed in seconds and Lucki was surprised to find that she'd completely settled in at the cat house. It had creeped into her system so that it had begun to feel like home somehow. She fell asleep to the sounds of the house settling, creaking and cracking, sighing and at times even groaning and woke up to the smells of Reuben's hungry-man style breakfasts—sausage, bacon, toast and eggs, fresh fruit and endless pots of tea. While she didn't actually have to nurse the cats in any way, she did take much pleasure in being surrounded by them at all times. No matter what room she walked into, there were always a handful ready and eager for petting and cuddling. At first it was weird knowing that the cats were actually humans, but Reuben had assured her that when they were cats, they were cats and should be treated as such. So, she did and she loved it.

With the help of Julian, Reuben, Ben and sometimes, begrudgingly, Wren, they'd managed to search the entire basement and the main floor and had yet to find Isabel's book, but that didn't mean defeat. The house was massive and there were still plenty of places to look.

Lucki's days were a bustle of things to do, which left nights to explore so many other things—like introducing Julian and Ben to the Internet...which led them, of course, to online porn...which led them to many new and inventive ways of bringing Lucki to orgasm again and again.

Reuben liked to read to her, and on quiet nights they'd sit in the portico with the stars shining overhead and hot cider in their mugs. She'd have her legs draped over his lap and an oversized fleece blanket to keep them toasty, and he'd read to her from his favorite books. They'd already finished *Northanger Abby* and had just started *Wuthering Heights*—books she'd always meant to read but had never found the time to. Those nights would end with deep, soul-moving kisses that would leave her gasping for breath and always wanting more.

None of those nights had ended with sex, which was fine with Lucki. She knew these men were questing for forever and guessed that sex was as important to them as it was to her. She could maintain a 'friend with benefits' relationship, no matter what the benefits entailed, but these men were too soft-hearted for that, too untainted by heartbreak or maybe too hopeful to give up on love, so crossing that line with them would make it harder to keep things simple. Lucki didn't push them. As much as she wanted the feel of their cocks inside her, she knew that they needed time to accept the deep truth of her convictions. She would not give them eternity, but she could give them a long time, as long as her life allowed, actually, because the more Lucki experienced Weeping Falls, curse and all, the more she wanted to stay.

Wren? He avoided her, often skipping out on dinner where they all sat at the large dining table and shared stories. He didn't touch her. He hardly looked at her. Of course, that made her want to seek him out more, which she barely managed to stop herself from doing. She had to respect his boundaries, especially since she'd erected her own.

"You'll need to dress warmly, beauty. It's cold out there tonight." Julian held out a soft, ivory-colored cable-knit sweater that looked about five sizes too large for her.

She was standing at the door of Isabel's sitting room, having stopped there on the way to the back hall for some unknown reason. She had a poking, nagging, annoyingly persistent feeling that she was forgetting something, but no matter how long she stared at the classically beautiful furniture in the sitting room, it wouldn't come to her.

"Thanks, Julian." She took the heavy sweater then slipped it on. "So, what *is* tonight all about, anyway?"

Reuben had announced at breakfast that they'd be eating dinner by campfire, because there was something special that needed to be done. He also insisted that everyone attend, including Wren.

"You'll see." Julian wrapped his arm around her waist and steered her toward the back hall.

The hike to the back part of the property was a little on the treacherous side, with jutting rocks and low-hanging branches, roots that came out of nowhere and brambles of needly plants that stuck to her clothes. It wasn't meant to be an easy walk, and Lucki found out why as soon as the campfire site came into view and the path evened out. There were colorful stones laid out, like a rainbow brick road leading to what lay ahead.

"This is..." More than words could say. *Breathtaking? Unexpectedly enchanting?*

"It's over two hundred years old," Ben said as he took her hand and hauled her away from Julian.

It reminded her of pictures she'd seen of Stonehenge. Towering boulders that were inhumanly positioned and looked precariously balanced were set up in a circle, with slabs for sitting or perhaps worshipping interspersed here and there.

"Come over, Lucki." Reuben had his apron on and his sleeves rolled up and was removing containers from a large cooler.

Lucki hesitated at the edge of the circle. This was a sacred space. She scanned the boulders again this time, noticing intricate designs and rune-like symbols etched in rows along their faces. "What is this place?"

"This is a place of power, Lucki," Julian said as he came up behind her. "Do you feel it?"

She held her hands up, just shy of crossing the invisible boundary of the circle. She'd experienced many magical things in her life—falling in love for the first time, holding her mom as the life drained out of her cancer-ridden body, hearing the rumbling purr of a hundred cats who lived to greet her day in and day out. Right now, as she closed her eyes and homed in on the circle of boulders, she felt the wisp of something more, a low vibration that tickled the pads of her fingers. She opened her eyes to find all the men staring at her.

"That's neat!" Lucki grinned.

"Neat?" Wren appeared out of the woods, his hair slightly messy and his eyes narrowed.

Lucki shrunk a bit under his stare.

He circled the boulders, his eyes never leaving hers. She didn't belong there. This was too sacred a place for a girl like her. *Leave. Now.* That was what Wren's eyes were saying to her.

"Go on, Lucki. The circle is meant for you." Ben's hand was on her back and he encouraged her to move forward, but Wren was stalking toward her, his body hunched, his fists clenched.

"I don't think —"

"Wren!" Reuben growled as he took a threatening lunge toward Wren.

Wren stopped his approach. He cut a scathing glare at Reuben. "She should be overwhelmed by the power, being this close to it," he growled back. "She shouldn't be thinking it's *neat*. I've changed my mind. She's not ready. I shouldn't have suggested she do this." His tone dripped with sarcasm.

Lucki flinched. So maybe they were wrong after all. Maybe she wasn't so special. "I should leave." She took a step backward — or tried to, anyway. Ben's steady hand was still on her back, holding her in place.

"No, you shouldn't. You belong here," he coaxed. "Inside the circle is where the real power lies."

She shifted her gaze to Reuben, who nodded, then to Ben, who smiled encouragingly. Julian took her hand and squeezed. She couldn't bring herself to look at Wren. She didn't have to. His frustration rolled off him in waves that she was sure everyone could sense.

She took a step forward. Julian released her hand. Ben patted her back. Reuben motioned for her to continue. She dared a glance in Wren's direction and found his scowl gone and, in its place, complete and open vulnerability. Entering this circle had great meaning for these men. She just hoped that whatever it was they wanted to happen, did.

Two more small steps put her past the invisible boundary line, and as she broke through, the slight vibration she'd felt on her fingers increased a thousand-fold. It was like she'd plugged herself into an outlet, the current of energy running from her scalp to her toes, so intense that she thought for a second she'd been struck by lightning. Her spine straightened, the hair on her body rose and her skin rippled. She forced herself to look down. *Am I glowing?* She felt like she must be. Every nerve ending pinged. Every snap of a twig, every chirp of a bird — all sound rushed into her ears. Her eyesight sharpened and static objects breathed. The massive tree to her left sighed and shivered. The grass and brambles gasped and waved. The breeze that she hadn't known was there mussed her hair, caressed her skin and carried bits of pine and dirt and moss.

She moved her head slowly, taking everything in as her senses were bombarded. It was too much at once and she wanted to close her eyes, but she couldn't, not now, not when she saw Reuben. His bear overlapped his human form. It flickered in and out of her vision and his aura shone yellow and red, so vibrant that she had to blink to see it. As she narrowed her eyes, she could make out the pulse of his blood and the steady, heavy beat of his heart. He was healthy and strong and completely fixated on her, shooting lasers of hope straight back at her.

She turned her gaze to Ben, whose aura was a blue and brown with an ebb and flow of orange. Julian's was similar, but with pink and reds mixed in. And

Wren...his aura was black and gray and purple, a swirling chaotic lightshow that flared when her gaze landed on him.

"It's so beautiful," she gasped. *So beautiful. So intense.* Her legs wobbled. Her vision darkened. Her hearing flickered. "I think I'm going to fain—"

* * * *

"Lucki, drink some of this. It'll help." Reuben's soothing voice brought her back to awareness. He pressed the edge of a warm cup to her lips, and she took a sip. Cider. Sweet and spicy. She took a bigger sip that coated her throat and cleared her head.

She was lying against Rueben's body, between his legs and propped up so he could hold her. Julian and Ben were hovering, looking stricken. Wren was out of sight.

"What happened?" she asked between sips.

"Too much too soon," Julian huffed. "We should have prepared you better."

"We should have at least told her," Ben grumbled. "But Wren said—"

Reuben *tsk*ed and Ben clamped his mouth shut.

"Wren wanted to test me." Lucki had seen it in his eyes. He'd wanted so badly for something to happen but at the same time hadn't believe it would. "Did I pass?"

"You did." Reuben jostled her a little as he poured more cider into her cup. "But your power is so great that we really need to work on control. We can't have you passing out with Angelica bearing down."

"No, I wouldn't imagine that would end well for me." She tried for a chuckle but ended up coughing instead. "What happened to me in there?"

"You became a conduit for the magic, as you were meant to be," Reuben said. "A tremendous amount of power rose, Lucki, and without a doubt, you are the one to truly challenge Angelica this time."

"I can hear a *but* in your words, Reuben." Lucki twisted her body so she could look at him. His smile flickered. She twisted back and looked at Julian, then Ben. "Just tell me."

"It's maybe too much power to harness without at least one bond," Julian said as he rubbed the back of his neck and looked at her with a grimace. "The battle with Angelica happens here, in this circle. If you can't control the power, you won't be able to defend yourself. We can't help you, either. We're stuck outside the circle until the battle has been decided."

His words struck with force.

It wasn't just that she had power she'd never known she had and that she had to enter a locked sacred circle with a powerful sorceress who wanted to harm her. It was that in order for her to use her power properly, she'd need to give one of these men her eternity.

Or she could just walk away.

She could get into her car, drive across the border, get back to her old life and forget about all of this.

"I can't—"

"We know," Ben said as he knelt down next to her, his eyes saying that he did know and did understand. "We'll find another way."

"We will, Lucki. We promise you." Reuben's voice rumbled through her.

"The cats can help." Julian made a face. "I mean, the townsfolk, in human form, can help. They've had to figure out how to harness their power so it doesn't consume them."

"They have the same kind of power?" Lucki shifted herself forward, ready to stand and shake off the lingering dizziness.

Julian winced. "Well, not exactly —"

"But we'll sort out how to apply it so it works for you." Reuben helped her up. "With the amount of power you have, Lucki, we'll figure out a way."

She looked up at Reuben, then at Julian then finally Ben. These three men were so good, so kind, that she wished she could give herself to them. "Let's start training now. By the time we get back to town, everyone will be in the tavern, right? We can make it back here before it's too late."

"First we eat, then we get to work," Reuben said in his all-business voice. "Can't have you fainting from starvation, now can we? Ben will fly into town to let them know."

When she started to argue about there being no way she'd ever starve with him around, he pulled her into his arms and cut off her words with a fierce kiss. Her legs wobbled all over again, and when he let her go, she spun into Ben's arms for a second heart-stopping kiss. By the time he let her go, she was breathless and panting, so when Julian held her in his arms, her head was spinning.

He cupped her face and stared down at her. "We will always protect you, Lucki, and we will always follow your lead." Then he kissed her too, and she swore she saw fireworks behind her eyes.

Chapter Twelve

Reuben

"Once you have better control, you'll be able to call the magic from the circle wherever you are." Reuben knew Lucki was growing more frustrated by the minute, but she was also doing really well, considering. "You barely singed that tree. It'll live."

In truth, the tree would make better kindling now that she'd blasted a hole almost clean through it, but Reuben was trying for uplifting, and besides, it wasn't her fault that the damn cats...er...townsfolk...who were acting more and more like feral cats, hadn't been overly clear on what she needed to do.

"Like I said, lass," Andy drawled from his perch on a nearby stump. "Think of the magic as a silky ribbon, floatin' in the wind — no, dancin' in the wind, toward its destination — "

"Oh, Andy, you fool!" Deb Brown had come along with Shep O'Hara, Stephen Lector and Silvia Booth.

The group of them had been interrupting each other for the last hour, which wasn't very productive. All were fine people and powerful cats, but their communication style left much to be desired. "It's not a dancing ribbon she needs to imagine. It's a fountain she needs to control."

"Or like a tap you turn on and off," Silvia added, motioning with her hands how to turn a tap on and off.

Big sigh.

Stephen turned to Lucki, whose hair was a nest of knots, thanks to all the magic swirling around her. "Sweetheart, you need to concentrate. Pull the magic up from the ground." He swept his arms from his feet to circle over his head. "Like you're pumping it up from a well, then push it out. And look where you're pointing! It's no good closing your eyes like you have been."

"I'm trying." Lucki sighed. Her cheeks were smudged with soot and dirt and her shoulders were hunched like she was carrying a thousand pounds. "As soon as I step into the circle, it's like a torrent. I can barely move my arms up to begin with."

At least she'd stopped fainting. That was progress, as far as Reuben was concerned. This had originally been Wren's suggestion, to test her in the circle. Like the rest of them, he'd grown increasingly concerned by the days slipping by with no book appearing and no obvious signs that Lucki could call her magic to the surface. They'd tried to walk her through making wishes and casting minor spells intentionally, but as familiars, they knew little of how to construct a proper spell and knew more about gut feelings, which was very hard to convey.

Now that she was in the circle and its magic had released hers, Lucki needed to get a handle on her powers—that or leave town and get as far away from Weeping Falls as possible. There was a small window left for either of those things happening without Lucki getting hurt in the process. Wren had been right to push them to do this, but all the same, Reuben wanted to knock him on his ass for taking off when things had gotten too traumatic.

"Maybe we should call it a night," Reuben said in the most authoritative voice he could manage. He'd tried twice before to shut things down, but Lucki wouldn't hear of it. "We've been at this for hours and it's beyond cold now."

"No, not yet." Lucki held his stare, blasting him with determination, challenging him to say no. "Just a few more tries, okay? I'm not too tired and I'm not too cold."

Reuben looked at Ben then Julian. All three men shook their heads but otherwise said nothing. Lucki called the shots. If she said she was okay, then she was okay.

"That's it, girl," Shep cheered. "You tell 'em boys what you want—and you do it." He smirked at Reuben before focusing back on Lucki. "Now, you do what ol' Stephen said. You think of it like a water pump and clamp down hard on that torrent. You control it, just like you control these boys." He winked at Lucki, obviously delighting in the pink hue that rose to her cheeks. "Squeeze on that power, then direct it where you want it to go."

"But maybe, lass, maybe try not to blast fire again?" Andy offered. "You have healing magic at your fingertips. You could try to repair the damage you did to that tree over there."

Lucki winced and Reuben felt the pain of that. She hadn't meant to harm the tree. It was on the tip of his tongue to defend her, but Lucki didn't give him a chance. She nodded, then stepped into the circle without a second of hesitation.

The magic funneled around her instantly, just as it had each and every time she'd been in there. It whooshed up her body, carrying leaves and dirt along with it. It pulled her hair into a tornado of twists and turns. She fought to keep her eyes open. She'd learned to keep her mouth closed. It was a wonder that the magic didn't pick her up and carry her away. She held her body with rigid determination, moving stiffly as she slowly started to raise her hands.

Then, like a lightning strike, a jet of magic erupted from her fingers and demoed the rest of the tree she was presumably trying to fix.

Andy hauled her out of the circle. This time she slumped against him, her legs no longer able to hold her body weight.

Reuben moved in. "I've got her." He scooped her up into his arms. *Light as a feather.* "You had enough yet?"

Lucki looked up at him through squinty eyes, then let her head loll against his shoulder. "Yep."

"Good." Reuben nodded to the townsfolk. "Thank you kindly for your assistance tonight."

"You'll get the hang of it, darling," Deb said with a pat on Lucki's arm as Reuben passed her. Lucki managed a weak smile in return before closing her eyes and letting out a long, exhausted-sounding sigh.

"That girl has got a lot of power in her," Andy mumbled behind Reuben. "It'd be a shame if she doesn't get control over it."

"There's a quick way to do that," Shep said, "but she won't have it."

Of course everyone understood the significance of bonding and how much it would help Lucki get a handle on things, magically speaking.

"We'll escort you folks back to town," Julian said, "so you don't get up to any mischief!"

Reuben smiled to himself at the sound of Deb, Andy, Shep, Silvia and Stephen all squawking at the same time. They were a mischievous bunch, but they were also the most patient and knowledgeable. A few more nights of training with them and Lucki would have the magic leashed and doing her bidding, he was sure of it.

But for now… "I'll draw you a hot bath when we get back and put the kettle on."

"Sounds good," Lucki mumbled, her eyes still closed and her head still pressed against his chest. She draped her arm around his neck and snuggled in closer. "Maybe we should read in bed tonight instead of in the portico. I don't think I'll be awake long enough for it to be worth walking down the stairs."

Reuben beamed to himself again. *Snuggling with Lucki in her bed? Hell yes!* "As you wish, Lucki, as you wish."

* * * *

While Lucki was getting all sudsy in the clawfoot bath, a mental image that Reuben found his body more than aroused over, he got busy washing up then preparing a pot of watermint-berry tea, one of Lucki's favorites.

His spirits were amped, even though Lucki had been less than successful out in the circle tonight. He knew that she'd get a handle on her power sooner rather than later. She was dedicated and determined, a combination that both delighted and awed Reuben. Although he had a secret hope that she'd change her mind about bonding with at least one of them, preferably him, he was reassured by the amount of magic she had flowing inside her. It was only a matter of time before she'd master it, which would give her a definite advantage over Angelica, whose magic had been waning over the centuries.

The house was quiet but for all the creaks and groans, sighs and cracks that happened every night as it settled. Wren had stalked off once he knew Lucki would be okay after her fainting spell, but Reuben had felt him hovering in the background back at the circle. As angry as he'd been that Wren had taken off, now that he'd had time to cool down himself, Reuben understood. Watching Lucki collapse had been heart-stopping for him as well and had conjured the memories of Isabel's death. He could only imagine how the sight of Lucki fainting had impacted Wren.

Ben and Julian would likely patrol for a while, leaving Reuben to have some alone time with Lucki.

Her cat, Mr. Whiskers, milled about, crossing in between Reuben's legs as he prepared a little plate of treats while the tea steeped. "You must be lonely when all your pals leave for the night," Reuben said to the mangy tabby. "I think that qualifies you for a special treat."

Mr. Whiskers meowed in a totally normal cat way, no hidden communication there. All the same, Reuben knew the little beast agreed. A treat was in order. He'd made some jerky just for the cats, which they all went wild for. Reuben used it mainly to bribe the pint-sized terrors when the need arose. Mr. Whiskers had been in the house long enough to know the sound of Reuben taking the jerky container out and was already leaping to the counter to get his portion. Reuben gave him a bit extra then petted his coarse fur, stroking from head to tail until he got the answering purr of contentment.

It was odd how only he could understand the rest of the cats in their meows and chirps. It had never been part of his shifter physiology to communicate with animals, but for some reason, these magical cats were able to get messages across to him. Sure, they were often a confusing mess of symbols and emotions—but give him enough time and he usually figured out what they were trying to tell him.

Not Mr. Whiskers, though. He was just a regular old boy who liked a good petting and an extra treat or two.

The tea smelled just right, so Reuben piled everything onto a tray then headed up to see if Lucki was ready to join him for a bit of bedtime reading.

He was in love with this girl already, his heart so full now that she was in his life. She was young, yes, and distant at times—especially, he noticed, when things got too intimate between them, but he didn't fault her for that. Even though she hadn't told him the details, he knew that whatever her ex-boyfriend had done had traumatized her, and that kind of wound was almost impossible to heal completely. He didn't take it personally and was content to let her lead their lusty romance in whatever way she wanted. Although, if he were going to be honest, his need to bond with her was tremendous. The ever-thudding pulse to protect her in the best way he could was a constant reminder of the sole purpose for his existence.

He was a familiar, born into his current shifter body out of mysterious magic more than two centuries ago, and his driving instinct was to seek out a magical creature and join forces. The curse had trapped him in Weeping Falls, and obligation had forced him to stay put, to not venture out of town and fight against the boundaries of Angelica's hex, so he'd been living for far too long without ultimately fulfilling his life goal. Now that Lucki was there, every instinct in his body screamed to claim her, but there was no way he'd force that on anyone.

He knocked on her bedroom door, precariously balancing the tray with one hand.

"Come in!" Lucki flung the door open and greeted him with a wide smile. "I could smell that all the way up here. My favorite!"

She was wrapped up in a plush robe, her hair pinned to the top of her head somehow. Her skin was flush with color, her freckles popping and her eyes sparkling with a hint of magic. Gone were the dark circles under them, and exhaustion was no longer radiating off her.

"I thought you might be hungry." He set the tray down on the desk in her room then offered her the plate of treats.

"Are those mini-eclairs?" She plucked one of the bite-sized pastries from the plate then popped it into her mouth. "Oh my Goddess, Rueben," she said between chewing, her fingers hovering over her mouth like she was scared the éclair would try to escape. "You are a master baker." She took another one.

It pleased him more than was reasonable to have her so thoroughly enjoying his baking. "I thought you might like them."

"Like them? Oh, Reuben, I might eat the whole plate!" She tugged his hand. "Come on. Let's get comfy on the bed."

That got him moving at lightning speed, which made Lucki laugh in her sing-song way. Within minutes he had them all set up, tea in hand, eclairs within reach, Lucki nestled against his chest, her head resting on his shoulder and his book in hand.

The scent of the watermint was powerful, but it didn't overshadow Lucki's natural perfume. Reuben was drunk on inhaling her unique mixture of cinnamon and vanilla. It wafted up his nose and tickled the back of his throat. It made his mouth water and his heart pound in all the right ways. He could get used to this. Having Lucki so close and so at ease with him was something he wished would last forever.

"Do you remember where we left off?" Reuben flipped open *Wuthering Heights*, one of his favorite classics. A funny thought, actually, considering that he himself was older than the book.

"With Heathcliff brooding over Catherine?"

Reuben laughed. "That could summarize the entire book."

"I know." Lucki sighed wistfully. She put her teacup down on the side table then nuzzled in closer to Reuben. "Why do people think this is a romance?"

Reuben frowned. "Do they?" It was far from a romance, with all its tragedy.

Lucki lifted her hand to stroke the side of his face as she looked up at him. "Some people do. They think

Heathcliff is the hero of their dreams. The tragic hero is appealing to some people."

She shuttered her eyes and Reuben knew it was partly because they were treading close to ex-boyfriend territory. He brushed some stray hair from her face and smiled down at her. "Dark heroes can be tantalizing to some, I'm sure, but I think you deserve a hero with a heart of pure intention and devotion. You deserve to be worshipped." Which he meant literally. Her body and soul deserved all that and more. He could worship her flawless skin with his tongue and his lips and his hands. He could worship her soul by making sure she was always happy, always cared for and always protected.

She nodded slowly, her eyes roving to his lips. "I like it when you say things like that."

He set his cup down then pulled her close enough to smell the mint on her breath.

"I will never hurt you, Lucki." His words rumbled out of his mouth with his heart tied up in them. "I will always strive to be the hero of your dreams."

She held his gaze for seconds longer and he hoped she saw the truth in his eyes. He was hers, body, heart and soul.

She slipped one leg over his hips and pulled herself higher, so she was eye level.

She kissed his forehead, then his eyelids, then each cheek before settling at his lips. "Show me," she said.

Chapter Thirteen

Lucki

Lucki was haunted by ghosts—ghosts of her past, ghosts of her broken heart and ghosts of her broken soul. The magic circle had awakened every sense in her body, even one she hadn't known she had. More than just a sixth sense, it was a sense of magic, and it was too much. She saw sparkles of it everywhere she looked now. It rolled off Reuben in pulsing waves of red. It coated every single thing in the mansion. Even when she closed her eyes, she still sensed it was there, ebbing and flowing in the air she breathed.

She wanted comforting, but not the usual kind that Reuben gave her. She needed his solid body pressed down on her, his hard cock pressed into her. And she yearned for his kiss—that deep, passionate, take-her-breath-away kiss that he was so good at and that would obliterate all other sensations.

He curled one meaty hand into her hair, cradling the back of her head tenderly. His soft eyes told her things she would rather not see. *Love. Loyalty. Limitless passion.* It was too much to handle in this moment, so she closed her eyes and let his kiss take her away.

With their tongues entwined, exploring and stroking, Reuben used his free hand to open Lucki's robe so that it gaped wide. Her nipples, already hard beads, stiffened even more from the cooler air of her bedroom, then more still from the brush of Reuben's hand as he eased her robe away from her skin.

His mouth pressed to hers and the heat from his hand as he cupped one breast at the side, rubbing his thumb over and over again against her nipple, made her shiver. He knew just how to strum her body so it sang.

The same euphoria she'd felt in the circle of magic stones spiraled through her, more manageable now than it had been earlier. She wanted to touch Reuben's body, to connect with him skin-to-skin so she could pull herself out of her head and all the spinning thoughts of the past, present and future.

She helped him unbutton his shirt, never once breaking away from their kiss. Even as he shifted out of his clothes then removed her robe, their lips somehow kept contact.

He roved with his hands first, wisps of touch along her sensitive skin, raising goosebumps in his wake. When he cupped her pussy, it was a cocoon of pressure, enveloping her clit in his huge palm. She gasped into his mouth, but he kept on kissing her. She spread her legs for him and he curled his fingers inside, rubbing against her clit as he did. She moaned and rocked her hips, urging him deeper.

His cock was too large to encircle with her fingers, so she stroked with her whole hand, shifting around his girth each time she slid from tip to base then back again.

When Reuben pulled his lips away, Lucki wanted to protest, but all words lodged in her throat because he'd only stopped kissing her mouth. He had no intention, it seemed, to stop kissing altogether. He moved her to the side, shifting so that his huge body hovered over her, still stroking her pussy and teasing her clit, but now also trailing his lips along every curve and dip she had.

He kissed a line along her collarbone, the hollow between her breasts and each nipple, all the while pumping his fingers deep inside, rubbing her G-spot, making the darkness behind her eyelids sparkle with millions of stars.

His kisses left a hot trail behind, and as he moved out of her hands' range, she let go of his cock and brought her fingers to her nipples so she could flick and pinch and tease herself into the stratosphere.

When his warm breath cascaded over her wet pussy, she arched her back, splayed her legs wider and offered herself to him. His answering grunt sounded like approval, so she held herself there until he wrapped his hands around her hips, his fingers spreading over her ass to hold her up. She opened her eyes and looked down her body at him. His gaze was on her pussy, devouring her before his lips had even touched her there.

He must have felt her looking at him, because he flicked his eyes to meet hers, a harpoon of lust shooting straight into her. She pushed herself up onto her elbows then let her head fall back, her eyes closed once again, reveling in the sensation of anticipation.

He lifted her hips higher and her body coiled. Her breath hitched and her heart pounded furiously.

She wouldn't beg him, not with her words, but she guessed her body already was.

She was wet for him, weeping need. Her flesh was taut, primed to be carried away on waves of pleasure.

When he licked her pussy from bottom to top, she groaned. He sucked her clit hard, and she cried out. When he held her up with one hand then used his other to slip his fingers back inside her, she lost her mind completely.

She came furiously fast and without warning. As Reuben sucked and licked, her orgasm made her fly along a rolling current, a hurricane of pleasure. And he didn't relent—even when her legs fell limp to the sides and she had to stop touching herself because her nipples were too sensitive, Reuben kept going. Her clit throbbed, her pussy spasmed, and just when she thought she might die from it all, the coil wrapped so tightly in her core released with a gush.

Reuben let her go. He climbed up her body. The bed swayed and bucked under his weight. She panted hard and lifted her hands to his chest once he was at eye level.

"I'm on the pill," she blurted. "Birth control." Not because she planned on having sex with all the men in Alaska, but because her periods were bloody awful without them.

"I'm immortal." Reuben's throaty voice was barely a sound. "I don't carry disease and I'm not susceptible to it."

"I want this." Lucki didn't flinch away, not even as Reuben's eyes showed his understanding, and how very, very much he wanted it too. "Not to bond."

"No. Not to bond," Reuben agreed, then he nuzzled into her throat and kissed down to her breasts once again.

She ran her fingers through his hair. His beard tickled her stomach and his mouth worked its magic on her nipples. She lifted her legs and wrapped them around his waist, urging him back up with a roll of her hips and a tug on his hair.

"I want this," she repeated then lifted her head so she could kiss him.

He pressed his cock along her slit, teasing her pussy just with his proximity. She rolled her hips again and Reuben's arms shook. He opened his mouth wider and deepened their kiss just as he slid his dick home.

She stilled for a moment, the girth of his cock stretching her beyond her wildest imagination. He let her be, not moving an inch until she coaxed him again, urging him with her tongue in his mouth and her legs wrapped around his hips.

One fluid motion and he was in to the hilt. Goddess, he filled her. There wasn't room left inside and she didn't know how he would move again—but he did. He rolled his hips and pressed his weight down, like he knew just what she needed, how much pressure it would take to chase away the ghosts in her head and let her focus solely on how their bodies fit together. He guided his dick out slowly, so she felt his tip moving as her body gripped him tightly. He slid his arms around her back, holding her up and close to his chest, then nuzzled his face against her ear so she could hear the thunder of his breath. He rocked into her again…and again…and again.

Reuben

Reuben had never been so close to heaven before. Lucki's sweet body cushioned his every move. Her curves fit like puzzle pieces against his muscles, and her legs around his hips held on so tight that he knew she needed him to fill her up, to pound her deep and to give her the release she so craved.

The rippling pulse of her pussy was like fingers stroking and squeezing against his cock. He could stay inside her forever, inhaling her scent, licking her skin, sucking on her lips and making her moan. Forever would be nice, but there was no way his body would endure. As it was, Reuben struggled to keep himself from coming. He wanted to make it last, to pleasure her for as long as he could.

But the way she purred.

The way she mewed.

The way her body writhed and flexed and stoked his fire.

It was too much to handle.

Even an immortal shifter had his weaknesses, and for Reuben, his was this beauty beneath him. It wasn't just her body, which was glorious, tight, flawless. It was her soul, her heart, her empathy and her magic. She was the complete package, and he was grateful that she was letting him in.

He sucked her earlobe and her body quaked. He crushed his chest to hers and her hard little nipples rubbed against his, sending sparks through his body that flashed from skin to core. His balls grew tight and hot. His cock stiffened almost painfully. He lifted her ass higher and drilled into her sweet pussy until he just couldn't take another second of denial.

"Lucki," he groaned. His whole body shuddered as he released a torrent of cum, spewing deep inside, coating her pussy. The urge to bond her pummeled against his restraint. He clenched his jaw and battled the impulse.

She is mine. She is mine. She is mine.

But she was not.

Lucki belonged to no one.

Reuben pushed himself away, withdrawing from Lucki's warmth. She tried to hang on, to keep him with her, but he couldn't. He just couldn't. She was too much for him.

"Reuben," she spoke softly, her hand out as if to stop him.

"I just need some time." He tried to keep his voice soft too, but he knew he sounded like a bear, because his bear clawed at his insides, desperate to get out, to assert dominance.

"I understand." But she reached out to him anyway and touched his shoulder. "I'm sorry."

"Your boundaries are clear, Lucki. This isn't a *you* problem. This is a *me* problem." He shifted back, because just that simple touch was enough to make his bear roar within. "I'm going to go for a run, to blow off some steam. You get some sleep. I promise I'll be fine in the morning."

She lowered her head, but not before he saw a flash of what looked like regret cross her face.

"Lucki, I can handle this." He forced himself to move close to her, to lift her face. He hoped with everything he had that his eyes didn't betray him, because her smell, her skin, her freckles, the way her eyes danced with a collection of unshed tears, all demanded that he kiss her again, and if he did, he'd never let her go. "I can handle this."

She smiled a little then nodded. She lifted her hands to his face then pressed her forehead to his. "I'll never do anything to hurt you, Reuben."

"It doesn't hurt. Promise," he lied. He pushed himself out of her reach again then bolted out of her room and away from her magnetic touch—like a coward.

Like a damn coward.

Chapter Fourteen

Lucki

Her hunting companion was Wren, and he hadn't spoken much beyond a few grunts all morning. They were searching the attic...top floor. It was the last section of the mansion to look, and like every other space in the massive house, the attic was massive too — although not as cluttered as Lucki had always imagined attics in grand old homes to be.

As with the rest of the house, there wasn't a spot of dirt or a bit of dust anywhere on the top floor. Reuben hadn't been joking when he'd said he kept a clean house. There were some large pieces of furniture that were stacked and draped with white cloth in the back portion, but otherwise it was set up like a large studio apartment. It had a plush king-size bed, a small office space complete with antique secretary desk, a decent-size kitchenette, a full bathroom and a seating area that was curl-up-on-a-rainy-day comfortable-looking. *Quite a little refuge.* Very cozy, even though it spanned nearly the whole footprint of the house and was all open space with high rafters that reached the various peaks.

"Do you know of any hidden nooks up here?" She'd been trying for the last twenty minutes to get Wren talking, because searching for hours wasn't exactly the most thrilling of jobs and she'd gotten used to the near-constant easy chatter she'd had with the other men while they'd been searching the other floors.

Wren stalked toward her, and for a second, she had the impulse to curl up into a ball and play dead. Even though he didn't resemble a wolf in any other way, his eyes always seemed to hold a sharp edge that warned her of proximity to a predator. Not that she thought he'd do anything to physically hurt her, but still... Call it instinct or whatever, but she always got a chill when he stared at her like that. And not a bad chill either, more like an intrigued one.

He got so close to her—which was jarring, because he always kept his distance—that she smelled his aftershave or whatever cologne he was wearing—cloves, oranges, maybe a hint of vanilla. She leaned toward him.

He reached past her and, with a screeching, grating, metal-against-metal groan, lifted a hatch she hadn't noticed was behind her.

"Laundry chute." He turned abruptly and walked to the other side of the room, moved two boxes then did the same thing with a larger wooden hatch. "Dumb waiter."

"Ah. Got it." Defeated, Lucki turned back to the chest of drawers she was searching.

"It's not that I don't think the book is here somewhere." His gruff voice startled her, if only because he'd never said so many words strung together all at once.

She froze and dared not speak in case he had more to say. *Goddess, I hope he has more to say.*

"Isabel wouldn't have hidden it in any place we would have looked. Not because she didn't trust us..." He huffed, so Lucki peeked over her shoulder to see him running his hand through his hair and pacing a small circuit in the middle of the room. "She just had a thing about her grimoire. She always said that it was only meant for a witch's eyes and that some things were too sacred to leave lying around."

Lucki turned fully to face him. "So, we're wasting our time?"

Wren stopped pacing and speared her with a different kind of sharp look, the exasperated kind. "That's what I've been saying for weeks, haven't I?"

Lucki frowned. "Um...no?" She crossed her arms. "This is the most you've said to me since I got here, which makes me wonder, since we're talking about it, why that is? Do you not like me? Do I bother you? Have I done something to offend you?" There was a sharpness to her voice that she didn't mean to let out, but dammit, she was just as frustrated as Wren seemed to be—maybe for different reasons, though.

"Sorry." He dropped his shoulders in a way that made him seem vulnerable.

It was not the response she'd expected.

"I'm not good with change," he continued, which shocked Lucki enough to dam up any more words from blurting out. "And you're just so"—he winced and rubbed the back of his neck—"here."

Silence hung between them like an iron shield. She didn't like it. It seemed impenetrable, but she also wasn't sure if it was her putting the shield up or him.

"I'm sorry if my being here is digging up painful memories for you." Which was what she assumed was going on. Wren had been Isabel's mate. He felt he'd failed her and that was why she had died. Lucki being here reminded him of that failure. It didn't take a psychologist to figure that one out. She swam in painful memories every day. While she was awake and while she was dreaming, she marinated in her pain. She understood how reminders could open wounds that were so deep she'd bleed to death right then and there. But she never did.

Die, that was.

"It's not." He shook his head and barked a laugh. "Okay, it is, but it's not your fault." He motioned to the other side of the staircase. "You want to sit for a bit? Take a break?"

Lucki couldn't help the beaming smile that cracked her face wide open. "I'd love to." Because really, that was all she had wanted to do since Wren had mumbled over breakfast that it would be him and her searching the attic. At the time, his words had made her think he was dreading the hours they'd spend together, but maybe he'd been dreading the feelings she would conjure in him.

Wren waited for her to select a seat, which ended up being a double-wide plush lounger that she sank into. Then he took the seat opposite her, which was kind of a bummer. It was silly, really, since the man had barely spoken to her in all the time she'd been there, but she'd gotten used to the free and easy way the others had been treating her. Even with the weirdness between her and Reuben after they'd had sex, he was still more affectionate and touchy-feely than Wren had ever been with her. She always craved that kind of connection, with friends, with lovers. She needed touch to keep her grounded in reality, to let her know where she stood with people.

"I've been difficult, I know." His face was deadpan serious. "I mean, Reuben has told me how difficult I'm being, that I should make an effort."

Ah, so this was because of Reuben. Funny, Lucki would never have pegged Wren for the type to follow orders from another man. "I understand why you want to keep me at arm's length. I don't like it, but I understand." Since he was being honest, she might as well be honest too. "I'm not exactly being easy when it comes to the whole bonding thing."

"No, you're not."

Even though she'd just said the same thing, she wasn't expecting him to agree so bluntly. "Well, I have my reasons."

"Right, the ex." Lucki didn't know if Wren meant to sound sarcastic, but the tone combined with his tight jaw and quirking eyebrow made it seem like he was.

"Shane." She hadn't said his name out loud in over a year. It tasted bitter on her tongue...like poison.

"What did he do to you?" Again, Wren's voice held a note of judgment, like whatever it was, Lucki had to be overreacting. He crossed his arms and leaned back in his chair so he could cross his legs at the ankle—very casual and yet, not casual at all. "Obviously he broke your heart, but what did he do that was so bad?"

So bad? Yep, definitely a tone. Anger boiled in Lucki's stomach, bubbling away like a simmering cauldron.

"Whoa, ease up there, cowboy!" Lucki held her hands up. "This is the first conversation we've ever had. Maybe we should start with favorite colors or something." She tried to keep her voice light, but she was straining and it was obvious that he could tell. If he was going to talk to her like that, then she wasn't going to give him anything more than necessary. Relationships were a two-way street.

He looked at her with wide eyes and a quirk to his lips that she thought meant she'd surprised him, but she didn't know him well enough to be sure. "You know about my heartbreak." Somehow, he managed to shrug sitting like that.

Good point. Yet she still didn't feel obliged to share.

"And *one day*, you'll know about mine." But not now. Conversation time was over. She patted her legs then stood up. "Better get back to it."

But before she could turn, Wren was up in her space with his lean, mean muscle-machine body, his delicious-smelling skin, his cascading hair that fell past his shoulders, his furious scowl — and kissable-looking lips.

Good Goddess, he was a spark to her gasoline. He was octane ready to detonate, and she was combustible just standing next to him. *What the hell do they put in the water around here anyway?*

He lifted his hands to her face, cupping her cheeks so he could stare into her eyes. His touch wasn't rough — his hold on her loose — but all the same, she dared not move. "What in the world did he do to you that would make you this way?"

His words were offensive. She *should* take offense, but instead, something crumbled inside her. A wall she'd been building and building all year cracked, splintered. It was like Wren's touch was almost enough to tear the whole thing down.

"He hurt me." But hurt was just a soft word for what Shane had done. He'd lied to her. He'd manipulated her. He'd taken her vulnerability and had twisted it for his own pleasure. He'd never hit her. He hadn't needed to. He'd wounded her deep inside — a sword to the gut that he'd slowly twisted and twisted for as long as they were together. He'd created insecurity and doubt.

Worse than all of that, he'd murdered her beloved cats.

Wren didn't tell her he wouldn't hurt her. He didn't attempt to sooth her relived pain. Instead, he held her stare and all he said was, "I understand."

And that broke her even more.

They called it quits on the search, because Lucki was on the verge of sobbing, and Wren had the sense to steer her downstairs so Reuben could make her some chamomile. After a barely hushed, furiously fast whispered argument, Wren stomped his way out of the house, even going so far as to slam the door behind him.

Reuben mumbled something that sounded like, "man child," as he got busy pouring water into the kettle.

She cradled her head in her hands, her hair falling like a curtain around her face. She hadn't had a chance to talk to Reuben, like really talk to him, after they'd had sex and he'd run away. At the time it had made perfect sense to her that he'd needed to bolt after their explosive sex, to cool off and gather himself. She'd kinda needed that alone time too, but she'd been avoiding actually talking to him about it in the days that had passed. Words died on her tongue every time she was alone with him lately, and an awkward silence usually hung around them until one of them broke it with something benign or neutral. So, they'd been talking about the cats a lot lately.

"I think I'm getting really good at upsetting everyone here." Self-pity was a default mood she didn't particularly like, but there it was, coating her thoughts right now and tainting her every word.

"No, Lucki, it's not you." Reuben clattered around in the kitchen, opening a drawer then a cupboard. "It's an adjustment for us, but we'll get there."

"Ugh!" Lucki rubbed her hands over her head, pushing her hair off her face. "Reuben! It *is* me!"

"It's up to us to adjust." Reuben turned toward her. "You didn't ask to come here and deal with the heavy story we laid at your feet. It's our baggage to carry, not yours."

But she'd definitely made things complicated by adding sex to the relationships. "Maybe we should all just be friends. No benefits." She hadn't meant to say that out loud, but there it was, right there, flopping on the table like a dying thing.

Reuben lowered his eyes then got busy with the kettle once again, but not before he pinched his eyebrows and curl his lips into a frown. "We'll follow your lead, Lucki. Always."

"You don't owe me anything, and you certainly don't need to be so accommodating." She pushed her chair back and winced as the feet screeched across the wood floor. "I'm sorry. It isn't like me to wallow in self-pity. It's just…well…you know…frustrating to hit so many road blocks. I want to help, but we can't find the book, and it seems like I'm the only one really messing things up here."

"Lucki—"

"No, Reuben, for real." She held her hand up and inwardly pleaded for him to understand her next words. "Should I go?" She didn't want to. She liked it here, with these men, with these cats. It had begun to really feel like home. "If I do, will Scout be free to find another Cat Keeper? Is me being here stopping another woman from being found…one who would be willing to…? Well…oh, never mind."

She started toward the hall, but Reuben was on her in a flash, just like Wren, but when he cupped her face and stared into her eyes, it wasn't lust that jammed up her brain this time—it was compassion and love. It radiated off him like a heater and warmed her in a way she hadn't realized she needed.

"There is no one who can replace you, Lucki. We don't want you to leave." He sighed deeply. "But we also won't force you to stay."

"I don't want to leave. I love it here. But I'm messing things up, aren't I?"

"You aren't messing anything up." He rubbed his thumb over her jaw. "You are the most important person here, Lucki. We will die protecting you if we must. It's you who doesn't owe us anything. All we want is friendship—with or without the benefits."

"But you told me that familiars need the bond of a witch." Many nights before, when they'd been in between books, Reuben had told her the story of his origin.

Reuben, along with many other shifters, had come to exist as fully-grown men with no memory of life before that moment more than two hundred years before. They'd been birthed into a guild of familiars, the Brotherhood of Shade, in an ice fortress way north of

Alaska. They'd spent time learning their place, honing their instincts and embodying the goals of the Brotherhood — protect a witch, bolster her power, serve her for eternity. According to the Brotherhood, the soul of a familiar never died, even if his body did. Each of them came to be after the death of their previous life. They retained no memory of their past one and were unburdened by lingering feelings for anything that may have come before this life.

"Yes, we do, but we've survived this long without one. Another few weeks won't kill anyone."

Which meant, of course, that if Lucki somehow managed to reverse the curse, Reuben, Ben, Julian and Wren would be free to leave — to roam the Earth and find a witch to bond with.

Her stomach twisted in a hollow way. Oh, how selfish she was being. The nerve of her to even feel an ounce of jealousy over that.

"Reuben —"

"Lucki —" He matched her tone then quirked an eyebrow.

She couldn't help but smile. "Fine." She threw her hands up. "Fine."

Reuben grinned, kissed her forehead, then let her face go. "Why don't you go sit down and I'll bring you your tea?"

Lucki rubbed her hand over her face. "You're too good to me." She waved off his protest then headed out of the kitchen.

Isabel's sitting room was directly in front of her. She hadn't actually gone in there for longer than a few minutes, because there was a weird energy hanging in the air. She stopped at the door. This was a proper tea room, and she imagined Lady Clover had often had guests in there, sitting with her, chatting about town events. Maybe she'd had fellow witches in here with her and they'd discussed how best to work a spell.

Lucki stepped into the room. Julian complained that the seats were uncomfortable, but they looked perfectly fine to her. There was a flamingo pink camelback couch that looked soft and well cushioned, and a peach Queen Anne, which she chose to sit on if only because it looked like the exact kind of chair that would be avoided by every man in this house.

The perfect tea-sipping seat.

And it was…stiff. She pushed herself up so she could look down at the cushion. It was bulky and looked like it should be soft, but it wasn't.

She sat down again.

As hard as a slab of marble.

As hard as a sheet of granite.

As hard as a… Her heart bounced in her chest. She jumped up then grabbed the chair arms. "Reuben!" She flipped the chair over as carefully as possible. It was so heavy, though, and took all of her strength to get it down on its side. "Reuben!"

His thundering steps vibrated through the floor. "What happened? Are you okay?"

There was a piece of wood that spanned the bottom of the chair and looked as though it was locked in place, but Lucki pushed on it anyway — and it moved…slid completely out of the back of the chair. Out tumbled a leather-bound book, right into Lucki's hands. It was heavy, almost unwieldy, but there was no denying that it was a book of magic.

The cat eye on the cover.

The tremor of barely contained power.

The answering call in her body like a magnet finding metal.

Reuben had his hand on his heart as he stepped across the hall to her.

She grinned up at him, her hands trembling, her heart thundering. "I found it."

Chapter Fifteen

Lucki

There were no visible words on any page of the book — not a letter, not a squiggle. Nothing. So, at first, Lucki was a little disappointed. Was this the long-sought-after spell book of the infamous Lady Clover? Or was this a decoy she'd planted in order to protect the actual grimoire she'd created?

The men all stood around Lucki as she hunched over the book at the kitchen table. She'd flipped from one end to the other but could find no evidence that this massive tome was actually full of spells.

But her skin prickled like every hair follicle was super-charged with static. Her chest was full with her drumming heart. Her stomach had bubbles brewing, ready to pop confetti all over the place.

There was something there. Lucki was missing it somehow.

"I don't understand." She ran her fingers along the edge of one page. Power snapped her nerve endings, making her hyper-aware of every sound, every breath, every smell around her. The men were crowded in, hovering, their confusion and concern sliding off of them like mini-avalanches to land on her shoulders.

"It would be just like Isabel to have a decoy," Wren mumbled before taking a step back so he could cross him arms and glower. "I knew it couldn't be this simple."

Simple! "We searched the entire house for this book! We looked in the sitting room. We gave up weeks in this hunt. There's nothing simple about where she hid it." Lucki scowled over her shoulder at Wren, who at least had the common sense to erase the grumbly growl from his expression. "I don't think this is a decoy. I don't know how, really, but I believe this is the book."

"It's empty, Lucki. The last I saw of this book, mind you, more than one hundred and fifty years ago, it was full — not a page left untouched." Reuben blew out his cheeks then let the air escape in a slow hiss.

"She did something to it then." Lucki ran her hand over a page and had the sensation of being plugged in, like she'd become a conduit but the power flow wasn't yet turned on. It was similar to how it was in the stone circle, but obviously more controlled and less intense.

One of the cats jumped up onto the table, a gray longhair with gem-green eyes, then two panthers, both with yellow eyes and sleek short fur and finally, a marmalade tom with hazel eyes and a Cheshire grin. The cats perched themselves around the book. They didn't lick their paws or make a sound. They all just sat like beautifully posed statues, their gazes full of expectation.

"What do I do?" she whispered. "You know there's something here too, right? You all feel it, don't you?"

If she had magic inside her and the book had magic hidden, shouldn't she be able to uncover it, reveal the writing somehow? Should the book speak to her in a way? If she were truly a magical being, a witch, then the secrets within the book should be available to her.

The tom cat touched her hand then quickly touched the book, so she laid her hand back down, palm flat and fingers spread over the page she had been staring at. She looked back to the tom cat, but he'd moved to the other side of the table and had begun licking his balls.

Nice.

Lucki shook her head. *Cats.*

The gray longhair moved in next. She nuzzled her cheek along Lucki's hand and purred so loudly that Lucki felt the sound tunnel into her and rattle her core. It was a 'wake-up' purr. A 'pay attention' purr. Lucki straightened her back and tilted her chin down.

The gray long-haired kitty licked her fingers, one after the other with her rough tongue, then bit deeply into her thumb.

Lucki yelped and tried to pull her hand away, but the gray longhair cat clamped down harder to hold her hand in place, its green eyes narrowed and locked with hers, which were quickly filling with tears.

"What the devil?" Julian reached over her shoulder to snatch the cat away, but Reuben stopped him with a low growl.

"Leave the cat."

"But the little bastard is hurting—"

"Leave it be!" Reuben growled again.

Lucki watched the droplets of her blood seep from around the cat's fang. The wound burned fiercely, like a hot poker was jammed into her skin. The two panthers slithered their way closer, taking up residence on either side of Lucki, so close that they were almost touching her. Almost.

A tremor rocked Lucki's body. Everything slowed down. Her breath caught. The grandfather clock ticked like drumbeats. She watched the drops of blood roll from her thumb to slowly fall to the page of the book.

The moment of contact, the seconds of splatter when her blood hit the page and was immediately absorbed inside was the moment that the magic was unleashed. It rose from the page, tingled through her fingers, electrocuted her muscles so they spasmed and travelled to the core of her body where she'd come to understand her own magic lay waiting. Once mingled, it was like baking soda and vinegar. It fizzed and bubbled, rushing up and out, sparking along every nerve and every vein, jolting her heart and forcing her lungs to work at hyper speed. Her vision flashed with fireworks, and her brain wobbled and blinked, like a shutdown was imminent. It was a torrent like the stone circle — a torrent that Lucki had no hope of controlling.

The black cats at her sides leaned into her, like they knew she was about to explode, and the second they made contact, everything going haywire inside her stilled. Time froze again. Her breathing settled. Her heart slowed. It was like she'd been plunged under water — but not in a terrifying way. It just slowed everything down so that when she turned her gaze to the book and the gray long-haired cat released her thumb then stepped away, Lucki saw the tight cursive scrawl of Isabel's spells. They bled into the page as she swept her eyes over the empty space then disappeared again when she moved on.

She couldn't help the gasp that billowed from her lips or the tears the tracked down her cheek. "Guys, are you seeing this? It's all here." She flipped the page and more words appeared — spells for enchantment, spells for love, spells for heartbreak. She quickly flipped through the book until she got close to the end.

"Try one of them," Ben said, his voice a little breathless.

Try one? Yes, she should. She definitely should. Lucki flipped back to a spell she'd seen near the beginning. The panthers at her side leaned closer, pressing their warm bodies into her upper arms. The marmalade tom was back, standing at the head of the book, his paw lifted just above the page she'd stopped on. She was taking that as cat approval. The gray longhair who'd bitten her was lying next to the book, stretched out leisurely and looking unconcerned.

Lucki sucked in a deep breath. Reuben put his hand on her shoulder briefly. She glanced up at him and tried for a smile. He nodded his encouragement. She didn't look at Wren, who was standing just behind Reuben. She didn't want to be swayed by his doubt.

"Okay then. Let's give this a try." She ran her hand over the page as the words popped up.

"Little beast, whose eyes doth glow. Rise up! Rise up! Let us see you grow." It seemed simple enough, and a swirl of magic wisped against Lucki's cheek and moved her hair.

"What's supposed to happen?" Wren asked.

Lucki opened her mouth, her shoulder half raised in a shrug, when the panthers at her side began to meow. They didn't move but Lucki felt a shift and, from one second to the next, they went from barely reaching her shoulders to purring in her ear.

The long-haired gray and the marmalade tom grew as well...triple their size. Still domestic cats in appearance, but more the size of large Maine Coons or Savannahs.

"They've grown!" Lucki looked over the cats in awe.

"You did it!" Reuben rubbed her shoulders, or tried to anyway. The two panthers were still guarding her sides.

"Well done, Lucki!" Julian leaned in and kissed the top of her head. Ben gave her a thumbs up and a beaming smile.

She flickered her eyes to Wren, whose arms were still crossed and eyebrows were still pinched together. As much as she knew what he was about to say, she still hoped it would be something else that came out of his mouth.

"And what, exactly, are we going to do with oversized housecats? Feed them more food, I guess." Then he looked at her pointedly, one eyebrow raised.

"It's not the cats' size that's important, you dolt," Reuben grumbled. "But you're too thick-headed to see past that. The *cats* have helped her control her powers. The cats chose this spell for her to show us." Reuben closed his eyes and rubbed one side of his head at the temple, like he had a sudden headache. "They want..." He seemed to be concentrating harder. "They want her to..."

The black cats meowed in her ears. One short meow. In unison. The stone circle flashed through Lucki's mind. "They want me to go to the circle."

Reuben blinked open his eyes to look down at her. "Yes. That's what they want." He held out his hand to her. "Let's go to the circle and see what happens."

With the larger cats leading the way, they all trudged out to the forest and headed to the stone circle. The smaller cats didn't stay behind. They came too, but they stuck together like a pack, trailing slightly behind, as though they were taking up the rear in case of an attack.

"I'm going to survey the area, just in case," Ben said, and in a dancing sparkle of color, he went from man to hawk, hovering in mid-air for a moment, his strong wings holding him at eye level before he craned his head upward and took off.

"I'll check the perimeter," Wren grunted. Then he, too, went from man to beast—fur flying and colors swirling, he transformed in seconds to his wolf.

"What are we worried about?" Lucki was high from her success. She was floating in euphoric triumph.

"Angelica." Reuben took Lucki by the elbow. "With the cats out like this, it could attract her."

"Oh." Her feet touched the ground once again. *Right.* Because there was a crazy-ass sorceress out there who wanted the cats, and here they all were, tramping along in the forest to help Lucki get a handle on her powers. "Maybe we shouldn't let them—"

"You don't really think the cats will listen to you right now, do you, beauty?" Julian came up to her other side and gave her a lopsided grin. "They do as they please."

As if to second his assessment, the larger cats who were leading each tossed her a sassy cat look over their shoulders before universally swishing their tails then trotting on ahead.

"Right. Well, what are the chances that Angelica will come right now?" Because she really, really didn't want a showdown with the woman before she actually had a chance to hone her power and learn the spells she'd need from the book. "I mean, the duel isn't for another month."

"She likely won't come." Julian gently tugged her hair. "But it's better to be aware of our surroundings. With the cats out, she might get curious. She can't breach the protection spell that Lady Clover created until the night of the Summer Solstice, but she can use her wiles to get the cats to cross to her."

Lucki didn't love the sound of that, but she knew that what Julian had said already was true. The cats did as they pleased and, right now, they were set on helping her. Reuben had wanted to bring the grimoire, but the cats had insisted that they leave it behind. They were all deferring to the kitties and their uncanny wisdom.

They were still a bit away from the stones, but it didn't matter, because every step Lucki took toward the magic space only intensified the jittering jolts that poked down her spine. Her brain was in squirrel mode as well, jumping from one thought to the next so that her eyes darted from here to there. It wasn't fear that had her so tweaked out, however. It was magic. For all intents and purposes, it was acting like a new drug to her system, making it almost impossible to focus on one thing at a time.

The larger cats bounded ahead, and as they turned past the next twisted, gnarly group of trees, the stone circle came into view.

Once again, Lucki was struck by how grand it was, how awe-inspiring, how ancient. It glowed with its own aura, a rainbow of shimmer that called to her. The bigger cats were already inside, sitting on different stone slabs, their eyes glittering with calculated thoughts that Lucki was already experiencing wisps of. *"Come,"* they said. *"We'll guide you."*

Lucki paused just outside the circle. Her hair blew off her shoulders. She blinked rapidly. Her hands shook.

The cats looked at her with expectation. *"What are you waiting for?"* their wry expressions and gargled thought-words said.

She sucked in a deep breath, filling her lungs to the brink of explosion, then let it slide out again. Rueben put his hand on her shoulder. Julian ran his fingers down her arm.

Both of them said, 'you've got this,' with only a touch.

"Okay then." She steadied herself, straightened her spine then stepped into the circle.

Chapter Sixteen

Julian

Julian froze the moment Lucki stepped inside the stone circle. He stopped breathing, even. He hoped, with everything he was made of, that it worked this time. She was the one. He knew in his soul that she was. Their antiquated way of bonding couldn't be the only method of bolstering and steadying her power, and if the cats had a way, he was all for it.

The magic rose in a funnel, carrying bits of dirt and dead leaves. Lucki's hair flew up around her. Her shirt billowed. She closed her eyes almost immediately and clamped her lips closed. She held her hands out, palms down, like she was trying to hold the magic in place and barely keeping it there.

"The cats, brother." Reuben pointed as the four super-sized felines encircled Lucki. The moment they made contact with her body, their auras aligned. Bright ropes of color—orange, gray and black—all exploded, then entwined, twisting and turning into strands. The twin panthers nudged against her calves. The gray longhair settled across her feet and the orange marmalade lounged against her heels. She was locked in with cats, like anchors holding her in place. Julian's heart walloped against his chest in great, heavy beats. *Can this be the way to make things work?*

The magic pulsed, a strobe of light that burned his eyes, making him raise his hand to shield his vision. It hurt to look at, but he couldn't shift his eyes away — not when Lucki stood in the center, not when her body seemed electrified.

Like the turn of a knob, the whirlwind of power dimmed. Lucki opened her eyes and looked down at her hands. They glowed with blue iridescence.

"What the...?" Lucki rolled her hands so she could look at her palms, then back again.

"What do you feel, Lucki?" Reuben leaned closer but, as he couldn't breach the circle, only got so far.

She snapped her gaze to him, a slow smile easing the frown from around her lips. "I feel..." She raised her hands. "I feel like I can do this."

Reuben nodded. Julian gave her a double thumbs-up.

Ben's hawk wailed from above, not a warning but a cheer, and by the crunch of nearby logs, Julian suspected that Wren had eyes on Lucki as well.

This could change everything. If she mastered this power, it could be enough to defeat Angelica.

She turned to face the tree she'd all but obliterated days before. It hung at an unnatural angle, nearly split in two where her blast of power had shredded the insides.

She lifted her hands like she had so many times before, but this time it was clear that she wasn't battling the power. Blue sparked along her fingertips and roped over her body, snaking into her hair, around her wrists and down her legs—ebbing and flowing over the cats, along their whiskers so their noses twitched and through their fur so they swatted their tails.

Lucki's chest rose like she had sucked in more air than her body could hold. She spread her fingers, fanning her hands in front of her. Then she let her breath go, and as she did, her magic flowed. Blue light emanated from her hands. It furled like large ribbons, trembling at first but quickly snapping to focus as Lucki brought her fingers together then slowly brought her hands together as well.

The tree rumbled and creaked. It groaned. The ground thundered. Bark shifted and cracked. Wood snapped. Julian couldn't pull his eyes away from Lucki. She was glowing like a goddess.

"The tree!" Reuben gasped.

Julian forced his gaze that way and lost his breath at the sight of Lucki pulling the tree back together—puzzle pieces that fit just right. Leaves greened like they'd never been stripped from their anchor. Roots dug back into the earth and branches snapped back into place. She'd made the tree whole. She'd repaired the damage she'd caused—and it all had taken less than a minute.

She was powerful.

Their savior.

This woman was going to free them all.

She closed her fists, and like a tap, her magic flow stopped. The cats mewed, each stepping away with a lazy stride, and as they moved, the rest of the cats, the regular-sized ones, all entered the circle. One by one, they brushed themselves against Lucki, marking her with their essence.

"They're bonding to her." Reuben's eyes nearly bugged out of his head. Julian guessed the big guy hadn't seen that one coming, for all his communication with the cats. "And look at the magic, it's binding to her. Do you see it?"

Julian did, and he grinned. "It was always about the damn cats."

The eerie howl of Wren's wolf echoed around them and Julian grinned even more.

"We're saved, brother." Reuben patted Julian's arm, then squeezed his biceps with one of his oversized hands.

"I believe we are, Reuben. Finally. I believe we've found the one."

* * * *

Julian and Lucki. Lucki and Julian. Sitting on the couch in man heaven. *Alone.* Finally. Watching a show about four older ladies living together. He liked the sassy one. Lucki liked the sweet one.

She still glowed with power—something he'd gotten used to, even though at times it made him giddy to catch a glimpse of it in his peripheral vision.

Lucki's display had no doubt triggered Angelica's senses. She would have felt that amount of magic being used. Surely, she'd come to investigate. The townsfolk were all holed up in the tavern, as they liked to be most nights, safe under the extended bubble of Isabel's protection spell. But Wren, Rueben and Ben were all patrolling, just to make sure none of Angelica's goons ventured past the border.

Julian was on Lucki duty—not that she needed his protection, really, not with her newly gained powers. Even if she had virtually no training as yet, she could defend herself on instinct, he was sure of it. Her power was that impressive. And it wasn't a chore to sit with her, cuddling together so comfortably as they watched what she called a must-see classic. But he wasn't going to squander his time alone with her, either.

"'No strings attached' just got a lot less complicated." He brushed his fingers down her arm. "I'm sure you've been feeling the weight of our expectation and our urgency to bond, if only to protect you."

Lucki stiffened, but it was there and gone in the flash of a second. She clicked the TV off then angled herself almost out of his embrace. His hand fell to her knee. He cursed himself for being so stupid. There were plenty of ways he could have started this conversation, but he'd gone with the one that was sure to upset her.

"I didn't want to hurt any of you." She looked down at her hands, which still held a tint of blue iridescence, then shifted so that she covered his hand with hers. "I didn't want to send the wrong message." She leaned closer, lifting it as she did. "Did I?"

With her eyes downcast and her brows pulled together, Julian knew she must have had something happen between her and one or more of the other men. Had they pushed her? *No. Never.* Had they said something to make her feel guilty? *Unintentionally, maybe.*

"Lucki—"

"But I also am so attracted to you all." She put his hand against her breast then climbed onto his lap, forcing him to adjust himself so that she could straddle him.

He thumbed her budding nipple through her thin cotton T-shirt. He'd discovered that she often went braless. It was a lovely surprise some mornings when she sat in the kitchen nook, sipping tea with the sun shining through her various items of clothing, showcasing her small, luscious tits. It was a thrill to notice at different points of the day when her little nipples budded against her shirt. It made his cock hard all the time and drove him wild.

She arched into his hand and rolled her head back. This woman was always so sensual, so willing to express her needs. Now that they no longer required the bond in order to protect her, Julian knew their relationship would only grow. He was looking forward to that. He had no possessive desires. If Lucki was attracted to them all, then they would all enjoy her company as she saw fit. He had no hang-ups about that. Even though he'd be able to leave after the curse was lifted, he didn't think he'd want to part from Lucki, not while she was still willing to be with him.

She rubbed her crotch against his groin. They'd yet to make love. He'd kissed and licked and tasted every part of her glorious body, but he'd yet to penetrate her. His cock wept for the chance.

He slipped his hands underneath her shirt then slid up her torso, following the curve of her waist and the smooth muscles of her abs to her pert little tits. Her nipples grew harder as he rolled them between his fingers and thumbs, and she rocked against his crotch more persistently.

She snapped her head forward. Her eyes danced and her lips parted. "I want to ride you — *now*."

Those words were music to his ears. He helped her take her shirt off then couldn't help but lean up so he could lick each nipple in turn. He swirled his tongue over her pink peaks as he slipped his hands to her yoga pants then pushed them over her hips.

She lifted her legs — one after the other — so he could pull the tight pants off.

"Lucki," he breathed against her flesh, his eyes riveted to her calves.

She shifted back to look at her lower legs. "Oh my..."

He hadn't expected the cats to leave a bonding mark similar to what the shifters' marks would look like — but they had. Like shimmering ribbons, Lucki's legs were covered in magic marks. They moved on her flesh, a ripple beneath her skin, and, as she ran her fingers across them, they glowed like her hands.

"Wow." She whipped back to face him, her lips split into a wide grin. "That's pretty cool."

"It's amazing...like you."

"Wait a minute," she gasped as she glanced at her legs once again. "Does this mean...I mean...am I...?"

"Immortal?" Julian brushed his fingers over the swirls of magic. "I think it does."

She flashed him a grin. "No sickness? No aging? No death?"

"The only thing that can hurt you, kill you, is magic. But you're so powerful, Lucki, that I really don't think that's a concern."

She laughed in a sexy, throaty way then got to work stripping his clothes off in a frenzy of movement.

They were skin-to-skin—hers glowing and warm, his a hot mess of need. He had to calm his heart and control his urge to sink into her and fuck her silly, because if he did that, if he took control, he'd come in a millisecond.

She hovered over him, her hot, wet pussy mere inches from his aching dick. He reached up to fondle her tits again, to fill his hands and play with her pretty nipples. She ran her fingers down his abs to his cock, and he hissed out a 'holy shit' seconds before she wedged him deep inside.

Her pussy clenched him tight. She ran her hands up her body and along her curves to squeeze her tits as she started to move…slowly, very slowly. She lifted her hips, arched her back and stroked his shaft. He stared up at her, unable to do more than hold the sides of her legs because his brain misfired again and again. It had been centuries since he'd been with a woman like this. To feel her heat, to be cushioned by her slick pussy, was too surreal, like a dream or a fantasy. He didn't want to wake up. He didn't want to ever not feel this way.

Her rhythm rocked the couch, and when she looked down at him and parted her lips, her eyes incendiary, he knew all over again that he wasn't dreaming. This was as real as it would ever get between them—and he was all in.

She leaned forward so she could brace her hands against his chest then increased her speed. Her panting breaths hit him with climbing urgency. He lifted his hands to play with her tits, rolling her nipples between his fingers, rubbing them until she moaned. He took her mouth, probing inside her heat there, tasting fresh mint and a touch of vanilla. His cock ached to go deeper, to thrust harder, but this was all her right now. He would follow her lead.

She pressed herself against his body, tits crushed to his chest, arms around his shoulders, and encouraged him to sit up, moving with him as he grunted his way to an upright position. He had his hands on her ass, never once breaking contact with her mouth or her pussy.

The sitting position gave her leverage, and she increased her speed even more, taking him deeper, harder. She squeezed her fingers between them to stroke her clit and let loose a deep, vibrating moan that he felt along his cock. He sucked her nipples, one after another, and held her ass, marveling over and over that this goddess had chosen him tonight.

As much as he wanted to hold on, to hold back, his orgasm had other plans. As her moans grew more desperate and her ride more aggressive, his cock hardened beyond tolerance. Every synapse was primed and ready to explode.

Her pussy squeezed his dick, undulating like waves until he couldn't take it for one more second. His balls were heavy and tight, and his body coiled like a snake as she slid down his shaft one more time. Comets blasted behind his eyes. He came like a geyser, spewing his load deep inside her.

She rode him until every spasm and wave and spurt of cum had ended, then she collapsed against him, her forehead sweaty and hair damp, her body hot to touch and her magic swirls still chaotic.

He knew he would do anything, *anything*, to keep this woman in his life. And for the first time in centuries, he knew he'd finally come home for good.

Chapter Seventeen

Lucki

The biggest change for Lucki, other than being able to hear the thoughts of all the cats in the house, was that wherever she went, whatever she did, the magic went with her. And it was not just roping around her legs as a symbol. No, it was more than that. When she called it, it came. When she tugged its multi-colored threads or even so much as brushed up against its vibrant edges, it responded instantly.

She'd learned pretty quickly that just thinking about her bath water going from tepid to hot-tub temperatures was enough to get the water near boiling. She also learned that she could change the channel on the TV and radio with a blink and an intention. She could light a candle with her breath, and she could stir a pot by staring at the water. Neat tricks, for sure, but what she still hadn't been able to figure out was the complex spell that Isabel had created to banish Angelica.

"What do you think she meant by '*a storm of fog will cloud judgment*?'" Lucki hunched over the grimoire, her hands threaded through her hair, holding her head up and pulling her face into an exaggerated lift.

"No idea. What even is a 'storm of fog'?" Wren knocked against the top of the kitchen table. "You've been at this for hours. Maybe a break will help things make sense."

Lucki blew out a long breath, ran her fingers down the length of her hair then closed the book. "My eyes are crossing." She picked up her pencil and retraced the lines she'd already decoded...or at least thought she had. "I think I have all the ingredients she lists now." She and Reuben had spent many afternoons out picking the herbs and flowers that Isabel had listed along the sides of the spell. There were notes all over the place in Isabel's book, some that made no sense to the spell that was written. It was possible the herbs and flowers that she'd listed weren't connected to the spell at all, but no one wanted to take any chances when it came to defeating Angelica. She tapped the pencil along the notebook. "I still don't understand how the mixture links to the spell, though." Was she supposed to throw the liquid on Angelica? Make the sorceress somehow drink it?

"She listed belladonna, right? She'd have to get Angelica to ingest it for that to have any sedative effect." Wren reached across the table and stilled her hand. "Break time."

"The duel is in two weeks." Isabel's grimoire had a list of protocols for the solstice battle.

Rules of Engagement.
Thou shall issue a duel notice at least two moons prior to battle.

Thou shall honor the code of sisterhood, the rules of witchkind that state do no malicious harm to those unsuspecting. Thou shall not launch an attack outside the solstice witching hour.

Thou shall allow each witch to enter the circle unmolested.
Bound in blood, so it shall be.

Lucki found it hard to believe that Angelica would follow such rules, but the men had assured her that for the last two hundred years, she had.

Wren shrugged. "You won't get to it if you don't take breaks."

It was jarring to have this version of Wren spending time with her, and his kindness, which was ever-present, was something she stutter-stepped over still. Ever since the cat bonding had happened, he'd been lighter, easier to talk to. He'd even willingly spent time with her—watching some movies, playing a few card games. No fooling around at all though, despite the fact that the chemistry between them was as off the charts as it was with the rest of the men. But Wren had made it clear that they'd be friends...*just* friends. She could handle that. It was nice to be surrounded by these men who were all so different and yet who all wanted to spend time with her in one way or another. They made a pseudo-family for her still-grieving and battered heart.

Being able to hang out with Wren was a treat after all the pushing away he'd been doing since she'd arrived. She figured he was at ease now that he knew she didn't need a bonding mark from him. She had to admire that he was so true to his long-dead love. There was something so tragically romantic about that, and of course, deep down, that made her want him more.

Complicated matters of a lustful heart.

"Come on. I want to show you something." He stood and held his hand out to her.

She only hesitated for a millisecond before picking up the grimoire then shoving it back into the safe that Reuben had installed under the breakfast nook window seat.

"Let's go!"

Instead of heading out of the back door as she expected, Wren led her out of the front. Because it was midday, the cats were all safe and sound inside the house, which meant the town's main strip was quiet...ghost-town quiet. Normally that would disturb her on some level. It was eerie to walk through a town knowing that no one was around. But today, with Wren striding beside her, she didn't have any of the creepy crawlie sensations of being watched or of imminent danger descending on her like a pack of wild, feral cats.

"I've been meaning to talk to you" — Wren shot her a side-eye glance — "about my behavior before."

"It's okay," she rushed to soothe, then cursed herself when Wren's lips clamped into a thin line. "I mean, I understand." She nudged him with her elbow. He'd said the same words to her not too long before.

His lips quirked. "Touché."

"There was a lot of pressure on all of us," she added.

"There was." He walked on, his strides long and powerful. Lucki didn't have to run to catch up, but she did have to push herself in a way that would have made any cardio fiend happy.

Not that she had to worry about gaining weight or losing muscle tone. She was immortal now, frozen in place while still moving forward in time. It had taken a few deep-thinking meditations to really come to peace with the reality of that. She'd been witness to her mother's cancerous decline, though, so Lucki was grateful to never have to worry about the same thing happening to her body.

Wren veered down the alleyway next to the barber shop. "I'm going to shift. Follow behind. There's nothing to be scared of."

Which of course meant there probably was something to be scared of. "Sure, for a big bad shifter."

Wren paused and waited for her to catch up. "I promise that you'll like this."

In a whirlwind of flying fur and a few grunts, Wren went from large man to extra-large wolf. He nudged her hand before bolting down the alleyway.

Lucki sighed, then followed cautiously. The alleyway ended at the forest line with maybe four feet of clearing separating the two worlds. She stopped when she reached the grass, but Wren was nowhere to be seen. Was she supposed to follow him into the forest? That didn't seem wise. Angelica and her wild cats could be lurking in there.

She heard a yip and a yelp, high-pitched and angry-sounding. There was a ruckus to the left, twigs snapping, things rustling. Creepie crawlies raced up Lucki's spine. Maybe this wasn't a great idea. Maybe she should head back. Maybe—

Out of the tree line burst a furball the size of a small dog, then another and another, all running straight for her. Little furry balls of... She crouched down as the excited little things barreled right into her, knocking her onto her butt. They climbed all over her, licking, nipping, yipping, wanting to be petted but not really. Three excited little wolf pups. "Oh my, aren't you all adorable!"

Wren stalked out of the woods, his wolf form appeared menacing as he paced a perimeter around Lucki and the pups. But the pups caught sight of him and raced to barrel against his huge body. They bounced off, of course. They were pint-sized and he was a beast.

Joy welled deep inside Lucki—pure, unfettered joy. Watching baby animals play was always a favorite pastime for her. Watching these mini-wolves prance around, rolling into one another, nipping at Wren's legs and overall causing havoc, lightened her in ways she hadn't realized she'd needed.

Wren roughhoused with them for a bit. He got down on his back to let them pounce on him, climb his body and tug at his ears. He growled a few times, warnings that the little ones didn't really pay heed to. Then they noticed Lucki sitting there watching and all came racing back to play with her again.

She was so caught up in petting the little monsters that she didn't realize Wren had shifted back to human form until he settled down next to her.

"I found them in an abandoned den."

"So, they're not yours then?" Lucki poked him with her elbow and grinned.

She always marveled at how these men could shift their clothing as well as their bodies. Ben and Julian never did. Their discarded clothes always ended up in the strangest places—flung onto high branches, tangled in brush, lining the bottom of a robin's nest. Wren always shifted with clothes and always came back with them on, except for today. Today, despite the chilly temps, Wren only had on a pair of jeans. Lucki tried with everything she had to keep her eyes averted from the smoothness of his chest and the abs that she so badly wanted to trace…with her tongue…and the line of dark hair that went straight down to his—

"Not mine. Not biologically, anyway." Wren nudged her hard enough to let her know that she'd been caught, then grinned at the blush that burst over her cheeks. "They're still too young to hunt on their own, although they try. That one, the female, managed to catch a rabbit on her own, but the two males? Useless right now."

She watched the playful things romp around in the taller grass—rolling and tackling, running and leaping, pouncing and stalking.

"What I wanted to say earlier," Wren began, his eyes straight ahead, focused on something just past the pups, "was that my behavior was unacceptable. Scout had sent word days before your arrival, and in that moment, I'd slipped into some kind of denial that it could be true…really, really true. He'd sent so many Cat Keepers in the past who didn't work out, who were so far off the mark that it was obvious just from the first hello. You came and it was instantaneously apparent that you were different. I felt you enter the town. No, I felt you drawing closer to the town and for days before you came." He turned to look at her and his eyes were full of vulnerability. "It scared the hell out of me."

Lucki didn't dare speak this time. She nodded and touched his arm briefly but let the silence work its magic on the ever-reserved Wren.

"I had hope for the first time in centuries."

Centuries. Lucki let that sink in, the impact of his words like boulders in her gut.

"Then I came to realize that you weren't like Isabel at all."

A lump grew in Lucki's throat. Being compared to a dead woman, a dead lover, partner, powerful witch, was both intimidating and unfair.

"You had convictions about relationships that didn't mesh with our old-world reality or the curse that was cast two hundred years ago. Why would you want an eternity, bonding to men you'd just met? Or bonding for eternity with anyone, for that matter. You didn't need us. You were always free to leave."

"I wouldn't have left—not without helping you all, though."

"I know. I realized that quickly too, but obviously I had my doubts about the effectiveness of your strategy, not that I blame you for rejecting the idea of bonding or fated mates or anything as archaic as that. I didn't have faith that your desire to help would actually translate into helping, if you know what I mean."

"I think I do."

"Like I said, I felt you before you got here, though. I felt your power coming toward me days before you arrived. I didn't know that was what it was, that the magic I was sensing was coming from you. But after I met you, I should have had more faith in what you were saying. I'm sorry I didn't."

Lucki touched his arm again, this time lingering for a minute. When she started to pull away, Wren took her hand and entwined it with his. "I respect that you are free and open. I understand that you've been hurt." He nudged her. "Don't get my acceptance of that to mean I'm not attracted to you. I am. I'm not stone-cold or stupid. I know there's chemistry between us that could light the world on fire."

Lucki's whole body heated like a hot coal was glowing deep inside her belly. The boulder that had been there minutes ago dissolved into mush.

"But we both have baggage that might be too heavy to heave onto one another, you know?"

Lucki nodded. They sat side-by-side, their hands entwined, watching the little wolves romp around, and it didn't feel awkward or forced or heavy. It felt safe and comfortable and familiar.

"My mother died when I was twenty-three." Lucki couldn't keep the memories from floating into her mind—of the way her mother's body had broken organ by organ, of how frail the cancer had made her over the agonizing course of years, of her dying breath and last words. *"Just be you, Lucki. Just be you."*

"I met Shane as that was all happening. He was charismatic and kind. For a time, he filled the hole in my heart. We shared the same beliefs. I'd seen him around at the Wiccan festivals, so he wasn't a complete stranger. I trusted him quickly and looked past the red flags that cropped up."

"He hid himself from you. His real self." Wren squeezed her hand.

"Yeah. Not that I was really looking that hard at him in the beginning. By the time I woke up, I was so entrenched in his world that it took more than a year to extricate myself. In the time that I'd been blind, he'd shifted me away from all my old friends. He'd isolated me. I was alone, knowing that something was wrong—but it took so long to wake up. When I finally got away—" Lucki's eyes filled and her heart thudded. New memories flooded her mind. The smell of smoke.

The heat of fire. The helplessness and defeat and the depth of grief that had crushed her all over again. "He set the cat sanctuary on fire. He knew that would destroy me. He killed all those precious cats." Except for Mr. Whiskers, who had somehow escaped the flames. "It was my fault," she croaked.

"You can't control the actions of others, not when they're set on destruction like that."

"I knew he was possessive and that he'd become hateful. When I left, he threatened me, so I called the police and got a restraining order."

Wren snorted but said nothing.

"It didn't work. It didn't keep him away."

"It usually never does." Wren nodded. "Makes it hard to trust someone like that again."

"I can't." Lucki wiped her eyes with her sleeve. "He really did almost destroy me."

"I do understand, Lucki." He wrapped one arm around her. "I failed to protect Isabel. I couldn't bear to have that happen again. But you..." He pulled her close then kissed the top of her head. "You're powerful enough to protect yourself. More powerful than Isabel was."

Wren's vote of confidence dried up her tears. Her heart thudded for an entirely different reason. He wrapped his strong arm around her shoulders and pressed his hard body to her side, sharing his warmth and comfort and friendship. It filled her up and gave her hope.

She closed her eyes and squared away any lustful urges she had for Wren. The chemistry was there—maybe always would be—but he was right that they both had way too much baggage to carry for themselves and they'd want too much from each other because they were too similar.

The pups had curled themselves up in a furball heap and were lounging in the sun.

"Are they safe in the forest alone?"

"I watch over them. Hunt for them. Try to teach them to care for themselves." He shrugged. "But yeah, there are dangers out there for them. I found their mom's body…or what was left of her body. Her heart had been removed. Maybe eaten, but maybe salvaged for a spell."

Lucki shuddered. "Angelica?"

"Perhaps." Wren watched the little wolves sunning in the grass. "I wanted your opinion. I thought it would be better to keep them in their natural habitat, but I can't watch over them all the time."

"Can you domesticate a wolf?"

"I'm not proposing setting them up in the house." Wren laughed. "But maybe we should lure them into the town, keep them fed until they grow bigger."

"Merrrow!" Mr. Whiskers jumped into Lucki's lap.

"Oh no, Mr. Whiskers, this is not the best place for you."

She started to get up, to protect her cat from the ever-curious wolf pups who now came bounding toward them, their glassy black eyes set on the cat. Mr. Whiskers jumped out of her arms and stood his ground right in front of her.

The pups closed in and Wren made to snatch them up while Lucki bent to get the cat out of harm's way.

Mr. Whiskers puffed, his fur sticking straight up his back. He turned to the side and hissed. It was enough to freeze two of the pups from coming closer. Wren and Lucki both stopped their attempt to grab the animals.

When the third wolf lunged, Mr. Whiskers swatted with awe-inspiring accuracy, catching the pup across the nose. The little beast yelped then lowered down to its forepaws.

"That cat has a wicked right hook." Wren rubbed his nose where Mr. Whiskers had scratched him all those weeks ago.

Mr. Whiskers mewed at the wolves then turned his back and trotted off. The pups immediately followed him.

"Well, I guess that decides that," Lucki said.

Wren touched her arm, and when she swung her eyes to meet his once again, she couldn't help but notice that the wall he'd used to keep her at arm's length was no longer there and all she saw in his eyes was pure, unfettered love — the same kind of love she felt for him.

Chapter Eighteen

Ben

Ben could be a culinary genius when he wanted to be, and breakfast in bed with Lucki was very motivating. He'd spent all night patrolling the air while Reuben and Julian had covered the ground, ensuring that all the townsfolk were safe in the tavern. But he'd broken off early, so he could beat Reuben to the kitchen and make Lucki a wake-up fit for a goddess.

He steeped her tea while he quickly fried up some eggs, toasted a bagel and shredded cheese. Okay, maybe culinary genius was stretching it a little, but he did decorate the plate with sprigs of fresh parsley…at least that was what he thought the green stuff was. He knew she had a sweet tooth, so he pilfered a few of the caramel nut muffins Reuben had made the night before to add to the breakfast tray as well.

It wasn't until he was just outside Lucki's door that he had an inkling of doubt. Maybe he should let her sleep. It was just dawn, and the sun had barely peeked over the horizon.

"I can smell something delicious out there. What are you waiting for, Reuben?"

Ben grinned as he opened the door. "Surprise!"

Lucki sat up in bed, her hair nicely tousled and her tank top straps slightly dipping off her shoulders. All the creamy skin made his cock pulse immediately.

"Ben! You cooked."

"I did. Beat Reuben to it." He brought the tray to set on her lap. "A meal fit for a powerful sorceress."

"Is that what I am?" Lucki grinned. "There's way too much food here for me. Why don't you climb in and share it with me?" She lifted the duvet and motioned him in.

She'd get zero resistance from him. He hopped into bed next to her.

Domesticated life had never felt so good. "I haven't had the pleasure of such a soft mattress in a couple of hundred years."

Lucki gasped as she pulled apart one of the muffins. "Not at all? Come on!"

"It's true. The last comfortable bed, human-made bed I slept on was filled with hay." He took the offered half and shoved the whole thing into his mouth. Caramel nut was one of Reuben's best.

"Do you even need to sleep?"

Ben shrugged. "I need to rest—and at times I sleep. I have been doing so as a hawk though. Safer that way."

"Because you're high up?"

"Yes. I can see for miles around me when I perch in a tree."

"It must be so wonderful to be able to fly." Lucki tilted her head and popped a hunk of muffin into her mouth.

"Wonderful is one word." He crinkled his face to downplay the sarcasm. "I mean, it would be nice to be one of the big guys too. To stomp around and roar with tremendous might."

Lucki pulled her brows together and frowned. "Being bigger isn't always better."

He stuck his tongue out and she laughed.

"No, seriously, who else can get the vantage point that you can? Or swoop in quickly to any situation? If I've learned anything from you all, it's that each of you brings unique talents to the group. You're all different, and everyone has their thing, you know? It's impressive. All of you are so amazing at what you do. I feel protected."

"With powers like yours, you don't need our protection." He waved his hand. "They didn't tell us about witches like you when we were training."

"Well, two hundred years ago probably meant there was a lot of chest pounding, 'me man, you woman', kind of stuff, right?" She giggled when he flexed his biceps then pounded his chest.

"Yeah, something like that."

"What was it like? Being born a fully formed shifter with no memories?"

"We all understood our existence inherently, I guess. No one questioned the whys or the hows. Some of the elders believed that we were created from the death of a witch—like a phoenix rising, a witch's soul reborn—but no one really knew for sure. What we all did know was that we were created to bond with a witch and that we had to make sure she was the right witch, with the right powers, because if we bonded with someone evil, we'd be tainted and would never be reborn again."

"Like Angelica and her wild cats? If one of those furious beasts dies, he doesn't come back?"

"Correct. Dead and gone. Good riddance." He motioned to the food. "Eat up. It's getting cold." And he hated to think what that would do to his culinary masterpiece. "I almost wish you could take Angelica out now, save us all the wait, get it over with so we can all move on."

Lucki snorted. "I'd rather have more time to spend with Isabel's spell. There are still some spots that I can't quite work properly and the words I wrote to end it are maybe too weak."

"You've tested the spell?" Now that was news to him. He'd thought that would be done with all of them present.

"Not in its entirety. Just parts. Some work great, others are still a little wonky."

He patted her leg. "You'll get it."

"I know. I mean, I hope I know. I'm still not sure what it's supposed to do exactly, but I'm sure I'll figure it out." She winked then pushed the tray off her lap. "Now, there's definitely one place where you're the biggest." She slipped her hand under the covers and over his thigh.

His cock perked to full attention. "Oh yeah?"

She nodded eagerly. "The biggest." She rubbed her hand over his dick and he moaned. The dulling sensation of his clothing only intensified his lust.

"Not too big for your mouth, though." He was dying — dying to get her lips on him again.

"Oh, I don't know...maybe... We'll have to check again to see."

He pushed the covers away and undid his pants in a hurry. "Yes, let's see."

She curled her lips then bit the tip of her tongue as she wrapped her hand around his shaft. Her warm, soft hand against his pulsing dick... Goddess, he could die right there and be happy.

She leaned down, her breath tickled his cock tip, her lips less than an inch away. He ran his fingers through her tussled hair, closed his eyes and —

"Ben, man, you in there?" Wren's bellow nearly rattled the walls.

Lucki snapped upright.

"Yeah, I'm here." Ben was already doing up his pants, somehow managing to get his cock back inside. "What's going on?"

He left the room to find Wren heading back downstairs. "What gives, dude?"

Wren cut him a hard look over his shoulder. "We're missing three cats."

"Shit!" He shouldn't have left patrol early. That was what Wren wasn't saying with words, even though his expression said it all. "Shit!"

"What's wrong?" Lucki was at the door.

Ben silently cursed his loud voice. "We're missing some cats. It's okay. It happens sometimes. They get a little tipsy and wander off then fall asleep in a barn or something. We'll find them."

"I can help!" Lucki bolted back into her room. "Let me get dressed."

"No, no." Ben followed her so he could grab her arm. She spun around and he kissed her. "You stay here. We'll find them. Don't worry. We can cover more ground and air. Better for you to mind the cats who are here."

Lucki nodded, frown firmly in place. "Are you sure?"

"Yes, definitely." He kissed her again. "I'll be back in a flash, then we'll finish what we started."

Her lips quirked. "Okay but if you're not back in an hour, I'm coming to find you."

"Deal." Ben squeezed her arm then left, all trace of his smile gone. Those cats weren't sleeping it off anywhere. If they'd wandered, they were in danger, or worse, already dead. It was too close to the Solstice for any other suspicion. He had to find out either way.

No matter what, it was his fault.

Chapter Nineteen

Lucki

Of course, Lucki wasn't going to sit around and wait for the men to find the cats. She wanted to help search too. After throwing on some warm leggings and a cowlneck sweater, she headed to the back of the house where she kept her hiking boots.

The cats crowded her every step of the way. "It would be helpful if you guys gave me some clues." Cats were jumping over one another to get to the back door. "And don't think you're coming with me, either."

Images flashed into her mind in rapid succession. The stone circle, Marmalade licking his balls, the stone circle, a flash of power, Marmalade lounging in the sun, the stone circle.

"Okay, got it. I was planning on going out there first anyway." She scanned the group. Marmalade, along with the twin panthers and the long-haired gray, were seated in the hallway behind the rest of the cats, watching her with what could only be described as full on cat-itude. "I'm not taking you." They'd all shrunk back to their original sizes now, but it had taken days for that change to occur and Lucki had the suspicion that they wanted her to cast on them again. Their extra size and weight had meant they got first dibs at all the food bowls for a few days simply by pushing the others out of the way.

She shook her head and walked to the back door. "No cats allowed past this door, not until I'm back." Iridescent blue flowed from her finger to the doorknob and her intention locked in place.

The cats yowled and hissed once they realized she'd locked them in, so Lucki slipped outside quickly. "It's for your own good." She'd give them extra treats when she got back, but all the same, the sight of almost a hundred cats jumping and clambering, scratching and meowing, frantic to find a way out of the glass portico flashed back memories of her poor darlings she'd lost to the fire. "I'm sorry, but you're safer there." She rested her hand against the glass for a moment, added another layer of protection to them then turned and headed into the forest.

The wolf pups surrounded her in an instant, jumping and rolling, nipping at her leggings, trying to convince her to come down to their level so she could pet them and they could maul her. "You three are staying here too." She brushed each one from head to tail with wisps of magic, compelling them to guard the house and protect the cats. Being the little pups that they were, the spell took instantly and they all trotted off to stand by the back door.

"Murrrow!" Mr. Whiskers came slithering out from under a bush, looking like he'd just woken up.

"You're to stay here too." But Mr. Whiskers blinked at her slowly, yawned widely then bolted into the forest.

Lucki sighed. *So much for that.*

She didn't know which three cats were missing, but if she were to guess, she'd say it would be Silvia, Andy and Shep. Those folks seemed to get tangled up in trouble almost daily. They'd never wandered far, Ben was right, but all the same, it was best to find them quickly, and Lucki had a gut feeling they'd be near or in the circle, just as the cats had insisted. That place was like catnip to the townsfolk, whether in cat form or not.

June in Weeping Falls was cool but comfortable. While still chilly in the early morning, Lucki knew she'd be shedding her sweater in a couple of hours, especially if she was still searching. It was nice to walk alone, or kind of alone, even though Mr. Whiskers darted in and out of the bushes ahead of her. He was quiet and not in her head like the other cats tended to be.

She'd memorized Isabel's spell, however convoluted it was. She'd tested out a few of the spells embedded in her words. She felt confident that she could at least recite it in a pinch, but she still had no idea what it was meant to do. There were lines and stanzas that made no sense in the context of battling someone. What the purpose of the spell was baffled her and Wren, and she'd thought that Isabel's lover, her best friend and confidante would at least have some idea of what her words meant.

That it was intended for Angelica was even up for debate. The only hint that it had anything to do with the woman was in the title and side notes. *Summer Solstice Defense. For the battle to be won, Angelica mustn't see it coming*. The word 'banished' had been written and crossed out several times.

Mustn't see what coming? So far, Lucki hadn't found anything in the spell that could strike out or lash at an opponent—nothing to do with disabling or even killing someone else. Isabel's written words spiraled around darkness and light, the blurred lines between good and evil, how what was hidden could be found, what must be hidden could be tucked away again. The least confusing phrase in the entire thing was, *forgiveness will come like dawn each day* and even that was hardly crystal clear.

The spell was a riddle that confounded Lucki still, and that bothered her, especially since she was counting on it to work in two weeks when she went toe-to-toe with Angelica and neither she nor the boys could tell her what it was going to do.

The circle loomed ahead, and Mr. Whiskers sprinted along the path, finally visible for more than two seconds.

Would the missing cats have ventured out there? It wasn't impossible. The townsfolk did get up to mischief at times when they'd been drinking. Even though the circle was more dangerous at this time of year with the Solstice approaching, they'd still been found a few times frolicking there. Lucki had to assume that the boys had looked there, though.

"Meeerow!" Mr. Whiskers sat frozen at the edge of the clearing. The stone circle lay just ahead. Nothing seemed amiss. The circle was empty, the magic wisping on invisible clouds that Lucki sensed more than saw. As Lucki got closer, she had to step over Mr. Whiskers because he wouldn't move from the path to let her by.

"Silly cat." But as she glanced down at him to give him a smirk, Mr. Whiskers arched his back and puffed up before letting a low, menacing growl slip past his bared fangs.

Lucki whipped around, her stomach plummeted to her toes and her throat seized. *What?* What was the cat sensing? She scanned the tree line but saw nothing amiss. She strained her ears but heard nothing unusual. She reached out with her power, but her heart was hammering too hard and drowned out anything she might have felt. And still, Mr. Whiskers growled and hissed.

Lucki moved slowly around the circle and goosebumps exploded over her skin. The tiny hairs on the back of her neck rose and sent a shiver like an icicle piercing through her heart.

The birds had stopped chirping.

The forest seemed darker, oppressive even.

The magic wind gusted from the circle to chill her even more.

She peered into the shadows, and as wind pushed past her, a bush wavered to the side and underneath it was a tuft of fur.

"Oh Goddess!" Lucki rushed to the fallen cat. It was Shep, his white and gray spots matted with blood. "Oh, Shep." Her world tilted and she crumbled to the ground. His body was warm but his life was gone. His little chest had been ripped open. "What in the world got you?"

Mr. Whiskers growled again. This time he'd moved closer but still hadn't entered the forest. She didn't blame him. This was gruesome. And the oppressive weight she'd felt at the circle grew heavier, thicker. She breathed it in, and it soaked her lungs and made her whole body sink.

She slipped her hand under Shep's head and closed her eyes. "Rest, wee one. Be at peace." When she opened them again, it was to the horrific sight of another cat, tucked away under another bush, not far from Shep. "No!"

She gently laid Shep down then scrambled to the gray tabby. This was Silvia, had to be. There was a little nick on her ear that marked her out of the other tabbies. Her little body was ravaged but again, still warm. "What happened here?"

She needed to get Reuben or Wren or —

"Meeeeeow." A weak cry came from just ahead.

Lucki bolted up and ran toward the noise, not thinking of the danger or of defending herself. She was just thinking about a cat in distress and that this time she could do something about it.

When she burst into the small clearing, it wasn't a huge beast that confronted her. It was a hawk — a larger-than-normal hawk. A hawk with tawny feathers and brown eyes. A hawk that was eating the third cat alive.

"No!" She rushed the hawk, forcing her brain not to jump to conclusions. It wasn't Ben. It wasn't. She screamed and waved her hands, ready to launch a bolt of magic at the thing that *wasn't* Ben.

Her power sparked across her fingers.

It rushed through every vein.

Blue light danced over her skin and the markings on her legs heated.

She flared her hands.

She hit an invisible wall.

A boom reverberated through her body, rattling her brain, jarring every organ. The wall absorbed her impact then shot her right back off like a catapult. She flew backward until she hit a tree with a bone-crushing thud.

She lay crumpled on the ground, her face in the dirt, her body on fire, her breath gone.

"Be done with it, Benjamin." A cold voice pulled Lucki's attention to the other side of the clearing.

Not Ben. Please don't be Ben.

Wisps of air found their way into her lungs. She lifted her head slowly, pushing past the pain to see a tall monster of a woman. She had to be as big as Reuben in both height and girth. She wore layers of black that looked like swaths of linen wrapped around her body. Her hair was cropped short and uneven, tufts of brown sticking up and out. Her eyes were dark, cold and surrounded by smudges of shadow. This was Angelica. It had to be.

The hawk squawked once. The cat mewed its last pitiful cry before the hawk ripped it down the middle.

Lucki retched and bile clogged the back of her throat.

"Bring it to me." Angelica held her hand out. The hawk tore the cat's heart out then flew to Angelica, dropping the bleeding organ into her hand before perching on a nearby branch.

This can't be happening.

Lucki swallowed and swallowed, forcing the bile down her throat to sit like a boulder in her stomach. Her magic pulsed weakly, reminding her it was still there, even if it was busy working to repair the damage that the invisible wall had done.

Lucki pulled her strength inside, yanking hard on the tendrils of her magic to give her enough power to push herself up, despite the screaming pain even the slightest movement caused.

"I had to come see for myself." Angelica held the heart in her hand, watching the blood stream down her forearm with hungry eyes. "This new Cat Keeper with all the power."

Lucki got herself to her feet. Her legs wobbled and shook, and she used the tree behind her to steady herself. "Let Ben go." Angelica had to have bewitched him somehow. Ben would never harm a cat. *Never.*

Angelica snorted. "Oh, I'll be letting him go very shortly, but not because you've demanded it." She lifted the cat heart and muttered a few words.

Magic pulsed with incandescent light—the same magic Lucki had inside her. Angelica tilted her head back then dropped the heart into her mouth. When she zeroed her focus back to Lucki, blood dripped from her lips, coating her chin and dribbling to the ground.

"That's three cat hearts. A fine boost in normal times, but not enough with you around."

Lucki's own magic flared to full force as the last of her pain evaporated. She lifted her hand, fingers splayed. "I banish you—"

"You can't banish me from here." Angelica scowled. "You've left your protective shield behind. You're in *my* territory now."

She raised her hands over her head then brought them down and out. Power slammed into Lucki, shackling her wrists with shadows that pulled her to the dirt once again. Invisible hands gripped her hair and yanked her head up, pulling her in opposite directions. Pain ricocheted through her all over again.

"You're curious like a cat." Angelica nodded behind her. "And you know what they say about that."

She flicked one finger over her shoulder and the hawk tumbled from the branch it was on.

"This is your fault. Just remember that." In a flash of feathers, Ben was Ben. Fully human, writhing on the ground, his lips clamped shut, his jaw tight, his eyes closed. "If you hadn't come, nothing would have changed for your shifters — but desperate times and all that."

Two gigantic wild cats stalked out of the forest, yellow eyes darting from Lucki to Ben to Angelica.

Ben cracked his eyes open to slits then wider once he saw Lucki. "No!" He reached out to her just as Angelica's beasts pounced on him.

"Stop!" Lucki screamed, but she was stuck to the ground with invisible shackles and pulled so taut by her hair that tears streamed down her cheeks. "Please stop!"

"Oh, she begs. How lovely. Save that wonderful sentiment for your turn."

The wild cats shredded Ben's chest like his flesh was nothing more than tissue paper. They opened him up so fast that Ben didn't even have a chance to scream. He stopped struggling, one hand stretched out as if he could touch her, and his eyes were locked with hers.

I'm sorry, his eyes said.

"The cats' hearts were a delectable appetizer, but a shifter heart? That's a main meal." She snapped her fingers and the wild cats pulled back, leaving Ben's chest cavity exposed.

"Please don't." Lucki gaze was still locked with Ben's. He blinked. He swallowed, and his Adam's apple bobbled slowly.

"But I must. Benjamin's heart will give me all my strength back so I can deal with you."

"It's not the Solstice!"

Angelica laughed. "I'm the bad guy. Do you think I'm going to follow the rules?"

Rules? No one had even told Lucki that there were rules outside of the ones listed in Isabel's grimoire. In all the time that had passed, all the conversations she'd had with the men, no one had said anything about more rules.

Angelica reached into Ben's chest. His eyes shuttered and dimmed. Lucki held his stare until Angelica murmured a few nonsensical words then ripped his heart out and stayed with him until the moment the life faded completely from his eyes, just as she had for her mother, so that he would know that he wasn't alone.

"Such power!" Angelica's body shook. She tilted her head then, like a snake, unlocked her jaw and slowly lowered Ben's heart into the gaping maw.

Lucki didn't need her hands to cast. She didn't need anything but her mind. Her power roared through her — a freight train of intention and rage and thirst for revenge.

Chapter Twenty

Wren

Wren raced through the forest. Angelica was near. He smelled the stench of her magic — vile, repulsive, toxic. She would never risk a pre-emptive attack, a fortnight before the Solstice, not unless she felt confident that she could win. If she'd lured Lucki out of Isabel's protection spell, if Angelica injured Lucki before the duel, then Angelica would be able to finish the job when the true battle began, when she could pull from the Solstice's natural magic. Killing Lucki on the anniversary of the curse's creation would generate enough power to obliterate it.

Three cats were missing and Ben's hawk was no longer flying overhead. Anxiety gnawed like a beast inside Wren. He pushed himself to run faster, to leap over the roots and low branches and duck under all that he could. A low growl rumbled in his belly. He tasted blood on his tongue. If given the chance, he'd tear Angelica to pieces.

Lucki was close. Her signature power looped through the air as if carried on the breeze, calling to him.

He dove through a thicket, the thorny branches ripping at his skin. *So close...so close...* Searing pain ribbed down his middle, like claws tearing his belly. His front paws gave out and he skidded to a halt in the dirt. Without willing it himself, Wren shifted back to human form. He clenched his torso, expecting to find his insides torn out and his chest gaping, but his flesh was intact.

Ben.

As suddenly as the pain had come — as excruciating as it had been — it ended. The stillness that followed was one Wren hadn't felt for a very long time. He didn't breathe for a moment. He didn't move. That soul-crushing pain only had one cause. Another brother had died. Ben was gone.

Wren rolled to his side then got onto his hands and knees. The murmur of Angelica's voice seared his ears. He had to get to Lucki. He called on his wolf, but nothing happened. Panic lashed him. After the death of a brother, his body was too stunned to comply. He pushed himself to stand, got his bearings, then took off again.

Even though his human legs weren't as nimble as his wolf's, he still managed to race quickly to Lucki's location. He caught sight of her bent in an unnatural way, her hands held together and pulled forward, her head yanked back.

Her lips moved silently.

The loops of Lucki's power contracted. Her eyes were closed. She was casting—unaware of Angelica's approach or of the sorceress's own spell building. Angelica's power rolled off her in black and gray waves. It stretched inky tentacles that crawled and slithered toward Lucki.

If Wren were in his wolf form, he'd go for Angelica's throat. Being in human form meant he detoured, adjusted his angle and leaped for Lucki, ready to throw himself over her so he would take the brunt of whatever Angelica was about to do.

As he slammed into Lucki, throwing his arms around her, his body covering her head, shielding her from Angelica, her ribbons of magic grew. They thickened, then wrapped themselves around both Wren and Lucki like a cocoon, pulling in wisps of Angelica's magic with it.

Wren's momentum knocked them both over. Whatever magic had been holding Lucki in place released as soon as Wren had made contact. He held her for an extra breath to make sure she was alive and well, then jumped up and turned to confront Angelica.

But she was gone.

Just gone.

"Did it work?" Lucki's groggy voice had Wren spinning around. How could Angelica just disappear?

Lucki looked up at him through shuttered eyes. "Wren, did the spell work?"

"What spell?" Wren scanned the tree line again. Where was Ben? Had he not fallen here? What about Angelica's minions? The wild cats had to be around somewhere.

"I cast Isabel's spell. Did it work?" Lucki pushed herself up.

"I don't understand." Wren called his wolf and his wolf came. One minute he was on two feet, the next he was on four. He huffed toward Lucki, hoping she understood to stay put, then he darted into the trees. Angelica couldn't be far, and even if she'd used some kind of magic to escape, Wren should still smell her and her wild cats.

He lowered his muzzle and attempted to track her stench, but nothing rolled along his senses. Nothing. Not even the faintest of scents was there. He weaved in and out of the trees and through bushes. He leaped on top of a tall cropping of rocks but saw no evidence of movement.

By the time he made it back to Lucki, she'd gotten herself to her feet and was busy plucking twigs and leaves from her clothes.

He transformed mid-step, startling her from her task. "They aren't here."

"I know." Lucki brushed her hair down with her fingers. "I banished them."

"Banished them?" Wren scrunched his face up. "What spell did you use?"

"*The spell.* Isabel's spell. *Summer Solstice Defense.*" Lucki waved her hands around. "It worked. She's been banished."

Wren shook his head. It wasn't right. Too easy. "I can't sense her at all."

"That's good, isn't it? I mean, I didn't know if it would work and I was desperate but she'd just killed Be—" Lucki covered her mouth. Tears welled in her eyes.

"I felt it." Wren rubbed his chest with his fist. "I felt Ben die."

Lucki curled in on herself right where she was standing. She hunched her shoulders and wrapped her arms around herself, lowered her head and wept.

And Wren, like a fool, stood there frozen. He had to know where they were because there was no way Angelica would vanish, mid-attack, along with Ben's body. He scanned the area again. The trees looked different somehow. The area was slightly unfamiliar, even though he knew this forest better than he knew himself.

"Lucki, we have to go." Wren finally moved to her. He wrapped his arm around her and kissed the top of her head. "We have to leave *now*." He needed to get them back to the house, to find the others and warn them.

Lucki sucked down her tears as she leaned into him. "Okay. Okay." She sniffled.

He led her back to the stone circle, which stood as it always did. Nothing amiss there. Then he steered her toward the path.

"Wait! Mr. Whiskers!" Lucki pulled away and *pstpst*ed for Mr. Whiskers.

Wren frowned. Something was off about this place. The path to the house was packed dirt, not lined with the colorful stones that he and Reuben had ordered from Anchorage years ago to brighten up the place.

"Lucki—"

"I can't find Mr. Whiskers. Wren, what if Angelica got him too?" Lucki's body shook and her eyes brimmed with tears again.

Wren pulled her closer. "He's probably back at the house," he lied as he ran his fingers through her hair. Nothing about this was right.

"Yes, right. He's smart. He would have run."

"Let's go find him." Wren took her hand and led her down the path. His gut sank with each step and his anxiety rose to fill the space. The plants were different, wild-looking, unkept even. The trees were smaller, not as full, not as tall.

The house appeared just ahead, and Wren couldn't help but freeze once again. Lucki looked up at him and frowned. "What's wrong?"

Wren closed his eyes for a second, hoping that he was hallucinating. The house was the house, but it wasn't the house at the same time. When he opened his eyes again, he realized what had happened.

"You didn't banish her, Lucki. You banished us." That was what Isabel had been working on all those centuries ago. Not a way to defeat Angelica but a way for them to escape the sorceress forever.

"I don't understand." Lucki followed his gaze to the house and gasped. "What happened to the cat house?"

It was painted black. The stones and wood, the shutters and frames...everything was black. The portico wasn't plain glass. It was all completely stained-glass, depicting wolves in different regal poses.

"It isn't the cat house here." So many late-night conversations... So many plans, no matter how far-fetched... Wren and Isabel had built a fantasy house. They'd envisioned the way they'd redo the cat house if they could, how they'd make it their own—in a different world, in a different time. Wren had thought that it had been in their fantasies only. But Isabel had done it. She'd build a sanctuary for them there, wherever 'there' was.

"Wren, what's going on?"

"Do the spell again." Wren clenched his jaw so tight that his head hurt instantly.

"What?"

"Do the spell." He tore his gaze away from the impossible house to look at Lucki, and he knew his expression was harsh. "The spell. We need to see if it works to bring us back."

Lucki shook her head at the same time that she let a long breath go. "Okay, but I think you need to hold me like you did in the forest."

Wren froze for a millisecond. It was too intimate all of a sudden, especially being there, with Isabel's creation steps away.

"I mean, you need to hang on, because I don't know how this works. If we're in a different time or place, we need to go together."

He nodded then closed the distance. This might be Isabel's creation, but it wasn't her. Isabel was dead...long dead. He wasn't betraying her by holding Lucki.

He'd been naked after his initial forced shift when Ben had died, and now still was, so every part of his body was on high alert. He wrapped his arms around her and, this time, because he wasn't trying to save her and they weren't in imminent danger, he actually felt her in his arms. She slipped her hands over his shoulders but kept her head down so she was staring at his chest rather than his lips. He wanted her to stare at his lips. He wanted her to tilt her head up. He wanted her to press her body against his.

"Do it." He didn't mean for it to come out as a gruff snap, but he needed to be away from her as quickly as possible before he did something stupid.

Lucki tensed but said nothing.

He wanted to suck his words back, to apologize again and again.

Lucki sucked in a deep breath, and as she exhaled, she unleashed her power. It rolled up his legs, brushed against his skin and wrapped around their bodies, uniting them like it had in the forest. She murmured the words of the spell, barely audible, even to his heightened senses. It floated like a string, adding to the ribbons of magic already encircling them. Her power was awe-inspiring. She was so much more a witch than Isabel.

Wren closed his eyes, knowing that even in his thoughts, he was betraying Isabel. He shut out the scenery and focused on Lucki's essence, giving his body permission to absorb everything she had to give in this moment.

The magic tightened, forcing Wren to pull her closer, making them melt into one another. Lucki put her head against his chest. Wren curled his body around hers. She uttered the final words and her magic swirled around them.

Heartbeats stretched into slow motion.

Wren opened his eyes. The black cat house was still there.

"It's not working," Lucki said.

Wren's world tilted sideways. He stumbled back, releasing Lucki from his arms.

The magic snapped away.

"It doesn't feel the same." Lucki scanned her arms like she'd find the answers there. "I don't understand."

"We need to go inside." Wren looked down at Lucki. "Isabel had planned an escape. That was what her spell was for, I think. She'd planned an escape to come here." And she'd died before she could make it happen – or she'd sacrificed herself instead of bringing him there.

They would have been safe. They would have been together.

She hadn't even hinted that this had been her plan.

Wren's heart sputtered and died all over again.

He'd lost so much already, but to know that Isabel had done this? He laid his hand on his chest.

"She planned to bring you here with her?" Lucki tore her eyes away from him to look at the house. "Without the others?"

Wren frowned as Lucki's words rattled in his brain. *Without the others?*

He didn't have to see inside to know that she'd taken every single idea he'd wished for and put it there somehow — for him, just for him.

He'd wanted her all to himself, even though he'd known he could never separate himself from the Brotherhood, not after everything they'd been through. He'd made it impossible for her to bond with any of the other shifters, if only because he'd asked her to vow herself to him only. He'd been selfish and stupid.

She'd planned to bring him here but not the others because that was what she knew he'd wanted deep in his soul — a wish he'd never said out loud to anyone but her.

"How did she do this?"

Wren shook his head and opened his mouth, but no words came out. He didn't know. Had no clue, but she'd had to have used a tremendous amount of power to build this place.

"Let's go inside. Maybe I can sense something in there, figure out a way to get us back from wherever this is." Lucki tugged on his hand to get him moving, but he walked on like a zombie on a leash.

Wherever this was.

Wherever did Isabel build this?

Alternative dimension? Another time? A plane of magic that only she knew about?

The reality of this place hit even harder as Wren realized that Isabel had kept a secret from him, a big, important secret. Perhaps it was because she'd wanted to surprise him or maybe because things had been heating up so much between her and Angelica that she'd planned this as a contingency. She would have known that he'd never leave his brothers willingly. He'd never betray the covenant to fight alongside them against the evil sorceress. Reality settled like a rock in his gut.

She would have had to bring him there without his consent.

Forgiveness will come like dawn each day.

She always used to say that it was better to beg forgiveness than ask for permission.

That was what all the ingredients she'd listed along the side of the spell were for. Belladonna was a sedative. She'd planned to drug him to get him there.

Had she brought him there against his will, she would have needed his forgiveness.

Forgiveness will come like dawn each day.

And he maybe wouldn't have given it to her.

Chapter Twenty-One

Lucki

Lucki found it strange to be in the cat house without the cats, to not hear Reuben's booming voice and Julian's smooth teasing. It was odd to be in Isabel's vision of perfection for her and Wren. Or maybe this was Wren's vision that Isabel had captured somehow. Either way, the house was eerily different—not so much in layout, which was relatively the same, and not so much in furniture, which looked antique, even though Lucki was sure that when Isabel had built this place, all the furniture had been considered modern. It was different in its essence. It didn't feel like home. It was missing the energy Lucki had come to know as unique to the cat house.

Her skin was tight and her head burdened with pressure. She kept throwing glances toward Wren, hoping maybe he'd unclamp his mouth and tell her what he thought was going on. But he was obviously shell-shocked—moving slowly through each room, running his hands over wood panels and marble hearths. His eyes were glassy and his mind clearly miles away.

He had found a stash of folded clothes at the entrance of the back hall and had put some on. Rather than his usual style of jeans and T-shirts, they were more a sign of Isabel's times—a button-up linen shirt that flowed past his hips and pants that were hilariously tight. An old-fashioned version of 'skinny fit'.

When he started his second lap up the main staircase, Lucki broke away from him. The house was empty, with nothing to see that would explain anything, but Lucki had an idea. She went directly into the front sitting room, which looked essentially identical to the one in the real cat house. This was Isabel's room in this world just as much as it had been in the other world. She zeroed in on the Queen Anne. If Isabel had hidden her grimoire in the chair once, she'd likely do it again.

Lucki eased the chair onto its side. The same wood panel was wedged into the bottom of the chair. She pushed against it, then slid it to the back. A leather-bound book tumbled out.

Not as big. Not as unwieldy. Not Isabel's grimoire...not exactly. It resonated with power. Not intensely like the grimoire, but a low vibration that tickled the periphery of Lucki's magic sense.

This book was half the size of its sister. The leather was a different shade of brown and it was embossed with vines and ivy rather than a cat's eye.

Lucki flipped the cover open. She expected to see blank pages again, but instead found that the first page held a simple inscription.

Wren, my love. Please forgive me.

Lucki closed the book. This was private, not for her eyes.

"What's that?"

She jolted then covered her mouth to keep herself from screaming. "Oh, Goddess, you scared me!" Wren stared at her blankly. He was void of emotion, locked up tight in his head. She held the book up to him. "It's for you."

He waved his hand. "What does it say?"

She looked down at the cover and traced her fingers along the vines. "She asks for forgiveness from you."

Wren snorted and shook his head.

Lucki ran her hand along the side then lifted the cover so Wren could see the inscription. He didn't say anything, so she kept going. The second page had more writing. It was jam-packed with writing. Not spells... No, this was more like a journal.

"It's her book of shadows," Wren murmured. "It'll probably tell us what the hell she's done."

Lucki stood with the book still open then carried it into the kitchen. Wren was already there, checking the windows and looking outside. "It's too foggy to see anything." He cupped his hands around his eyes. "I can't see past the front porch."

Lucki settled herself in her usual seat at the kitchen table. She expected to hear Reuben grumbling around. She expected to smell watermint tea. Wren turned from the window. "I don't think there's anything out there."

Lucki flipped through the next few pages of the book. Isabel's writing was a tight scrawl, but not unreadable. "Yes, there's nothing outside." *Nothing lies beyond these walls and garden. The magic demand is too strong.*

Wren pulled out a chair, the rumble of its feet scraping the floor like thunder in the empty house.

Her words were written like stream of consciousness. A purging of her thoughts onto the page. *This is what you wanted. This is what you needed — what we both needed.*

"I think you need to read this. I think it's for you." Lucki tried to shove the book toward Wren so he could see Isabel's words, but he put his hand out to stop it from sliding his way.

"I already know what it says." He shook his head. "I mean, I know what Isabel would have written in there." He tapped the table, lowered his head and sighed. "I wanted to possess her completely and she me. My jealousy was out of control, but so was hers. The time I spent with my brothers was time away from her. I wanted her all to myself, yes, but she wanted me all to herself as well."

The others had already told her that much. Lucki stayed silent, her gaze locked on the top of his head, but he didn't look up. He just traced an invisible pattern on the tabletop.

"I complained a lot about not having time to ourselves — of not having a space of our own." He flung his arm up and motioned around them. "That's why she built this place...for us."

"But the others..." A lump the size of a walnut was stuck in Lucki's throat, and no matter how many times she swallowed, the thing would not move.

"I wouldn't have left them." Wren snapped his eyes to meet hers. "I wouldn't have broken the covenant to the Brotherhood. It was fantasy Isabel and I had dreamt up that I knew would never happen. I wanted so badly for her to be mine, only mine, and she wanted me all to herself."

"Wasn't she, though? Wasn't she yours?" The lump in Lucki's throat grew. She knew that kind of possession. *"You are mine. Forever."* Shane had wanted her all to himself. He'd cut her off from everything and everyone she'd ever known.

"As long as the others were in our lives, we would always know what should have happened. Isabel should have bonded with all the shifters. She should have taken the magic they would have given her. It would have bolstered her. It would have saved her. If I hadn't been such a damn fool, I would have found a way to convince her…to protect her."

"But she didn't want that." *Like me.* She'd rejected the idea of eternity with all of them, not because of previous trauma but because she had loved Wren so much.

"We thought she was powerful enough."

Like me. Dread coated Lucki's nerves. Her stomach flipped. The lump in her throat wedged in tight, threatening to choke her.

"But no, she didn't want the bond from the others…only me. We'd both been short-sighted fools. We'd both been too love-blind. It was our fatal flaw." Fatal for Isabel.

Would it be fatal for Lucki as well? Suddenly all the confidence she'd had in the time leading to this moment evaporated.

Poof.

Gone.

"Isabel wasn't strong enough to defeat Angelica, but somehow I am? She rejected the bond from the others, and you said that killed her in the end. So, aren't we being fools as well?" She closed her eyes for a second. "Me? I'm the fool this time, right?"

Wren gulped. "You're powerful." Something that looked like doubt flickered across his eyes. "The cats have bolstered you."

"History always repeats itself eventually." Lucki shook her head as she scanned Isabel's words on the next page. *Safe haven. Refuge. Will Wren consider it a prison? Will he hate me for locking him here? Will he forgive me in time? Is it worth the sacrifice?*

Yes. A million times, yes.

That sense of dread flooded every part of Lucki's body. She slid her eyes over the words again. "I don't think we can leave here." She shoved the book his way, her finger under the lines she'd just read. "I think Isabel intended to lock you in here with her."

Wren read where she was pointing then continued to the next line. "Desert island. Oasis. Eternity together." He looked up at her, his eyes laser-focused, like Wren's brain had finally left the fog of grief and clicked into power mode once again. "You're not powerful enough on your own to take us back."

"I was powerful enough to bring us here!" She bristled, which caught her off guard. Why was she getting defensive?

"You pulled Angelica's power into yours. I saw her magic, black like smoke, entwined with yours as you finished the spell."

Her mouth dropped open. She hadn't felt Angelica's power invading hers, but Lucki had felt like her power had had a boost. She'd assumed that had been Wren in some way.

"Ew! Do you think her magic infected mine?" Lucki brushed her hands down her arms as though she could dislodge any lingering trace of Angelica's power.

"I think her power gave you the surge you needed to finish the spell that brought us here." Wren shook his head. "And I think we're stuck here unless we figure out a way to bolster your power again."

Bricks dropped, one by one, into Lucki's stomach.

They knew a way to bolster her magic.
Wren would have to mark her.

Chapter Twenty-Two

Reuben

Reuben tore through the cat house in search of Lucki. He kept his hand on his chest the whole time, partly because the gaping hole of Ben's death was raw enough to keep him from shifting and partly because he feared his fellow shifter's demise meant Lucki was in danger. He had to find her.

"Where is she?" Julian crashed through the front door, his face covered with dirt, his chest heaving, his eyes wild and darting erratically.

"I can't find her."

The cats were in a frenzy, racing up and down the stairs, trailing after Reuben, sending him incessant but incoherent thoughts. Many of the cats were at the back door, scratching and meowing to get out. As soon as Reuben swung around the banister, he realized why. A blue tint of Lucki's magic was all over the door.

Suddenly the messages the cats were sending made sense.

"She went to the circle." Reuben beelined to the front door, where there were fewer cats blocking his way. Julian was already there, holding the door and keeping the cats back so they could slip out without any of the felines escaping. They'd already lost three cats and a shifter to Angelica today, and there was no way he'd risk losing anyone else.

He and Julian took the side way into the forest, a slightly longer route to the circle with more obstacles to tackle, but they'd come at it from a direction that would give them a surveillance advantage. Not that Reuben thought Angelica had somehow breached the perimeter of Isabel's protection spell, but if Lucki was close enough to the edge, Angelica could lash out with her powers to hurt her.

Ben's sudden death throbbed deep inside Reuben's core. How had Angelica trapped him? And why hadn't she enthralled Ben just as she'd enthralled Alessandro, Camden and Rafi all those years ago? Why kill a powerful force? Unless her magic was waning so much that she didn't have enough left to transform Ben into a wild cat. As horrifying as Ben's death was, if Angelica was that weak, then there was a silver lining. It meant Lucki really did have a chance to beat Angelica in a duel.

A horrific realization slammed into Reuben's thoughts.

Angelica had killed Ben so she could consume his heart. Ben's heart, along with those of the three missing cats, would give her a tremendous boost of power.

With that amount of raw power, Angelica would be a force that Lucki would have a hard time defending against. She'd get injured, which Reuben was now sure was part of Angelica's multi-step plan to defeat Lucki. If she'd wounded Lucki, then the duel on the night of the Solstice, when Lucki's powers would be at their peak, would be much simpler for the wicked sorceress to win. It was foul play and the dirtiest kind of warfare, but Angelica had never been known for following the rules.

Reuben's bear stirred. *Come on, big guy. It's time to fight.* Reuben wasn't used to coaxing his bear to action, but losing a brother was soul-shattering for his inner beast. His bear took notice of Reuben's coaxing but didn't rise.

Julian approached the circle from one side, Reuben the other.

Angelica's magic was stronger here. Black smog trailed like a diesel exhaust all around the empty circle, but it wasn't coming from there.

"She's in the forest." Reuben cut through the clearing, no longer caring if Angelica knew he was coming. If she had Lucki, he would rip her throat out with his bare hands.

"Murrrrow!" Mr. Whiskers jumped into his path, then, with what seemed like a nod to follow, the cat raced off into the forest.

"This way!" Reuben took off after the cat and with each pounding step called his bear out. But his call, once again, went unanswered. His bear was still reeling. Panic surged up Reuben's throat. The air reeked of Angelica's magic, but mingled in the stench were wisps of Lucki's signature scent. *Cinnamon. Vanilla. Lavender.*

Pushing himself harder, he leapt over roots and knocked away hanging branches, like a freight train ramming through the dense foliage—nothing would stop him from his goal to protect Lucki.

He broke through the final wall of brush into a clearing and watched as Wren dove for Lucki. Magic swirled like a hurricane, Lucki's blue and Angelica's black. Knowing that Lucki would be safe in Wren's arms, Reuben redirected his body to the sorceress then called his bear one last time.

From one second to the next, his bear exploded from its grief and transformed Reuben mid-leap. He was inches away from barreling into Angelica and let loose a mighty roar that should have had her quaking in her skin. But instead of turning toward him in fear, she did so with a grin that rattled even his bear. With a flick of her hands, Reuben went from soaring toward her to suspended in mid-air, an abrupt full stop that violently jarred his body, snapping his bones like twigs. He grunted through the pain as his body quickly started to heal. He struggled to get free, but whatever he was caught in was tacky and sticky and his struggles only managed to tangle him more.

From his peripheral vision he could see Julian caught in the same snare. The lion chuffed and growled as it tried to bite away the invisible threads that bound it, but, like Reuben, the more he moved, the more entwined he got.

"Where is she?" Angelica growled.

Reuben attempted to crane his head and could just barely make out the spot that Lucki and Wren had been moments before. The now-*empty* space that showed no trace of either of them.

Reuben growled back, his bear none too pleased to be trapped in her web of magic. He had no idea where Lucki and Wren were, but he prayed that somehow Lucki had transported them to a safe place.

"Bring her back!" Angelica demanded.

Despite knowing it was pointless, Reuben's bear struggled against the bonds, using his teeth to chomp at the strands that coated and pulled on his fur.

Angelica moved closer to him. Her wild appearance was even more startling than in years gone by. Her eyes were black, lined by shadows and filled with malice. She'd descended even further into madness over the centuries until there wasn't a trace of her humanity left, not that there'd been much to begin with.

"Caught you in my web, big bear. You and your lion. Do you like it? I imagine not." Her laugh sounded like a hoarse cough. "I've learned many new tricks since we last battled." She leaned closer. "Many new magics that your sweet Cat Keeper will never see coming." She splayed her fingers and Reuben's body contorted so that he was spreadeagled. With a roar trapped in his throat, he attempted to fight against the bonds, but they were like iron shackles holding him open and completely vulnerable. The rumbling growl of Julian's cat let him know that they were both stuck and at Angelica's mercy.

It didn't matter, though. As long as she was busy with them, she wouldn't be busy trying to find Lucki.

"I ate your hawk's heart. Did you feel me doing that?" She circled Reuben, somehow not getting caught in her own sticky web. "I know you beasts are connected to one another." As she came back around, she pounded Reuben's chest with her open palm. His skin flayed like she'd just touched him with the sharpest blade. Pain exploded like a firebomb. His whole body jolted on the web. He refused to cry out and instead clamped his muzzle, clenched his jaw and called to his bear to fight, however fruitless it seemed.

"I've found a way to break the curse. Well, not so much a break as a transfer of ownership." She leaned in closer. "I'm going to find your little Cat Keeper. I'm going make it so she takes on the burden of this curse, so I no longer have to fuel it. I'm going to make her the

226

conduit of this blasted spell so that it's her power that is drained year after year, decade after decade. Although I don't think she'll last that long, do you? Tiny, weak thing." She touched his chest again and a searing burn ricocheted through his body. The fur, fat, muscle and sinew parted like a knife through butter.

"You're not going to be able to warn her," Angelica sang like a demented music box. "I'm going to eat your heart and the lion's heart too." She leaned in close again. "It's not the same as the kitty's, but it'll give me what I need to get the job done."

She slipped her hand into the gaping wound in Reuben's chest.

This time he screamed.

Chapter Twenty-Three

Lucki

"There has to be another way." Lucki tapped the book a little harder than necessary. "There's got to be something in here."

Wren pushed his chair back. "You read the book. I'm going to survey the area, see if there's anything beyond the fog out there."

"Wait! Are you sure that's a good idea?" She remembered a movie she'd once watched, a classic, where a couple who'd died were trapped in their house and when they'd tried to leave, they'd ended up in some desert wasteland being hunted by giant worms.

Would giant worms really be that surprising, with everything else that had happened in her life in the last two months?

No.

"I'll be fine." Wren stalked to the front door. "We need to know the boundary of Isabel's world. It's possible there's a gateway or a weak spot we can take advantage of."

"Oh, right, good point. I'll come with you." She was on his heels, so when he stopped and turned, she ended up crumpled in his arms. "*Oof!*"

He steadied her with his hands on her shoulders, pulling her away from his embrace so fast that she almost fell backward. "No, you'll stay here."

"I may not be powerful enough to get us out of here right now, but I'm still powerful."

"I know you are, but I can cover more ground as a wolf, and you need to find out what her book says." He didn't wait for Lucki to reply. He opened the door then shifted, going from man to wolf in a nanosecond.

Convenient. Don't want to talk about something? Just shift into a non-lingual animal. "Whatever."

As she turned to go back to the book, Wren's wolf nudged her hand. She looked down at him and could have sworn he was attempting to smile at her.

A wolf grinning. How very comforting.

Then he bolted out of the door and was swallowed by the fog. Lucki shivered as she closed the door. The fog outside had grown thicker in the time they'd been in the house, like it was closing in on them. She couldn't even see the back garden anymore.

Be safe out there.

She wrapped her arms around herself then headed back to the book.

Time slipped by. Hours maybe. It was hard to tell with no phones or clocks to mark its passing, and Lucki was so immersed in the book that she barely noticed that her neck was growing more and more kinked because of how she was bent over. Added to the effect was that Isabel had warned that time moved differently in this place, so Lucki didn't know if hours had actually gone by or if it had only been minutes.

The book was fascinating, like finally getting a glimpse into the mysterious Isabel Clover's head. Her hopes and dreams were in the book, her ideas and intuitions, her inner-most thoughts about Wren and the love she felt for him. All of it was scrawled up and down, sideways sometimes, like Isabel had grabbed the book to hastily fill its pages, no matter which way the words flowed.

She did explain why she'd rebuilt the cat house in this place, but it hadn't been a straightforward thought process. Lucki had found tidbits of explanation interspersed through the pages, and there was no continuity or flow. It wasn't until she read a notation about an alternative plane of magic that she realized Isabel was even talking about this version of the cat house. And like a key in a lock, Lucki finally understood the other things she'd read.

Isabel had built this house as an escape for her and Wren. She knew that he would resist, so she was working on a spell that he wouldn't be able to fight. If it was performed on the night of the Summer Solstice, then it had the greatest chance of locking Wren here and preventing anyone else from getting in. Her words expressed fear and urgency but didn't explain why. Could Isabel have been worried about Angelica? Or was there some other reason why she'd even consider tearing Wren away from his brothers and forcing him to live in this world with her? She didn't explain that on any page that Lucki had read so far, and she was getting close to the end of the scribbled pages.

It did mean that because the Summer Solstice was still two weeks away, Lucki could bring them home.

They weren't trapped here. The magic dimensional deadbolt hadn't been turned. *Yet.*

She had to find a way to harness more power, though.

Lucki flipped from back to front and front to back, quickly scanning for something she hadn't seen. There were no spells in Isabel's book of shadows, but there were ideas for spells. Maybe there was one that could help Lucki figure out—

Bile rose to the back of her throat. Her stomach pitched. *Oh Goddess.*

A shifter's heart provides significant power. From bonding most certainly, his love and protection extends like a warrior's embrace — but also if consumed. The heart of a shifter will fuel the most desperate needs of the truly wicked. The more hearts, the more unstoppable she'll become.

Lucki read the words again...and again.

Angelica had consumed the cats' hearts because it gave her a power boost. She'd consumed Ben's heart too.

Lucki covered her mouth. *Reuben and Julian.*

She jumped up from her chair, toppling it over in the process, then raced to the back door. The fog pressed against the window, so thick that Lucki couldn't see anything but the gray and white swirls. She opened the door then hesitated.

What if she went out there and couldn't find her way back? What if Wren was lost somewhere? What if—

An eerie howl broke the silence and goosebumps rose all over her skin. The fog rolled into the house, up her legs, around her arms. Everything it touched dampened, like dripping fingers were trailing over her clothes and skin. She shivered. She had to find Wren. It was time to take action.

She sucked in her fear and put it away, then stepped outside.

There was no way to see beyond the fog, no way to know if she was headed in the right direction. She made it to the edge of the backyard where the garden began to turn wild, but still, she wasn't sure if she was even headed the right way.

Everything quaked inside her. Her heart drummed hard and fast. She panted through each breath.

"Wren!" He had to be close. "Come back! We have to hurry!"

Reuben and Julian were in trouble. They'd go after Angelica. She'd find a way to ensnare them just like she'd done to Ben. Then she'd eat their hearts too.

"Wren!"

The rattling of sound echoed from all directions. Quick movement to her left, then her right. Something running, or pacing, crashing through foliage, crunching on leaves.

Lucki strained to see beyond the gloom, but even her hands disappeared in the dense fog when she wasn't holding them up close to her face. "Wren," she whispered, her throat all jammed up, fear licking its way down her spine. "We need to go."

A branch snapped next to her. She spun, hands raised and magic sparking along her fingertips. Wren stepped out of the fog, huffing and spitting past bared fangs. His eyes were feral. His teeth menacing.

Lucki took a step back. Then another.

Wren tracked her step for step.

"Reuben and Julian are in trouble." She didn't know how much he could understand as a wolf. "The book says time moves differently here." Her voice wobbled. "I think we can get back to almost exactly the same time we left." Her butt hit the door. She splayed her hands behind her. "As long as the intention is there, I'm sure I can do it."

The wolf's growl, low and deep, was just like that night all those weeks ago when she'd first met Wren in the alley. Was he even Wren right now, or had he slipped into his wolf so deeply that he didn't even know who she was?

She straightened her spine then pushed herself away from the door.

"Wren, stop fucking around! We need to get back home. We need to make sure Reuben and Julian are safe!" She dropped to her knees and held her hands out. "You need to bond with me." She stared into the wolf's blue eyes. "We need to do this."

In a flash Wren was human again. He gripped her face roughly. "You don't know what you're asking."

"I know that Angelica is eating shifter hearts because they give her more power than the cats' hearts. I know that our friends are going to die if we don't get back to them."

"She was going to trap me here." His eyes blasted pain and anger. "The fog just gets thicker and thicker. Isabel was going to keep me here."

"She thought she was protecting you because she knew it was a matter of time before Angelica figured out what would happen if she ate the shifter hearts." Why she was making excuses for Isabel she had no idea, but Lucki didn't want Wren to get hurt and she knew, based on what she'd read, that Isabel had loved him, possibly more than she had loved herself.

"If I bond with you — " His voice cracked wide open. He let her face go, hung his head and heaved a sigh.

Her heart clenched. *Oh, Goddess…* "Wren." She brushed his hair back from his face. "Wren, I'm not Isabel. I don't want to trap you. I wouldn't do that to you, and I wouldn't do that to your brothers." She coaxed him to look at her again. "We have to bond. I need your power to bolster me."

"You don't want this." His eyes were bloodshot and swimming in unshed tears.

"I don't want to live without Reuben or Julian" — she ran her fingers over his face—"or you. You're my family now." No truer words had ever been said.

"Lucki, the bond —"

"I'll handle it." She kissed him tenderly, chastely. "We have to save our friends."

With another deep sigh, Wren nodded. "We have to save my brothers."

Chapter Twenty-Four

Julian

While Julian was in his lion's body, he was aware of things on almost a pure animalistic level. He was caught in a web. The spider was Angelica. No matter how much he struggled, he couldn't free himself, and she was about to kill his brother.

The horror of watching her hand slip into the bear's chest was enough to make Julian writhe and growl and chuff with every ounce of strength he had, but that only seemed to make things worse. Hopelessness was like a steel lid closing on his coffin or a cage trapping him in the reality of what lay ahead. Reuben was going to die. He was going to die. And worse was the fact that Angelica would benefit from their deaths. She'd take their hearts and gain power from it. His lion understood her words enough to gather that as truth.

With her hand embedded in Reuben's chest, it was only a matter of seconds before she ripped his life away.

The wind whipped up fast and furious, sending dirt and leaves and twigs to tangle in the web with Julian. Angelica didn't notice or didn't care. She was so intent on her prize that she failed to register a change in the air. But Julian knew... This was no ordinary windstorm. This was magic — Lucki's magic.

Streaks of blue light sparked a short distance behind Angelica and a strange fog began to roll along the ground. Julian fixated on the pulse of that energy, how it gained strength with each of his heartbeats.

Come on. Come on! His lion roared.

Her wild cats slipped out from the forest, grunting at the fog.

Angelica snapped up her head, her hand still inside Reuben. She looked behind her, eyes wide and mouth slightly agape, then she flipped herself back to the task of removing Reuben's heart.

Julian blinked. One blink and the forest opened for a split second. The fog contracted around Angelica, moving up her legs quickly, while behind her, Lucki and Wren appeared. They were holding each other tightly, but the moment their feet touched the forest floor, they separated.

Wren immediately transformed into his wolf and went after the wild cats. Lucki raised her hands and, along with the movement, the fog rose swiftly, coiling like a snake around Angelica's body, freezing her and halting her attack on Reuben.

Lucki swooped in, her mouth working silently, her arms and chest glowing with markings... Wren had bonded with her. His power had bolstered her. She was a goddess. *So confident. So powerful.* Julian was in awe.

Angelica struggled and was able to move her lips to mumble something indecipherable, but Lucki pinched her fingers together and that noise stopped. She trailed her fingers along Angelica's arm and slid into the gaping wound in Reuben's chest, then slowly, so painfully slowly, she eased Angelica's hand out.

Angelica didn't have the heart, but her hand was coated in Reuben's blood.

Reuben's bear sighed. His eyes drifted closed and his body went slack.

Panic flashed across Lucki's face. She seemingly didn't know where to keep her attention, and she darted her eyes from Reuben to Angelica. It was clear she had to choose.

Angelica started to move.

Julian chuffed loudly as he struggled against his bonds and understanding dawned on Lucki's face. She murmured something as she twisted her hand like she was turning a knob, and Julian was suddenly free. He charged Angelica, who had sense enough to use her newfound mobility to run. He closed the distance between them quickly, but before he could strike, Angelica disappeared.

Lucki had Reuben's bear in her arms on her lap. It was an awesome sight to see such a delicate woman holding the head of such a massive beast. Her eyes were closed, her breathing steady. Her lips moved quickly and her hand, the one not cradling Reuben's head, hovered over his gaping chest wound. Her blue magic was streaked with black and gray and purple. It mingled together like it was meant to be. Wren's magic was entwined with hers. She was his now…and he was hers. That was the only way she would be able to heal Reuben.

Wren returned to the clearing looking unhurt. The wild cats must have disappeared along with Angelica.

Unspoken communication passed from predator to predator, an acknowledgment of deference to Wren and Lucki's bond. Julian would guard Wren's mate with his life. He would stand down in his quest to bond with her as well, since he knew that was Wren's preference. History would repeat, if only in that Wren would have his love and the Brotherhood would have their backs.

Lucki's voice pulled him from the intensity of his thoughts. "I need your bond, Julian. I can't save him without your bond."

Julian's animal brain registered what she was asking seconds before his human consciousness did. His lion forced the change from beast to man before Julian could ask for it. He ended up on all fours, staring at Lucki but not knowing what to say.

"He's dying, Julian." Lucki pleaded with her eyes, her hand still hovering over Reuben's chest, the magic swirling. "I need your bond."

"But Wren—"

The wolf grunted then nodded in Lucki's direction. *Do it*, the wolf seemed to say.

"I need you, too." Lucki closed her eyes, her forehead pinched. "Please."

Julian scrambled to Lucki's side. Wren's mark was black and gray and purple. It undulated over her chest and down her arms. Julian moved to her back then lifted her shirt. Her skin was creamy smooth and flawless. "Are you sure?" His lion clawed and clambered, urging him forward. *Mark her. Take her. Give her power.*

"I'm sure," Lucki croaked.

Julian closed his eyes and called his lion forward, not to take over and not to transform, but to guide him through the marking, to claim Lucki as well. Julian went on instinct as he ran his fingers over her soft skin. He curved and dipped and looped all over her back, using all the space, covering every piece of flesh she had there. It took no more than a few minutes, but as his power flowed through his fingers and into her, locks began to fall into place and click closed. One by one, they united and sealed their fates together. When he opened his eyes, her back shone with ribbons of color — reds and oranges and purples that moved beneath her skin.

She let out a gasp, her head tilted back, then her power ignited to a brilliance that hurt his eyes. He released his lion once again, then sat with his back pressed to hers, on guard as she worked her magic to save his brother.

Chapter Twenty-Five

Lucki

Lucki had thought she had magic before. Her own, the power from the circle, the bolstering from the cats, but it was nothing compared to what she received from Wren and Julian. Their magic was filled with love and, as strange as it was to say, that love bolstered her more than the magic did. It filled her gaping holes and it gave her confidence to do the unthinkable.

Like bring a giant bear back from the brink of death.

His heart was mangled inside his chest. Angelica had dug her fingers right in and her inky power had left residue everywhere, like sticky tar. By the time Lucki had extricated Angelica's hand, Reuben was bleeding to death and Angelica's magic was already poisoning him.

At first, Lucki had fashioned her magic into thread and had tried to sew his wounds back together, but the holes were too big, there were too many and Angelica's magic was toxic enough to hamper any healing. Reuben's own shifter magic was clearly at work as well, desperately trying to mend the damage but at the same time battling against the darkness that Angelica had left behind.

Reuben was dying. His eyes, though closed, were darting behind the lids, and his breathing was shallow and strained, rattling a little with each exhale. His heart pumped still, weakly, and with each contraction gushed more blood than seemed possible.

When Lucki accepted Julian's bond and his bright flare of power entered her body and mingled with her magic, she knew what she had to do.

A thread was too singular and too slow. What she needed was a net or something that would bind the wounds quickly and aid his own body's attempts to heal. She created a mesh and threaded it through the sides of Reuben's injuries, while at the same time directing Julian's colorful light to bleach away Angelica's gunk. Julian's power was perfect for that, with all its vibrancy, and Lucki's powers, mingled with Wren, were enough to mend the wounds.

With all that magic and all that power, she finally began to make headway. One by one, his wounds closed, starting with his heart, then his ribs, then the muscle and sinew, fat, flesh and fur. The toxic sludge that Angelica had left behind evaporated too, leaving Reuben as he had been before Lucki and Wren had fallen into the magic world that Isabel had created.

By the time Reuben was whole again, Lucki was wobbling, ready to collapse, even though she was sitting. If not for Julian's lion pressing against her back and keeping her upright, she would have splayed herself on the forest floor, unable to hold herself up.

With Reuben's head in her lap and his eyes tightly clenched, she willed him to live. She poured her love into his body. The men, without meaning to, had slipped into her heart and had given Lucki exactly what she hadn't known she so desperately needed…a family.

"Wake up, Reuben," she whispered. "We need you."

"Lucki." Wren's voice startled her.

She looked up and realized how bleary her vision was.

"It might be better to come away from Reuben. Let him wake up on his own. His beast might lash out when he comes to. He may think he's still under attack."

Lucki gulped, shook her head then looked down at Reuben once again.

It was surreal in so many ways to have this massive beast in her lap. She ran her fingers over his broad forehead and impossibly soft ears. His fur everywhere else was coarse, made for the harsh Alaskan weather, but not his ears. They were teddy-bear ears, soft and plush, just like Reuben.

She knew he was a beast and that beasts didn't always know right from wrong, friend from enemy. His fangs were sharp and pointy, his jaw powerful enough to bite her hand off. She wasn't afraid, though. Not a chance. Not just because she knew that Julian and Wren would always protect her, but because Reuben was family and, in her heart, even without a bond, she knew he'd never do anything to hurt her.

"Reuben, come back to me." She leaned down and kissed his eyelids. His fur tickled her lips, but that didn't stop her from kissing his muzzle.

He heaved a huge breath in, then out. His whole body shuddered. Then he shifted from beast to man.

When he opened his eyes, there was no confusion there. "Lucki." He gulped, touching his chest. Then he let out a laugh that instantly warmed Lucki and rejuvenated her energy.

"You're awake!" She leaned down to kiss him again, this time lingering on his lips as he slipped his hand into her hair and held her close.

"You are incredible." Reuben touched his forehead to hers. "So powerful."

"I'm bonded." Her heart galloped suddenly. "With Wren and Julian."

Reuben pulled away so he could look into her eyes.

"I'd like to be bonded with you as well." Her heart was in her throat. "If you want to, I mean."

A grin exploded on Reuben's face. "Damn right I do!"

Before she even knew what was happening, Reuben had curled himself into an impossible angle so he could lift her shirt and kiss her belly. His lips were on her skin, and he pressed his hands to her waist. It was more than just a touch and deeper than skin-to-skin. Reuben's mark seeped into her like a tattoo ink without the needles. The heat of his aura—red, orange, yellow—all combined like an incendiary mark that would keep her warm and light her up whenever she needed.

When he pulled himself away, she didn't mourn the loss of his touch, because he was inside her now. She'd always carry a part of Reuben and Julian and Wren with her.

"So, I guess you're stuck with me." She laughed at the thought of that.

Reuben brushed his big hands over the sides of her face. "You're stuck with us, and we'll do everything, always, to show you how much you mean to us."

Julian leaned back and licked her neck with his huge kitty tongue. Wren tilted his wolfie head and howled in what Lucki understood to be heartfelt agreement, and Reuben kissed her lips, fully, completely taking possession of her just as surely as she was taking possession of him.

Chapter Twenty-Six

Lucki

They'd cremated Ben in the circle of stones on an altar of wood. Lucki had been joined by the cats and the wolf pups inside the sacred place, while the shifters stood guard along the border. She'd used her magic to light the flame that would release Ben's familiar soul and, hopefully, give him another chance to become a shifter and part of the Brotherhood once again. She hoped that one day he might find his way back to them, to her, but she knew he'd be reborn with no memory of his time in Weeping Falls.

They'd honored his death with a night of stories, and even though Lucki had only known him a short time, she had some too. Like the time Ben had tried to make her egg salad sandwiches but hadn't thought to take the shells off the eggs then somehow managed to mash the lot up and shove it into a pita. She'd gotten quite the surprise when she'd crunched her way through the first bite.

They'd spent more time laughing over Ben's funny ways than crying over his loss. She knew that the men would mourn quietly and in their own ways, as she would in hers. She always had a white candle burning in her window for her mom, and now when she said her evening blessing, she added Ben's name as well.

Lucki and Wren were alone again. He was in his room and she was in hers. Twice now she'd opened her door to peer down the hallway. Twice, she'd chickened out then closed it again.

Five days had passed since the bonding. Five days of recovery and resting.

Everyone was suddenly super shy about spending time alone with Lucki, despite the fact that she knew they had to be feeling the same intensely magnetic pull toward her as she felt toward them. Yet they were all walking on eggshells.

These men were infuriatingly considerate. They were giving her space and time, no doubt thinking that she had to mourn the loss of her single-woman freedoms. She had no regrets. Not one. Well, okay, maybe one. She wanted to be with Wren, alone, at least once, before she embraced all three men together.

And they *would* all be together — but not tonight.

Tonight, she wanted Wren to herself.

With a deep, steadying breath, Lucki opened the door again.

Wren was right there with his fist raised, as if he were seconds away from knocking. His eyes flew open, as did hers.

"Oh, hi!"

Wren lowered his fist. "I, ah, thought, I'd…shit." He rubbed the back of his neck then looked at her with a wolfie grin. "I wanted to see you…alone."

"Me too!" She took his hand and yanked him inside.

His startled-sounding, rough bark of a laugh made Lucki shiver all over. His aura rubbed against hers as he passed, and that sent a whole different sensation through her body. Like steel to flint, his aura ignited her core and triggered her markings to flare.

He noticed, of course, the swirling black and gray and purple ribbons he'd left on her chest and arms. His pupils dilated. His lips parted. "Lucki," he said, his voice a hoarse whisper as he finally, *finally* reached up to touch her.

He cupped the nape of her neck and pulled her close. She locked in on his eyes, seeing no doubts, no confusion. He was here with her, now and forever. The bond made that a certainty. For the first time since she'd arrived in Weeping Falls, Wren kissed her, and for the first time, he reached into her soul and caressed her damaged parts. His lips were firm, his kiss insistent, demanding, taking possession of her as surely as she was him. He probed her mouth, entangled her tongue with his, poured himself inside her and filled her up in all the places where she still had gaping holes.

He lifted her shirt and helped her take it off. She unbuttoned his, brushing her fingers along the dips and curves of his six-pack. He unhooked her bra, and as he slipped it off, he cupped her breasts and thumbed her aching nipples. Her brain had short-circuited as soon as his lips touched hers, so she was melty all over and desperate to have his body pressed against hers, his cock buried deep.

She unbuttoned his jeans and dropped the zipper. He slipped his hands into her yoga pants and squeezed her ass cheeks before sliding the pants all the way to her ankles. On his way down, he kissed along her belly, pressing his lips briefly to the cleft of her pussy before helping her slip her pants off one foot at a time.

She ran her fingers through his hair. He lifted her leg and slid her foot onto his shoulder then, with one hand on her ass, brought his heavy, hot breath to her slick, aching pussy. She moaned as soon as he touched his lips to her clit and dabbed his tongue along her hole. He slurped and sucked and licked and grunted his way along her pussy lips to her clit and back again, until her hips were rocking to the steady beat of her throbbing need. She pressed her palms to her breasts and rubbed against her hard nipples, and he slipped his fingers deep inside to rub her G-spot. Goosebumps broke out all over her skin. Her pussy clenched up tight and her body coiled until all it took was one more lick, one more stroke. One more grunt and she was exploding against Wren's face and squirting into his mouth.

He helped her shift her foot from his shoulder to the floor and kept her wobbly legs from giving out completely by guiding her to the bed, but before he could ease her down, she dropped to her knees and gave back what he'd just given her.

His cock was long and hard and curved. She wasted no time sliding it into her mouth, taking him all the way back, her eyes locking with his, then, with a little adjustment, she worked him deep into her throat. He groaned, his eyes shuttering, his hands roving in her hair as he guided her back out. She cupped his balls and gently kneaded them while she pumped his huge dick, coating him with her saliva, stroking him with her tongue. She could suck his dick all day. She wanted to swallow his cum, to feel it hit the back of her throat and slide down as his jets filled her. Even though she wanted this, it was Wren who stopped himself from finishing.

"I want to be inside you the first time," he grunted.

The thrill of his words, the promise of his cock filling her up, stretching her out, had her scrambling to do as he wished. They had an eternity for her to suck him off, but only once to christen their first time.

He helped her stand, brought her closer then kissed her hard. He pressed his body along hers and held her tightly, her breasts mashed firmly against him as he devoured her with his lips.

He eased her onto her back. She wrapped her legs around his waist and grabbed his ass, urging him closer, coaxing him to hurry. He paused, pulled his face back then looked down at her as he ran his fingers through her hair.

"I've wanted this so much." And his eyes said that no matter how he'd acted, he'd always wanted it.

Lucki's voice was trapped in her throat, so instead of speaking, she lifted her lips and kissed him once again. As he sank into her, with his tongue and his cock, she couldn't help the long moan that slipped past her lips and into his mouth.

He rolled his hips and pressed his weight into her, and she tightened her grip with her legs then urged him deeper. She ran her fingers through his silky hair and kissed him as he slowly, agonizingly slowly, pumped his cock into her again and again.

They were one — a rolling wave of passion, their kiss unbreakable, their bond eternal. Her magic markings were alight, glowing as her body revved and roared, building to a climax that promised fireworks.

She couldn't take him in deep enough. She couldn't taste him enough. The press of his body against hers wasn't enough, either. She could do an eternity of this with Wren – an eternity and more.

Her climax catapulted her past the clouds and the sun, past the Milky Way and out to deep space where she floated on waves of ecstasy and wished never to return to Earth.

Wren roared his release, and the hot jets of his cum filling her pussy brought her back in a daze. When he stared down at her, his eyes full of love and desire and possession, she knew he saw the exact same thing shining back at him in hers.

"I'll never let you go." Lucki brushed his hair back from his face.

"Me neither." He leaned in to nuzzle her neck, and the pulse of his cock stirring had her body revving all over again. Now that they'd made love, she was going to fuck this man's brains out and ride him like a bronco until they were both too exhausted to move.

* * * *

Satiated and sweaty, Lucki lay sprawled on top of Wren's slick body, her head on his chest, one leg draped over his hips, one arm curled along his waist. Wren ran his fingers gently over her sensitive skin, which teased new jolts of arousal to the surface. But she was too tired to do anything about it.

"Tell me again what happens the night of the Solstice," she murmured against his chest. The rise and fall of his body as he breathed and the constant thud of his heart were peaceful rhythms that could lull her to sleep, but she wanted it to be his voice that she heard last when she drifted off to dreamland.

"The veil parts, Isabel's protection spell wanes and Angelica will be able to enter the circle to access its magic."

"Which will bolster her power."

"That and the hearts she has consumed. Ben's, the cats', will make her more powerful. Her experience too, will give her advantages." He squeezed her closer. "But you have the mark of three shifters and ninety-seven cats. You have more raw power to wield, and her power is constantly siphoned by the curse. You are the greater sorceress. You'll win."

Lucki huffed out a strangled laugh. "If I don't do anything to mess it up."

"You'll use your instincts. You'll know how to counter anything she throws at you and you'll lash out with more power. You'll win this, Lucki."

"And you?"

Wren laughed. "I'll be battling the wild cats, as I usually do. All that magic flying around gets them riled up. We'll keep them in line and away from our cats."

"No one else can enter the circle."

Wren squeezed her again then kissed the top of her head. "We would never let you step foot in the circle if we thought you were at risk of losing. You have our bonds, and our magic will bolster you. We have the advantage."

Lucki pushed herself up so she could kiss him. "I feel like maybe we should knock on wood, just to be safe."

"Oh, if it's wood you want, I've got some right here."

Chapter Twenty-Seven

Wren

The Solstice duel was an hour away and Wren didn't know who was more nervous — him, Reuben or Julian. The three of them had been sharing fretful looks all day. He knew who wasn't nervous…Lucki. She was cool, collected and ready to kick some ass. Having grown tired of her mates' fussing, she'd sent them all out of the house to wait for her at the circle. She'd said she'd be along shortly, but as the time ticked away and Lucki had yet to make an appearance, he'd grown more and more wary. Was she having doubts? Was she crying in the bathroom? Should he double back and make sure she was okay?

He needed to give her space. They all did, but Wren, as usual, wanted to make sure she wasn't upset. He had his concerns about the impending battle, and anxiety had crept up on him as he lay with Lucki through the night, listening to her light snoring and holding her as tightly to his chest as she could bear.

Angelica was facing her greatest foe in Lucki since Isabel, and she'd barely made it through that battle two hundred years ago against his former mate. Angelica would do whatever she had to in order to win, which meant that Lucki had to be confident. She had to be on her game, because even with the men bolstering her, she was still going to be pushing herself to the limits of her power in this battle. They should have done more training. They should have prepared her more. His confidence the night before had been a product of post-sex bliss, and now, with the battle approaching, he felt like he'd over-promised on her success.

"I should go back and get her." Wren didn't wait for the others to object. He started walking toward the path to the house. Maybe he could whisk her away, get her out of town before Angelica could do anything about it.

But Lucki was right there.

She was in the ceremonial dress, Isabel's dress, and she was stunning. The dress was white lace and flowing layers that moved like fairy wings all around Lucki as she walked toward them. On her face was Isabel's battle mask, also white, with two curled horns and a sparkling crystal between her eyes. The white would offer some protection from Angelica's dark magic. The crystal would help keep Lucki focused on the battle. Lucki's exposed skin danced with her markings, swirls of color that represented all her bonds — to the cats, to the men, to the circle.

Trailing after her were the cats — all of them — as well as the wolf pups. It would be safer for them at the house, but he couldn't fault them for following Lucki. The magnetic pull toward her was so powerful that even he couldn't keep back. He closed the distance between them before the other men could, and that gave him a rush of possessive triumph.

She took his face in her hands and her magic jolted through his body. Her lips on his lips made his knees wobble.

We are one. You are mine, her kiss said.

When she released his face then turned to kiss Reuben, any trace of jealousy or possessive need was gone from Wren's mind. *We are one. You are mine.*

She kissed Reuben the same way as she'd kissed him, and when the big guy staggered back, she turned to Julian then kissed him too.

The stone circle was considered safe territory and under the protection of Isabel's spell until midnight of the Summer Solstice, which was minutes away. At midnight, the veil lowered, and Angelica would be able to enter the circle with Lucki. She would also be able to harness its power if she were strong enough, which she usually was. Lucki could take advantage. She could strike out at Angelica before the appointed time. Wren almost wished she would. But Lucki wouldn't break the rules. She'd play fair. That was more than he could say for Angelica, who'd already violated the duel protocols by attacking Lucki and Ben days before — not that he'd expect anything less from such a wicked woman.

The wind picked up, carrying with it a darkness that muted the light of the moon and stars and silenced the night creatures.

"She comes." Reuben's deep voice reverberated through Wren.

Wren called his wolf, and before Angelica appeared, he was on all fours and baying to the inky night sky.

Angelica wasn't the only creature who could cast fear on the surroundings.

Reuben and Julian transformed as well, then spread out on their side of the circle. The time would come for them to take up a battle with Angelica's wild cats, but not before the duel had started.

Angelica, cloaked in shadows, stepped into the clearing. Wren sniffed the air and swiveled his ear, straining to find a hint of where those blasted wild cats were lurking.

"Midnight is upon us." Angelica's booming voice echoed off the stones. "Your presence must mean that you've accepted my challenge."

"I have," Lucki responded.

Wren left his appointed post to sniff the air closer to the forest. Where were her damn wild cats? Julian chuffed, his cat ears shifting this way and that, obviously trying, as Wren was, to detect the beasts.

"We will enter the circle at the same time." Angelica had moved to the edge of the circle. "Then the battle will begin."

Lucki raised her hands, readying herself for an instant attack from Angelica, just as they'd prepared.

"Your protectors can stand down. They will only be spectators tonight. My boys were put to better use."

Wren turned his head to stare at Angelica. *What?*

Angelica grinned his way just as she stepped into the circle. "They sacrificed their hearts to a worthy cause."

Reuben's roar shook the trees. Wren ran toward Lucki, hoping to stop her from entering the circle, but it was too late. The shock of Angelica's confession registered on Lucki's face seconds before the first blast of magic ripped into her chest. Angelica had eaten the hearts of her wild cat shifters. She was much more powerful than they'd ever anticipated.

Chapter Twenty-Eight

Lucki

Angelica's power hit Lucki like a crossbow. It pierced her skin and sent her reeling. As much power as Lucki had available to her, it would do no good if she didn't anticipate attacks. Angelica had caught her off guard, yes, but her first shot had only caused minor damage to Lucki's body. Wren's markings had forced the magic out almost as soon as it had entered through the wound. Lucki's flesh had started knitting back together before she could blink.

She lowered her stance and called her magic, a reinforcement of purple and orange and red swirls that rolled up and down her arms and sparkled along her fingers.

Angelica mimicked her position, a wry grin on her face, like she was toying with Lucki. Her own magic jolted from one hand to the other, black fuzz that was hard to focus on and hurt Lucki's eyes if she tried to.

"I see you've bonded with your shifters. Pity you only have three." Angelica circled right. "Had you not wasted time with the fourth, you'd probably have a chance here today, but as it is —"

Lucki had heard enough. This wasn't a game. She tossed out a wallop of power, aiming high so that Angelica moved to block her face, then Lucki followed with a low, fast-rolling stunner which she hoped would knock Angelica on her ass.

But neither spell hit. Instead, Angelica barked a startled-sounding laugh, swept her arms over her head and somehow sent those spells reversing back at Lucki.

She barely had time to dive out of the way before the spells backtracked to her.

Shit. Not good. Her face slid into the muddy ground and dirt went into her mouth.

Angelica lobbed another series of short bursts, flinging them out haphazardly. They dug into the dirt all around Lucki as she struggled to get back to her feet.

The spells Angelica had sent into the dirt had produced snaking vines that rose with grabbing tendrils, reaching for Lucki's legs. The cats' mark kept them from taking hold, offering Lucki protection against Angelica's attempt to bind her.

Lucki called up Wren's power. Black like Angelica's, it offered darkness to match her darkness. She entwined it with the chaos that swirled within her own natural powers, the magic that she'd fought so hard to contain at the beginning. She didn't pause, she didn't hesitate — she zeroed in on Angelica's core and let her magic flow.

Concentrated lightning strikes of sheer magic jolted from Lucki's fingers. Her intent was to obliterate

Angelica, just as she'd obliterated that tree weeks before.

Once again, Angelica somehow deflected, sending the lightning right back at Lucki. She was ready this time, though, and volleyed it back, adding more force, more power until her lightning strikes were conduits of even more magic, tightly wound threads that pulsed so quickly that not even Angelica could deflect them all.

Angelica staggered, growled then came back swinging.

Hit for hit, Lucki continued to pull more and more of her magic from her core, from her bonds. Hit for hit, Angelica did the same. After what seemed like hours, Lucki felt like her body might collapse right out from under her. Angelica didn't seem to tire or slow down. She kept up the punishing drill of spells, pushing Lucki back, forcing her to swing harder each time she counter-attacked.

The strategy was a good one, tried and tested. Angelica was trying to wear her down — and it was working.

Lucki didn't know how much longer she could hold out. Her magic sputtered within and her body sagged under the pressure to keep the battle going.

One of Angelica's spells slipped past Lucki's defenses, and even her markings couldn't stop the hit from penetrating. It struck her belly like a sledgehammer and brought her to her knees.

"Get up, Lucki," Reuben bellowed.

Of course, she'd get up. Except, when she tried to push to her feet again, her belly screamed, and instead of getting up, she crumpled. Angelica didn't waver. She sent more pounding magic to strike Lucki, pushing her deeper into the ground, pinning her in place.

"Lucki!" Wren screamed.

Lucki shifted her eyes to look at him, knowing that the only way to win was if she took Angelica out for good.

It was the night of the Solstice, the night when Isabel's spell would lock someone into her alternative world.

Angelica hit her with another round of jolts, moving closer so that each jab was an earthquake of pain.

Lucki began the spell.

The first few words brought the fog rolling in. It stuck to Angelica like glue then snaked its way to Lucki. Angelica kept moving, not noticing the fog, so intent on striking Lucki that she had no idea.

But Wren knew. "No, Lucki. Don't."

She closed her eyes, blocking the tears from falling, and continued the spell. This was what she had to do to keep her men safe. She had to take Angelica to Isabel's other realm and lock her there.

"Have you had enough? Are you ready to concede?" Angelica hovered over Lucki's prone body. "My intent isn't to kill you, girl — only to transfer this curse to you. Now you're so weak that it'll likely kill you. If only you'd just cooperated from the start..." She sighed. "Well, there's no use crying over it now." She raised her arms to the night sky.

Lucki slapped her hand to Angelica's ankle, her grip firm and unwavering.

Angelica snapped her gaze down just as Lucki finished the spell.

The fog rolled over them like a freight train, consuming them both.

Just as the first time, Lucki was falling — falling through the fog, unable to see. The disorienting sensation of magic swirling over her skin, of pushing her in the direction she needed to go, almost knocked her out. She knew what was coming—a hard jolt and her new reality. Trapped in Isabel's magic realm with Angelica, for an eternity.

She mourned the loss of her shifters—of her life, of the pain that was sure to come.

Angelica's furious scream echoed in Lucki's head.

At least she knew her sacrifice would release her shifters and the cats from Angelica's torment, even if she couldn't end the curse for them.

She landed with a thud then released Angelica's ankle and tried to roll away.

"What have you done?" Angelica shrieked. "Where have you taken me?" Magic crackled around them.

Lucki braced herself for Angelica to strike, but before anything could hit, Lucki was yanked backward, her mask ripped from her face, her dress torn almost completely from her body. She fell through the fog once again, this time totally unsure where she was headed.

Chapter Twenty-Nine

Lucki

For the second time that day, she landed in the dirt and ate a bunch of it on impact. Before she could wipe it from her face, wet rough tongues were doing it for her. She cracked her eyes open to find three happy-looking wolf pups eagerly lapping away the stuff from her face.

"Ugh, thank you. Thank you. I've got it." She brushed the saliva from her cheeks as she pushed herself up. "What happened?"

Reuben in his bear form and Julian in his lion form were running the perimeter of the clearing, their noses to the ground. Wren stepped toward the circle and as he did, left his wolf behind.

"You did it." Wren took a step toward her, only to hold his hand up and freeze.

A low, menacing chorus of hissing started up around Lucki and she lifted herself more so she could see what was going on.

The cats had surrounded the circle—every single one of them.

"They brought you back." Wren turned into his wolf then made a second attempt to get to her, snapping his big teeth at the cats who insisted on protecting her. They finally parted so he could stand at the edge of the circle.

Lucki scanned her body, both outside and in, for any sign that Angelica's attacks had caused permanent damage. "I locked her in Isabel's world."

Wren shifted to human again then held his hand out for her to take. "The witching hour has passed. If Isabel's spell holds, Angelica is locked in that world now."

Lucki pushed herself to stand then stepped over the circle's border. Wren pulled Lucki straight into his arms and she melted on contact.

He brushed her hair back from her face then rubbed his thumb over her bottom lip. "I thought we'd lost you."

Lucki gulped down her heart, which had bounced up into her throat. "For a moment, I thought you had, too."

"The cats anchored you. Brought you back. One second you'd disappeared with Angelica, and the next you were back."

"With my face full of mud."

Wren barked a laugh. "The pups got that all off."

They grinned at each other.

Reuben and Julian joined them in human form. All three men crowded around her, cocooning her in their warmth and love. Her heart was full and her body was primed, ready to embrace these men in all ways. Her magic swirled to attention all over again, but not readying for combat. No, it was preparing for something far more important.

"Come into the circle with me." She tugged Wren's hand as she looked from him to Reuben to Julian. "Honor me the way it was done centuries ago."

How she knew that, she couldn't say, but in her gut was the truth. She could bring her mates into the circle. She could protect them from the overwhelming power and use it to bolster their abilities. She could take them in the sacred place and cement their commitment to one another and to her.

"We can't—" Wren choked on his next words.

"If Lucki wants us there with her, we can." Reuben's voice was grumbly gruff and delicious to her ears.

She shifted toward Reuben then took his face in her hands and urged him down so she could kiss him. "I want you." Then she turned to Wren, held his hands, leaned up his body and kissed him. "I want you." When she turned to Julian, she draped her arms over his shoulders and stood on tiptoe to kiss him. "I want you."

"Forever," Wren said.

"Yes." As she led them past the border of the circle, the cats all dispersed, wandering away to give them privacy. There was no need to fear an attack any longer. Angelica was locked away and Lucki and her familiars were free to do as they pleased. As they entered the circle, Lucki let her intention be known. She would have her shifters here with her. They would not be harmed. The magic circle would gift them with more power, a reward for their dedication, bravery and honor. The magic responded to her call and reacted to her demands. It enveloped all four of them in colorful waves of blue and pink and yellow. It filled Lucki with electric sparks and fizzed along her familiars' skin. Wren gasped. Julian groaned. Reuben laughed a sound from deep in his belly that made Lucki grin.

"I've never felt such a thing." Reuben flexed his hands out for them to see. Threads of magic weaved around his fingers and caressed his skin. Markings etched along his arms.

The other men experienced similar effects. Lucki urged the circle's magic to do more…to give more. These men deserved it. They'd given so much to her — their power, their protection, their hearts. Now it was her turn to give them back even more.

Lucki guided them to the altar stone. It stood seven feet high and was long enough and wide enough to hold her body. Wren lifted her then set her onto the cool, smooth slab. She shivered against the cold surface, but Wren kissed away the chill. As he pressed his soft lips to hers, a fire ignited in her belly and spread to her limbs, heating her so that she was sure she was radiating a glow. Julian began to strip away what was left of her gown. Reuben ran his fingers through her hair and gently tugged away the debris that was tangled in it.

Magic surged with the pulse of her desire for these men. As they helped her strip to nothing, she helped them do the same. Before long, they were all naked and their bodies were all primed and ready and waiting for her next move.

Lucki wanted this more than anything in the world. She wanted to worship these men just as they had always worshipped her. She kissed Julian, entangling tongues to stroke and tease. She ran her fingers along Wren's shaft, which was jutting and hard, ready for her in every way. She shifted to Reuben so she could kiss him too, alternating between him and Julian while she stroked Wren until he moaned.

Julian knelt in front of her while she kissed Reuben. He parted her legs and touched her aching pussy. She gasped into Reuben's mouth when Julian's hot breath wafted over her clit, when his fingers entered her slick hole. Reuben continued to kiss her as he lowered her back so she could lie down. While she was busy kissing him, she worked her hands all over Wren's cock—rubbing his long shaft, caressing his tight balls. He teased her hard nipples, rolling them between his fingers, making her arch to beg for more, which of course, he obliged. He licked each nipple, before sucking each one deep into his warm mouth then rolling the buds against his tongue and his teeth. Julian sucked on her clit so powerfully that she cried out and Reuben swallowed that cry with a more punishing kiss.

Her body was aflame, crackling and sputtering along every nerve ending. She demanded more—more pleasure, more sensation. She broke the kiss with Reuben and transferred her hands to his cock while she turned her head and motioned for Wren to move closer. While she stroked Reuben with her fingers, she took Wren's dick into her mouth and sucked him off. He filled it while Reuben filled her hand and Julian her pussy, his deft fingers propping her G-spot expertly.

This was bliss, perfection wrapped up in magic and muscle and men.

Wren clenched her hair to help steady her lips as she took him as far back as she could into her throat, her mouth entirely full of his cock. Reuben flicked and teased her nipples as she pumped his dick from tip to base then back again with her hand. Julian's relentless attention pushed her to the brink of explosion again and again before pulling back, kissing his way over her hip, distracting her from the looming orgasm that was just out of reach.

She wanted to be penetrated — to be fucked.

Julian read her mind when he entered her, wedging his giant cock deep into her pussy with one great thrust. She shifted her mouth from Wren's dick to Reuben's, taking him in as much as she could while she rubbed her saliva over Wren's shaft and pumped him like Julian was pumping her. Her orgasm continued to build, like a dam filling to the brink of overflowing. She filled and filled with pleasure, her body primed, pulled taut with desire and need. Without direction, without need for words, the men shifted positions. Julian moved so Wren could take his place. She felt the loss of Julian's cock for mere seconds before Wren stuffed her full of his dick and continued to pummel her. He stroked her clit. Julian licked her nipples and she sucked on Reuben's crown.

There was no beginning and no end to their connection. Every part of Lucki's body was touched, teased, stroked, pounded. Wren held her hips and lifted her ass so he could drill into her deeply. Julian snaked his hand to her clit while he tended to her tits, and Reuben stroked her hair while she licked her way down his shaft again and again.

If they were giving some signal, she was unaware, but somehow, they knew when it was time to shift positions, and once again the men moved. Reuben gave her pussy a giant lick before gliding his massive cock into her. She attended to both Julian and Wren this time, alternating between their cocks, which glistened with pre-cum and saliva and her own creamy juice. She used her fingers, her lips and her tongue to stroke them, to love them. Their hands on her body became unidentifiable. She didn't know who was stroking her clit or who was pinching her nipples, but it was like a thousand sensations all at once, tongues licking and teasing, fingers plucking away at her so that her orgasm continued to rise, to build so high that her body was floating, it had to be.

With no warning but a guttural groan, Julian bucked into her mouth and exploded with cum. It hit the back of her throat and slid down. Wren moaned. His cock jerked in her hand, then he too began to spurt all over her tits. Lucki's climax brought her to the edge of a cliff, tilting, tilting, ready to push her over. She arched up to meet Reuben's thrusts while Wren continued to rub her clit. As Reuben's cock detonated inside of her, her body finally tipped over the edge.

She was flying, her body soaring, catching the wind and riding the currents. Her brain sparked again and again as her orgasm rippled and squeezed her pussy tight. Her body quivered and quaked as Reuben filled her up with his hot cum.

She couldn't imagine another version of her life that didn't include these men — not now, not for an eternity.

Epilogue

Lucki

"One more round!" Andy shouted with his beer mug spilling foam as he swung around to address the crowd.

"Oh, Goddess, if I have one more round, you're going to have to carry me home." Lucki laughed. Her vision was already beyond blurry, and her sense of gravity was lopsided.

"You've got three very capable escorts to ensure you get there." Reuben carried over an apple caramel martini, his newest specialty. "Besides, I made you another one." He handed her the cocktail.

"Oh boy, this is going to be a fun night." She took a sip, because there was just no way she'd let a signature Reuben cocktail go to waste.

"Isn't it always a fun night?" Julian winked as he gulped down his wine. He held the glass up to Reuben just as he was lowering himself into one of the chairs at their table.

Reuben rolled his eyes but took the glass anyway, then headed to the bar.

"It is always a fun night with you guys." And that was an understatement, because it wasn't just fun and games between Lucki and her shifters. It was also love, respect and a growing sense of family that she'd so badly missed since her mother had died.

"I'd like to make a toast," Scout said, his glass raised as he stood from his stool. "For a hundred and fifty years I'd been searching for the Cat Keeper who would save us from our captivity. One hundred and fifty years of finding the wrong kind of Cat Keeper."

"We did think you'd gone mad, Scout." Deb laughed. "All those magicless humans you sent to us."

"It wasn't easy to find the right one, but I did." Scout nodded toward Lucki. "She came. She stayed. She conquered. And now...now we're free!"

"Free to shift as we please," someone said.

"Free to come and go."

"Free to live without fear."

"Here's to Lucki, our powerful, unbeatable, brilliant Cat Keeper."

The whole crowd cheered.

Lucki had done that, hadn't she? She'd saved the cats from Angelica. She'd removed the threat and had also somehow broken the curse — or at least had put a dent in it. The townspeople didn't have to spend all day as a cat and all night as a human. Like Scout, they could change at will and did so when it suited them. Like, for example, when Lucki had needed help in the garden, a chore which none of the townspeople seemed to love. If she went looking for someone to help, all of a sudden there were too many cats and not enough humans to lend a hand. It always fell to her strong shifters to weed and hoe and carry big bags of dirt wherever she needed it. And they hardly grumbled about it.

No one had ventured beyond the border yet. Everyone was a little too afraid still to explore, but Reuben had told her that the pull he always felt to the town was diminishing as each day rolled on.

They'd be free to travel soon enough. And yes, she'd done that too. Somehow, she'd broken a curse that had plagued these people for far too long, managed to end the terrible reign of an evil sorceress — *and* she'd found love, and her heart had begun to truly heal, because in that love she'd found peace.

Two months ago she'd thought she was coming to Weeping Falls to be a Cat Keeper, but what she'd really become was herself.

"Best job in the MFing world," she whispered with a grin.

Want to see more from this author? Here's a taster for you to enjoy!

Wicked Distractions: Wicked Disclosure
Angela Addams

Excerpt

"Someone will see us," Trent breathed out the words, half a moan, as Sabine opened his pants.

"Yeah, maybe." She licked her lips, her hand on his cock making him jolt. "But no one will talk about it."

He opened his lips to mutter some other stupid shit then closed them again. Sabine licked him from balls to crown and he thought he was going to come from that alone. He tilted his head back, groaning when she sucked him, slowly gliding her lips over his shaft, swirling and flicking her tongue before easing his dick in. She pumped him, taking him past the gate of her throat, fucking him with her entire mouth. His brain misfired, thoughts fading to nothing but electric impulses of pleasure. She gently massaged his balls with her fingers, her moan vibrating along his cock. Everything coiled—his gut, his sac—ready to blow.

She slid his dick out of her mouth, slowly, pressing her tongue hard against his shaft, lingering to give him another couple of flicks just under the ridge of his crown. He sucked in a deep breath and looked down at her, her lips glistening and a wicked smile greeting him. His body uncoiled, pulling him back from the edge enough that he could think again. It would have been some embarrassing shit if he'd lost his load so quickly.

"I probably shouldn't be doing this. Conflict of interest," he said, then chastised himself. *Shut up, you stupid fucker. Shut up, shut up, shut up!* There was Sabine Cowan, CEO of an escort empire, heiress to a multi-corporation legacy and notoriously *hot* bad girl, on her knees with her lips...*oh fuck*...her lips wrapped around his... "*Fuck!*"

She popped her mouth off him again, the suction making him want to follow her, his dick bobbing, begging for more. "You're not working tonight," she said. She sat back on her heels and slid her hand up his chest, pushing him to sit down in his chair. "I wouldn't have invited you to my party if I thought you were on the clock."

"Why am I here, then?" His brain was exploding, lust driving his every thought. He watched her lips move, her tongue darting to lick the corner of her mouth.

"Well..."

She moved between his legs, pushing against his thighs, nipples popping like they'd explode out of her low-cut dress. He wished they would. He kept his hands gripped to the arms of his chair, not trusting himself to move and break the lusty spell she was weaving.

"You're here to see how I keep secrets, aren't you?"

"I'm here to get you to sign a confidentiality agreement." He nearly choked on those words. *Could that be any more of a buzz kill?* She'd refused to sign the agreement at their meeting earlier, scoffing at idle threats made on behalf of his boss.

She smiled, batting her lashes. "Well, I guess you're just going to have to convince me then, aren't you?" She took his balls into her palm, stroking one then the other. "You wanna fuck me, messenger boy?"

"Yeah," he croaked. *Screw the confidentiality agreement.*

She released him, pushing on his thighs to stand, her hand out to help him up. In a daze he took her offer, standing on wobbly legs, dick rock hard, leading the way.

"You might want to tuck that bad boy back in." Sabine chuckled. "We've gotta walk through a few crowds to get upstairs."

Confused, Trent glanced down, realizing in a daze what she was saying. He pushed his aching dick back into his pants and zipped up. He'd had blow jobs in his life. Many. But he'd never had one like that. It seemed as if Sabine had enjoyed it just as much as he had. Maybe he'd just gotten so used to his mundane sex life that he'd forgotten how good things could be. Either way, he wasn't going to put the brakes on this. He couldn't. This was a fantasy-in-the-making of epic proportions. And he believed Sabine when she said that discretion was a guarantee. Off the clock or not, he knew his boss would not be happy to hear that Trent had not only partied with the enemy but fucked her too.

And that potentially sobering thought—the risk of blowing everything he'd worked his ass off to achieve, a corner office as Morgan and Miller Limited's newest lead communications officer, a stellar and solid reputation for innovative promotional campaigns and the bank account to show for it—still wasn't enough to derail his lust.

The temptation was just too great.

Sabine had been a socialite first—a wealthy heiress who'd attracted the media spotlight for not only her stunning looks but also her outrageous behavior. Drugs, parties, sex tapes… She'd done it all. Done it and reveled in it. Her celebrity status alone made her a trophy bang, but add to that her smoking-hot body—voluptuous and plump in all the right places—combined with her I'm-gonna-fuck-your-brains-out aggression and Trent was a goner.

Sabine took him up the grand staircase, leading him, walking just a little ahead so he felt like her hand in his was more like a leash, guiding him in the right direction. Adam, her very watchful bodyguard, was standing a few steps up, flicking his gaze from Trent to Sabine, his frown firmly in place. Sabine paused long enough so she could lean in and say something quietly to the giant brute. Adam gave a tight nod, shifting to look straight ahead, like Trent didn't exist. With another sly smile over her shoulder at Trent, Sabine continued up. His dick was literally weeping for her.

There was another staircase leading to the next floor, probably where the master suite was, but Sabine didn't continue upward. Instead, she took him down the hall, wall sconces lighting their way. It was quieter up here, the sound of murmured voices from the many conversations muffled as they moved higher and deeper into the house.

The room she led him to was bigger than his hotel room, even bigger than his condo. But there was nothing suggesting a touch of Sabine, nothing that made him think she'd invited him into her own bedroom, her sanctuary. He didn't know why that bothered him. Why it would matter that she wanted to fuck in a generic room?

"Is this a client room?" He pushed away the feeling of jealousy that had reared, surprised that it was there at all. While downstairs had been all about socializing and harmless flirting, upstairs was a different story. If there was any doubt in his mind that her legitimate escort business was a cover for more nefarious shit, the multi-room traffic of girls and older men they'd passed on the second floor had been enough to tell him otherwise.

Sabine smiled when she faced him, her hand on the door to close it. "This is a guest room."

She shut out the rest of the party then moved toward him to run her hands up his body and wrap her arms around his shoulders, pressing her lips to his. He melted into her kiss. Finally, he could taste her. Any other thoughts dissolved when she slipped her tongue into his mouth, exploring, entangling. He moved his hands to her hips, then over her ass, lifting her so she could wrap her legs around his waist. Her skirt hiked up under his hands and he brushed flesh. *She isn't wearing any panties.*

"You're bare," he said as he pulled away from her mouth.

She cocked her head in a coy gesture, one he didn't believe for a second. "Yeah, I was hoping you'd figure that out sooner and slip your fingers in for a bit."

"Downstairs?" He was taken aback then chuckled at his own shock. "Finger you in front of everyone?"

Sabine wiggled her way out of his grasp, kicked off her shoes then climbed onto the bed, facing him on her knees. "You'd be surprised how few people notice those kinds of things. And the ones who do either enjoy the view or look away."

Trent yanked off his jacket and shoes then crawled onto the bed, invading her space, making her move so that she was holding herself up, leaning back on her hands, her legs partially spread.

"Well, it would be a good show if they did watch." What he was really thinking was, *I sure as shit hope no one recognized me.* Instead of blurting out his panicked thoughts, he distracted himself with Sabine, letting his dick do the thinking from that point on. He ran his hand up her calf then down her thigh, slipping the skirt of her dress back to her waist.

She laughed, dropping her head back, and opened her legs wider. He ignored her offer, bypassing the view of her pussy, those plump lips bare of hair with the glint of a piercing on her hood, in favor of her luscious fat tits. Finding her peaked nipples hard, he lowered his mouth, sucking her through her dress before nipping her between his teeth, taking her by surprise so that she whipped her head back up to meet his gaze. Something sparkled there—intrigue, curiosity. She watched him move from one breast to the other, latching on to the top of her dress, yanking it down so that her tits spilled out.

She moaned when he nipped again at the lush bud that was hard, impossibly hard. He flicked his tongue against it, sucking while he fondled her other breast with his hand, cupping as much as he could, her ample flesh spilling out of his palm. He alternated between the two, flicking and teasing. He could play with her nipples forever, sucking them until they were hot and rosy red, throbbing against his tongue.

"Eat me, messenger boy." She rocked her hips, nudging against him, making his cock pulse.

He pulled away with a smile, feeling cunning, triumphant. Sabine Cowan was as good as begging him to lick her clit. He obviously had to oblige. He spread her legs wider, holding her knees as he lifted them, pushing back until they were nearly touching the bed. Her pussy was gloriously splayed, wet, glistening, the piercing a diamond stud, hot as hell. He licked his lips and she moaned, the sound enough to make his cock throb. He lay down between her legs, flicking at the piercing, rolling it around with his tongue before moving to her clit to give her a good suck. He licked his way down, probing her hole, lapping her juice. He glanced up and caught her watching him as she played with her tits, teasing herself, her eyes hooded.

He slid his fingers deep inside, stroking her G-spot, giving her the right kind of pressure, servicing her with his tongue and his lips, so that her orgasm would rise just as his had. And right when he got her writhing, groaning, her breathing hard, her eyes closed and back arched, he stopped.

It took her a few seconds to realize what he'd done. She cracked open her eyes, watching him, snaking her hand down to finish the job he'd started.

"Nah uh, sweetie." He gave a shake of his finger while he unbuttoned his pants with his other hand. "You're going to come around my cock."

Sabine froze in place and gave him a slow, knowing smile. She wiggled herself out of her dress, tossing it over his shoulder to land in a heap on the floor. He pulled his pants off, then his boxers and socks, followed by his shirt. After giving him another once-over, she crawled to the other side of the bed, swaying her ass in a tantalizing manner. She opened a drawer on the bedside table and pulled something out. Turning to face him, she tossed it against his chest.

Condoms. A row of them.

Trent smiled, his cock jolting, eager to be sheathed. She crawled to him, slipping her mouth over his dick at the same time that she ripped a condom from the row.

When she sucked her way off, he mourned the loss but knew something much better was coming. She slipped the condom on him then spun around, wiggling her ass. He didn't need more of an invitation. With hands on her hips, he thrust into her, his balls smacking her skin. He moaned as her pussy gripped him.

She lowered herself so her face was against the mattress, his thrusts rocking her, her tits swaying. She slipped her hand down her front, likely to rub her clit. He couldn't actually see her fingers, but the thought of her touching herself had his orgasm rising fast. He reached one hand around to play with one of her breasts, cupping it then gliding his thumb down to flick her nipple. She cried out, her pussy spasming hard and fast, her moans bringing him to climax and cum spewing into the condom. It was a great release after months of nothing but his hand.

He pulled out of her, sitting back on his heels as he caught his breath — or tried to, anyway. She was on him in a flash, pulling the condom off, slipping her lips back on. Sabine soon had him hard and wanting her all over again. She slid another condom on then pushed him backward, nearly toppling him off the bed so she could straddle him. He knew he was in for the night of his life. With her eyes locked on his and his cock buried deep, she gave him a slow ride. All he could do was stare up at her and think that Sabine-fucking-Cowan was a goddess.

* * * *

He woke up with a sex hangover. His dick was sore, every muscle in his body felt strained — and he was smiling like a madman. *What an unbelievable night.* He shifted, rolling to the side, not really surprised to find himself alone. He pushed himself up on his elbows, noting that the bathroom door was open, the room itself dark. Sabine hadn't stuck around. That wasn't surprising, but, if he were honest, it was disappointing. He collapsed back onto the mattress with a sigh. It wasn't that he was complaining. He'd had an amazing night of hot sex, more times than he'd thought was possible. It had been wild, crazy, uninhibited, no-rules kind of sex in every possible position. Sabine's body and what she could do with it—he moaned at the thought—was like the best porno fantasy times a thousand. *No, times a million.* It was a story for the record books. His friends would likely do just about anything to hear about it. But no one was going to hear about it. That one was locked in the vault, meant for only his enjoyment.

He pulled himself out of bed, making a half-assed attempt to find his clothes, hoping that maybe Sabine was just downstairs getting coffee for them. His phone rang, a muffled sound from across the room. He narrowed his eyes at the pile of clothes, flung haphazardly on the floor. It took him a few seconds to find it, but by the time he did the call had gone to voicemail. There was a text from Roy, a link and nothing else. With a sinking feeling, Trent clicked it.

"Oh fuck," he breathed. The link opened to a popular tabloid where a grainy photo showed Sabine on her knees, looking up at Trent. *"Morgan and Miller Golden Boy Caught with His Pants Down."* There was a spread and a half dozen or more photos. Trent wanted to barf.

Another text came from Roy.

Not good.

Trent closed his eyes briefly, nausea sweeping through him. He typed a response.

I was promised discretion.

It sounded lame. He wanted to take it back the second he pressed Send.
No response.
Fuck. Trent typed.

I'll fix this.

Damage is done. Get your ass back here. I sure as shit hope you got the confidentiality agreement signed.

Trent cursed again. He dug into his pile of clothes, searching for the agreement. He found it crumpled up where he'd left it in the inside pocket of his jacket—unsigned, of course.

His phone dinged again. He looked down, expecting to see another text from Roy, but it was from Sabine.

Had to fly out this morning. Early. Didn't want to wake you.

A second text came.

Had a great time last night. XX See you around.

"Fuck!" Trent threw his phone against the wall, satisfied when it busted to pieces.

Home of Erotic Romance

Sign up for our newsletter and find out about all our romance book releases, eBook sales and promotions, sneak peeks and FREE romance books!

About the Author

Angela Addams is an author of many naughty things. She believes that the written word is an amazing tool for crafting the most erotic of scenarios and likes telling stories about normal people getting down and dirty and falling in love. Enthralled by the paranormal at an early age, Angela also spends a lot of her time thinking up new story ideas that involve supernatural creatures in everyday situations.

She is an avid tattoo collector, a total book hoarder, and loves anything covered in chocolate…except for bugs. She lives in Ontario, Canada in an old, creaky house, with her husband, children and four moody cats.

Angela loves to hear from readers. You can find her contact information, website details and author profile page at https://www.totallybound.com

www.ingramcontent.com/pod-product-compliance
Lightning Source LLC
Chambersburg PA
CBHW021513240626
47154CB00002B/618